I0549775

STRIKETHROUGH

LOUISE DAWN

Copyright © 2021 by Louise Dawn

All rights reserved.

Strikethrough

Cover Design by Sweet 'N Spicy Designs

Editing by JRT Editing

ISBN: 978-1-7363041-2-9

This book is a work of fiction. Names, characters and incidents are products of Louise Dawn's imagination. Any resemblance to actual events, people are purely coincidental.

All rights reserved. This book or parts thereof may not be reproduced in any form, stored in any retrieval system, or transmitted in any form by any means —electronic, mechanical, photocopy, recording, or otherwise—without prior written permission of the publisher.

Thank you for respecting the hard work of this author.

This book contains elements of: Assault. Violence. Murder. Kidnapping. Threats of violence. Sex (consensual). Bad language. Guns.

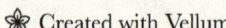 Created with Vellum

To Derek—a brave Special Agent
who dealt with my endless questions, text messages and phone calls.

When violence erupts, DSS Special Agents thwart extremists,
rescue locals and U.S. personnel, and respond to danger.

This series is dedicated to the brave men and women serving in Diplomatic
Security.

Colorado.

K neeling in the same spot for hours resulted in cramping muscles and a dampening forehead. Shifting positions would show weakness. Sweat burned the eyes, not ideal when staring down a scope.

"Any moment now." Papa's whispered words drew Jona's attention back to the bird's eye view of the school.

The empty tenth-floor apartment in the partially completed residential building afforded the best vantage point at the perfect distance. A couple of school kids pushed open the doors from the auditorium. Around Jona's age, they seemed carefree while galloping down the stairs. Spoilt Americans.

"Remember what I have taught you." Papa's warm hand touched Jona's shoulder. "I would take the shot, but my hands are no longer reliable."

This assignment was Jona's first kill—first human kill.

Animals didn't count, although Jona had hunted alongside Papa in the Finnish woodlands for ten years, since the age of six. That was when Papa was in-country and not on assignment. Otto Kivela was a legend and a mystery to many. And now, he'd become a shadowed soul.

The crossover to Tuonela wasn't long coming. Papa grew weaker every day as cancer ate away at his once fit body and his rapid decline was a worry. As a neopaganist, Jona should feel comfortable with losing Papa, but that was not the case. Otto spoke about the balance of nature and returning to the earth, but where did that leave Jona? Alone on a callous planet.

"Relax. You are white-knuckling the weapon."

"Sorry, Papa."

"Concentrate. 400 yards. Wind—five klicks left."

"Yes, sir."

Otto pushed up to look through his binoculars. He'd used the same pair for over twenty years—a green rubber, armored Leica Vector pair, with a built-in laser range finder. Like a sniper's rifle, a good pair of binoculars was vital to the trade. Jona stroked the AI AW rifle with the tactical suppressor and folding stock that could easily fold into a suitcase for a quick escape.

This was the first time that Jona would fire the Arctic Warfare bolt-action sniper rifle on the job. Jona's humble rifle back in Finland wasn't up to the challenge. Otto refused to use any other model and had relied on the weapon's accuracy for over thirty years.

His firm relations with cartels and criminal syndicates meant easy access to weapons. Otto had never missed a mark with the AW. Over the years, he'd bought and stashed this same model in safe houses in various countries. Back in Finland, on the range, Jona had practiced for weeks with an AW rifle. Finally, the moment of truth was upon them.

"Do not rest the barrel—that will affect the fall of your shot."

"Yes, sir," Jona replied, although Otto had said that many times before.

"Aim for a strikethrough. If you can't take the headshot, aim for the chest."

"Strikethrough" was Papa's reference to a clean kill when a bullet enters the skull's front and blows out the back—the same went for a shot to the heart. Accuracy meant slicing straight through the organ. A perfectly placed round entered at an exact angle and the mark was dead before they hit the ground.

Jona forcibly relaxed as crowds pushed their way out of the school hall and flooded the parking lot. Many made their way to their vehicles. Some milled about as the dipping sun cast shadows on the lot. Still, Jona waited another fifteen minutes. A limousine pulled up, and Jona let out a trembling breath. The targets would never climb into that car.

Two bodyguards led the way. The tycoon followed; his arm wrapped around his teenage daughter. They were far enough away that Jona could barely make out facial features but could feel the daughter's excitement with her performance at the school play. Her stage make-up highlighted in the telescopic finder as she smiled up at her father.

"Base centered of auditorium," Otto whispered, alerting Jona to the first mark's position.

"Seen."

The mother followed, pausing beside her husband and daughter, her erect posture clothed in a pale-blue designer suit.

"Fire."

Jona followed the command with a squeeze of the trigger. The first target was the father. Jona aimed for the head, knowing the wealthy magnate may be wearing a ballistic vest. The mark fell.

Now came the hard part—readjusting aim to the mother.

The gun fired again. She dropped but kept moving. Jona swore, as a bodyguard pulled her down the stairs to cover. The limousine now sat in the way.

The daughter... Jona focused on the kid and hesitated. Her screams weren't audible from a distance, but Jona could feel her palpable anguish.

"Pull the trigger!" Otto yelled.

Jona fired just as a large guard shoved the girl to the ground. They rolled down the steps.

"I missed." In frustration, Jona took down the nearest watchdog. A headshot dropped the blond warrior.

"You don't say. We need to move. There will be immediate heat. Pack up! Now!"

"I'm sorry, Papa."

"We get paid for the three deaths—not one. I should have taken the shot!" Otto used the table to climb to his feet.

"I killed the rich bastard! The wife will die from her injuries."

"You did half a job." Papa's voice sounded thready.

"Let me stay and finish," Jona begged. "They're crouched behind the transport. I'll pick them off."

"There's no time. Stop sniveling and help to pack the gear."

"I'll ruin your legacy." Jona scrambled to help.

"My fault. You're too young—only sixteen." Face paling, Otto swayed.

"Papa!"

"I'm fine."

Jona caught the frail man as he fell.

"Leave me."

"Never, Papa! No."

"My life... is over. Let me have... the last victory."

Jona tried to pick up Otto and strained under the weight.

They wouldn't make it. The tycoon's protection detail, along with local law enforcement, would track them down.

"Go. That is a command." Otto shoved a palm into Jona's chest. "We waited too long…. not strong enough."

"I love you, Papa." Tears streamed.

"Grow up, child. You know what I expect."

"Do you want me to…" Jona stared at the rifle in dismay before swiping at a wet cheek. "I can't shoot you!"

"Let them arrest me. I'll gloat in those federal pigs' faces before I die." Otto smiled weakly.

After adjusting the plans, and hurriedly wiping down the rifle, furniture, and equipment, Jona propped Otto against the wall near the weapon and kissed his clammy forehead.

Leaving without Papa's beloved binoculars wasn't an option and Jona tucked them beneath a thin jacket, along with the expensive laser range finder.

Papa's last order came—the words barely whispered. "Bide your time. Finish the job and kill both bitches."

"Yes, sir." Jona never looked back.

The descent rushed by in a blur. After exiting into an alley, then detouring and backtracking, Jona finally sat behind the wheel of their rental car. It smelled like Papa's cigarettes, and childhood memories came flooding back.

God, Papa stayed behind. Otto should never have come on the hunt. Jona should have insisted on leaving him at the rented cabin.

The entire fucked-up operation was all Jona's fault. That's what happened when a sixteen-year-old kid stepped into an assassin's legendary shoes.

2

Twelve years later.
The U.S. Embassy, Colombo, Sri Lanka.

"Taylor, what time is it?" Ignoring the burning pain radiating down her left arm, Ambassador Connie Durant sped up as they entered the quiet passage. Her assistant battled to keep up.

"Eight-thirty in the evening."

"And my daughter decided to go straight to Martin." Although Connie trusted Martin Roberts with her life, it annoyed the hell out of her that Chantal hadn't come to her mother first. Why would she? Their strained relationship lacked the affection they'd once shared.

"He is the RSO."

Which was why Connie should feel gratitude. In the past, she'd worked with Martin in DC—established a friendship— and when he'd landed the job at her embassy as the Regional Security Officer a year ago, Connie had breathed a sigh of relief. With twenty-two years on the job, Martin was a seasoned agent with a stellar reputation within diplomatic security, who now protected her and her embassy and American personnel from possible threats. He headed up the RSO section, which was responsible for running day to day security.

The Regional Security Officer worked under constant pressure as the principle security attaché and security advisor to an ambassador—ensuring that all mandated security programs were carried out.

Connie needed good people on her team so that as an official envoy, she could get on with the business of diplomatic troubleshooting. She wasn't leaving Sri Lanka without making a difference. There were two ways to be an American ambassador. Through wealth—hefty donations to the U.S. presidency led to comfortable rewards and serving ambassadorships in top-notch embassies like Paris, Madrid, or London. That wasn't Connie's way—she chose the hard road. Although she was an extremely wealthy woman, she'd risen through the ranks of the State Department with driven ambition.

Dedicating her life to foreign service had always been her goal, and she was now in the running for Regional Director. She'd made enemies along the way. Striving for patience in every aspect of her job wasn't always easy. She'd worked hard on that aspect of her personality her whole life—more so, when fighting the daily pain. Her body rarely stopped screaming. Connie had lived with the relentless waves of agony for twelve years.

And the torment blocked out any niceties she once had—a constant reminder to accommodate others when all she wanted was to curl up in a dark space and whimper. But Connie was a rising star in the Foreign Service and refused to be taken down by a damaged body.

"Confirmation—Rajin Bandara's ex-wife is in Martin's office, with my daughter."

"Yes—Pearl—Pearl Bandara." Taylor scurried ahead and swiped her card to open a door as they neared Martin's office.

"And her life's become a sudden crap-storm?"

"Seems that way. She has her daughter with her—the girl looks to be around four years of age."

Connie smiled. "I'm sure Martin will have a full rundown on Pearl's background by morning."

Finally, they entered the RSO block, which lay quiet— aside from the soft light coming from under Martin's door. Taylor knocked before opening the door and placing additional files on Martin's desk. She exited and departed down the passage. Connie stepped into the RSO's office, and her dear friend offered her a warm smile. She didn't respond, ignoring the handsome older man.

Martin was the only individual on the planet who could ruffle her composure. She hated how her palms grew clammy in his presence and how she ached to walk into those burly arms. She'd avoided the urge for years and would continue to resist the temptation.

Connie focused on her daughter's friend. She'd once met Pearl at the Marine Ball and remembered her as a statuesque stunner on the arm of an ambitious husband. Connie remembered her sparkling personality. The woman before her looked like a paler, thinner version. Bare-faced with her hair pulled up in a messy bun; Pearl clung to the child in her lap.

Connie turned her attention to her own beautiful daughter, sitting with a perfect posture in a leather chair beside the pair. Chantal had inherited her good looks and effortless elegance from her father's French side of the family. She even wore her hair in a striking bob haircut, highlighting her large brown eyes and classic bone structure. Unlike her mother, Chantal had little need for heavy make-up.

Connie needed a lip-liner for her thinner lips and heavy concealer for a tired face. A decade of pain had turned her hair gray and added premature age lines. Connie covered the gray with blonde highlights but wasn't vain enough to consider surgery for a face that wasn't pretty to begin with—at least in her eyes.

Ankles crossed elegantly, Chantal rested her hands in her lap and smiled at her formidable mother.

"Don't smile at me. Where did you go in the middle of the night and why did you rush back like your hair was on fire?"

"Seven o'clock isn't the middle of the night, Mom. I'm twenty-eight years old. I'll come and go as I please."

"And yet, here you sit. After pulling in diplomats in a flurry of dramatics."

"You know this is important," Chantal shot back.

"I don't know anything except what Martin has told me in his brief summons. Your friend is in trouble?"

"I am… Madam Ambassador." Pearl stood, lowering her child to her side, who watched Connie with huge eyes—a sweet girl with golden skin and dark hair. Looking sleepy while clutching at a stuffed teddy, she wore pink pajamas.

"What's your name, angel?" Connie directed her question at the kid.

The girl looked up at her mom, who smiled down reassuringly.

"Aysha… and this is Shreddy." She dangled the raggedy bear in the air.

"Nice to meet you both. Do you like hot chocolate?"

Aysha nodded enthusiastically.

"Chantal will make you some—with marshmallows." Connie wanted to talk to Pearl without distraction—aside from Martin's broad form, which now took up space near the small window.

Chantal rose. "Are you going to be okay?" She directed her question at Pearl.

"I'll be fine. Don't give Aysha too much hot chocolate. I

don't want her wetting the bed when we eventually find a place to sleep."

"Can I have ten marshmallows?" Aysha asked Chantal eagerly.

"Oh Lordy—the impending sugar rush." Pearl rolled her eyes and called out to the kid. "Hey, Ladybug! Half a cup and a couple of marshmallows."

"Five!" Aysha splayed out her tiny fingers. "And I'm not a bug!"

"Three and you're my love bug."

Chantal nodded and led the now excited little girl from the room.

"Everything is a negotiation with that child." Pearl smiled tiredly.

As soon as the door closed, Connie got straight to the point. "What have you got my daughter involved in?"

"Madam Ambassador—"

"Sit."

"Ma'am—"

"I said, sit." Connie wasn't usually this short when it came to guests at the embassy, but she always trusted her instincts and Pearl's fear felt palpable. The prickling at the back of Connie's neck had her rounding Martin's table and taking a seat opposite the dark blonde.

"You're recently divorced." Connie didn't need a dossier on Pearl's public separation. It was common knowledge in Sri Lanka, thanks to the media and Pearl Bandara's former husband, a popular presidential candidate in the upcoming elections. Rajin Bandara—the Minister of Law and Order— was the people's favorite. However, the local media had vilified his American ex-wife despite her tireless work with Sri Lankan charities.

"From what I gather, this late-night meeting involves intel

on your ex-husband? Don't drag my embassy into a marital war."

"That's not why I'm here." Pearl rubbed her palms on her jeans. "I'm seeking protection."

"From Rajin Bandara?"

"Yes. Contrary to what the media says, we've had an amicable split, and secretly separated a long time ago but still lived together for the sake of Aysha. I only recently moved out."

"Why did you separate?"

"Rajin has a wandering eye and had many illicit affairs throughout our marriage."

"And you're still on friendly terms?" Connie raised her brows.

Pearl fidgeted—rubbing a now ringless finger. "We are— were. He makes a better friend than husband. And my perspective has changed in the last week."

Pounding pain in her left arm intensified, and Connie shifted to get comfortable before waving her other hand. "Go on."

Pearl swallowed before continuing. "Rajin gets Aysha on the weekends. We worked out an informal custody agreement. He loves her dearly, and I wanted her to spend time with her father. Two weeks ago, I picked her up on a Sunday, and later that evening, when I walked into Aysha's room, her backpack sat open beside her, and she played with an odd object. I bent to take a closer look and spotted a camcorder cassette. Aysha had jammed one of her Lego pieces into the spool. When I asked her where she got it from, she said, 'daddy's office.' From what I'd understood, she was playing hide and seek with the au pair, ran to his study, and hid under his desk. That's when Aysha found a hidden drawer."

"At his residence?"

"Yes."

"Where was Rajin?"

"When I asked, Aysha said that daddy went out. At first, I wasn't concerned. I told her that she couldn't bring daddy's things home to mommy and I brushed it off, intending to return the cassette. But I got to thinking about why he'd hide it away. I assumed it was a taped sex act with one of his lovers. He likes to tape himself." Pearl shifted uncomfortably.

"Would you like some water?" Martin opened up his bar fridge and when Pearl nodded, he handed her a bottle. They waited for her to take a sip and continue.

"I have an old camcorder in storage—in the spare room. One morning, in the early hours, I dug it out and watched the tape. The video is horrifying—I couldn't watch to the end."

Martin pulled up a chair beside Connie and spoke. "It's a tape from 2012. Rajin Bandara participated in the torture and murder of three victims. There's an hour's worth of footage. I've skimmed over the contents."

Connie rubbed her forehead and tried not to think of the victims or the impending shit-storm. "This was three years after the war ended?"

"Yes, ma'am—Madam Ambassador." Pearl's pale complexion spoke of the horrors on that tape.

Sri Lanka's 26-year-long civil war ended in 2009 and still cast a dark shadow over the diverse ethnic communities. Forty thousand civilians, were killed during the war, bringing the death toll to more than a hundred thousand from a population of around twenty million. And even though the civil war ended in 2009, not only did grievances remain unaddressed, but the covert torture of ethnic minorities had been an ongoing issue. Civilians dragged off the streets and shoved into unmarked vans were never seen again. Some that survived had escaped to India or the UK. A presidential candidate torturing prisoners would stir up old tensions and new conflicts.

Pearl continued with her story, and Connie hung on her next words.

"I needed to know if that was the only footage. It haunted me for days. This evening, I turned up at Rajin's home to drop off Aysha, but I'd left her at home with a friend. I told him that she felt ill and was in bed but that I'd like to chat about joint custody and our future if he became president. I brought along Rajin's favorite wine, and he invited me in for dinner." Pearl glanced nervously between Martin and Connie.

"Go ahead. Tell the ambassador what you told me."

"I drugged him."

Connie raised her brows.

"It wasn't a large amount—a sleeping tablet slipped into the wine."

"Drinking even one alcoholic beverage in combination with sleeping pills can be dangerous."

"I know. It was foolish, and I checked Rajin's breathing. I couldn't risk getting caught—not after seeing what he did to those poor men."

Rubbing her eyes, Connie encouraged Pearl to continue.

"When his staff had retired for the night, and he'd nodded off, I searched his office and found the drawer."

Martin pointed to a ziplock bag filled with cassettes on his desk. "She found the motherload."

"Have you checked any of them?" Connie twisted to face Martin.

"Yes. We need to sift through the footage, but from what I've seen so far, it's brutal."

For Martin—a seasoned soldier—to use that descriptor...

"Show me."

"Connie." He switched to an informal address, which indicated his concern.

"I need to know what we're dealing with." She picked up a

cassette noting a more recent date from three years back, taped to the device.

"They're all dated, which makes our job easier." Martin opened his hand, and she placed it in his palm, ignoring his warm touch. He placed it in a camcorder and fiddled with an RCA audio cable before pressing play.

Connie watched the video roll with growing horror and disbelief. Two men hung upside down—naked from a ceiling as three plain-clothed men beat them with batons. Finally, when they stopped, a fourth man stepped into the frame. Rajin carried a gasoline container. Kneeling, he poured the liquid into plastic shopping bags, stood, and tied a bag around one of the victim's heads.

Rage had Connie wanting to reach through the screen and stop the sick bastard; instead, she sat helplessly and watched.

"Wait a sec." Martin paused the footage and zoomed in on the second victim. "Do you recognize him?"

Connie blinked before sitting back in her chair. "Jeewana Cooray—the junior diplomat that went missing. He was from…"

"Mumbai." Martin leaned in. "The Indian diplomat walked out of a UN General Assembly meeting after challenging Sri Lankan policy on further disenfranchisement among minority Tamil groups."

Although his later disappearance had made global news, Connie hadn't been assigned to Sri Lanka at the time and hadn't followed the story as closely as she should have.

"Did they ever find his body?" Martin swung to his laptop.

"I'm not sure." Connie shook her head in disbelief. "Your ex-husband is a monster."

Pearl nodded. "I didn't know what to do and contacted Chantal because of her U.S. diplomatic connections; she's the only friend I can trust. But when he discovers what I've done. I have to protect my daughter."

Connie considered her options. "You'll be handled by ACS —American Citizen Services. We'll get you back to the States, which is where I assume you'd like to be?"

"I haven't been home in so long. I met Rajin six years ago while on vacation. We married that same month. Rajin will want Aysha; he'll search for her. Oh, my God!" Pearl stood and paced. "He has both her American and Sri Lankan passports."

"ACS will sort out her travel documents," Martin volunteered.

"And then what? Rajin was the Inspector General of Police before he became the Minister of Law and Order. He has connections! With this evidence, his presidential aspirations are dead in the water. What I've done—in his eyes—is unforgivable. He will find us, and if he doesn't kill me, he'll take Aysha, and I'll never see her again."

"I can't assign a protection detail." It wasn't standard protocol for non-diplomats, and Connie could land in hot water. Especially with the upcoming fight on her hands.

"But I can." Martin acknowledged Connie's confusion with a reassuring smile. "Not in a formal capacity. Agent Torres is returning to the States tonight." Martin smiled reassuringly at Pearl. "He's a Diplomatic Security—DS—agent who's finished with TDY. He's highly trained in security and combat and also Former Special Forces."

Pearl frowned. "What's TDY?"

"Temporary duty. Agent Torres flew over to fill in for a colleague on emergency leave." Let me talk with him and see if he's willing to accompany you back to the States. He's heading to DC in a few days—perhaps we can shift up his flight."

"Martin, we do not involve our people." Connie stood and flexed her aching fingers.

"Agent Torres won't be on company time. Mrs. Bandara and Aysha will be exfiled out of the country as soon as possible.

Rajin doesn't know where she is, and hopefully, he's still unaware of the deception."

"This stays between us—and carefully selected members of our team." Connie didn't want Pearl's blood on her hands. And Chantal was now involved. The thought of her daughter getting hurt had Connie tensing, causing her to wince. Her damn shoulder.

"Connie, are you okay?" Martin stepped forward.

Cursing her rare display of weakness, she nodded and turned for the door. Striking out, she re-established boundaries. "Watch your address, Agent Roberts."

"My apologies, Madam Ambassador."

Ignoring his resigned tone, she opened the door and turned to Pearl. "Good luck. We'll get you to safety." And Connie would be left to deal with the fallout. Because she refused to let a psychopathic brute like Rajin Bandara rule the fragile country she'd grown to love. He'd pay for his veiled murdering sprees—she'd see this to the end.

Three months later.
Colombo, Sri Lanka.

G age Hendrix headed across the soft sand with his friend and teammate, Jason Webb. They carried food and paper cups from the nearby street stall and slowed as they reached the rest of his MSD team. The sun hadn't yet topped the horizon, and aside from a few fishermen, the beach lay quiet.

"Wakey, wakey. Eggs and Bakey." Gage kicked the prone body stretched out on the dunes. "We leave you for five minutes, and you're already snoozing."

Gannon sat up and yawned, running a hand through shaggy blond hair. "Fucking jet lag is already kicking my ass. I'm not a Spazmanian Devil, like you." He glanced at the watch on his muscled wrist as Jason walked to the other men at the shoreline. "And you were gone for twenty minutes, bro."

Gage passed his Deputy Team Leader a cup. "Stop

whining like a girl. You're on a beach in Sri Lanka, and we're staying at a sweet-ass hotel." Gage thought back to their previous deployment. "We could be back in Lagos in those prefab barracks."

"Hell to the no." Gannon took a sip and grimaced. "This is tea."

"Sri Lankan tea, which is good stuff. You had enough coffee on the plane."

"You can never have enough coffee."

Gage handed him an egg hopper and grinned at the raised brows.

"What is this?" Gannon asked.

"Hoppers are savory crepes made with rice and coconut milk—like a taco. And they drop a soft boiled egg in the middle." Gage dug into his breakfast.

"Is it spicy?"

"No, dude. C'mon." Gage wiped his chin with a napkin.

"I hear everything is spicy on this island. You know I don't do chilies or curries."

Yeah—Gage knew. He'd served with Gannon for many years. They'd both first worked as U.S. Marine Division Recon operators before retiring and joining Homeland Security. Now, they operated as specially trained Diplomatic Security Special Agents in an elite tactical unit, known as the Mobile Security Division, or MSD.

Looking down at his best mate, Gage smiled. They were similar in personality and yet physically different. Gage rubbed at his dark, short hair. He hated dealing with thick, wavy hair in this damp heat—it was a lot to handle while focusing on the job. Less time in front of the mirror meant more time in the field.

Gannon, on the other hand, encouraged his shaggy growth which made him look like bloody Conan, the Adventurer. Both men were tall bastards, but Gannon was built like an ox and had gained even more meat in the last month. Gage, on the other hand, preferred to pack on leaner muscle and was known for speed and agility in the field.

"Eat up, bud. We should already be heading to the embassy. It's going to be a long-ass day. We have that briefing at nine." Gage sat beside his large friend, settling in the sand, and watched the rest of the team shoot the shit down the beach.

"The new medic is a knife guy—from Vegas." Gannon directed his nod at the bearded operator who wolfed down his breakfast, ignoring the waves dampening his boots.

"You're from Vegas."

"The hell I am! Carson City ain't Sin City." Gannon looked briefly offended before switching his attention back to the new guy. "Earlier, he waved a custom Benchmade knife around like it was a machete. He has 550 rope cord in his pocket, which he's been slicing up. Let's ignore the serial killer vibe. What's his name again?"

"Kohen Block." Gage watched the man's every move. They'd met the new agent on Sri Lankan soil after their previous medic resigned to take care of an ailing father. "And I'm pretty sure he has a collection of machetes and multi-tools stashed away. I hear he throws knives."

"I prefer a firearm. You can't 'Block' a bullet or bring a knife to a gunfight." Gannon stood. "Aside from your sweet-ass Ka-Bar." He pointed at Gage's vintage combat knife clipped to his belt. "Now that's a knife."

"Hands off my blade. I'll kick your heavy ass."

"Yeah, yeah." Gannon cupped his mouth and yelled at the medic. "Hey! Blockhead? Do you love on your big guns as you do on your pointy sticks?"

Everyone laughed, and the bearded agent looked pissed. Gannon had a big mouth—like Gage. Thanks to their wild ways, they were both known as troublemakers in diplomatic circles, but they also got the job done.

Rising, Gage signaled to the team. "Let's rollout. The sun is up, and we have shit to do."

Over the roar of the surf, Gage heard someone yell his name. The team turned and faced a fit, older man walking towards them from the Royal Marine Inn.

"I pull up at your hotel... and the first thing I see is my security guys playing lifeguards on the beach. Where's your fancy bathing suit, boy?"

"Ah, shit," Gage swore softly and headed Martin's way. It had been a year since he'd seen the man who'd been like an uncle to him—more of a father for nineteen years. Back in the day, Martin had been dating Gage's aunt, and he'd taken the twelve-year-old kid under his wing after Gage's father had committed suicide. Gage owed Martin his life. His loyalty. His love. For now, he'd settle on not fucking up their first deployment together. In the four years that Gage had worked DSS and MSD, Gage and Martin never worked the same deployment in the same country. Until now.

"We were about to head your way." Gage walked ahead to greet the only person—aside from his teammates—who mattered in his world.

The men hugged, and Martin smiled as he punched Gage in the arm. "Good to see you, son. I hear you're still rabble-rousing."

Gage shrugged. "I take after the old man."

Martin dropped his smile and squeezed Gage's shoulder. "Never. You're a great team leader with a stellar reputation."

"He's the golden boy!" Jason stepped up beside them and Gage shook his head at the MSD nickname which he'd earned, due to his lightly colored amber eyes.

"Thanks to Gage, we haven't had a training mission yet." The general rule of thumb in the world of MSD was that if a team leader had a good reputation, his team got better assignments. A weak team leader meant they'd be stuck with training missions, which were no fun.

Martin smiled proudly at Gage. "How have you been? Are we doing Christmas this year?"

"Depends where we are."

Gage's MSD deployments and the long assignments that Martin served weren't conducive to family life.

To say that Gage loved his job was an understatement. Team Five—his six-man team of Special Agents worked in high-threat environments, serving to protect members of the U.S. Federal Government and their families. Fighting terrorism on foreign soil, protecting consulates and embassies, and evacuating U.S. citizens were par for the course for a well-run MSD Team.

His highly trained, heavily armed agents focused on dignitary protection and security operations. They specialized in hostage situations, civil wars, political coups and securement after terrorist attacks.

"I hear this might be a complicated mission."

"Sensitive politics in an unstable pre-election environment." Martin sobered. "Let's head to the embassy, and I'll brief your team."

Gage took one last look at the rising sun—a red ball on a misty gray horizon. A storm brewed to the north, and he shook off an ill sense of sudden foreboding as he headed for their transport.

The MSD men waited in the briefing room for Martin and his RSO team to join them. Happy to be in an air-conditioned facility—deep in the bowels of the embassy, Gage powered up the basic cellphone and tossed the packaging at the trash can.

"Ya missed, bro." Gannon grinned and threw his empty box in the same direction. "New guy cleans up the mess."

Kohen shrugged and stood. Local comms were crucial in the field. MSD agents couldn't miss a beat when it came to enabling varying and reliable devices. After the briefing, they'd check weapons and their kit, which always remained at the embassy unless in use.

"So, what's the deal?" Kohen tidied up their mess. "We're playing babysitter for 'Chanel Five?'"

"Chantal. Her name is Chantal, and we'll get the lowdown in ten." Gage eyed the newer agent, not liking his conde-scending tone or the nickname.

The medic lowered his voice. "I hear she follows her mama around like a lamb... hangs with the locals... gets to travel for free."

"And if the Anaconda hears you disrespecting her daugh-ter, she'll nail your balls to the wall." Gannon popped a stick of gum in his mouth.

Ambassador Durant was known in diplomatic circles as the Anaconda—for a good reason. Rumored to latch onto an adversary and squeeze them into submission, whether through diplomacy or sheer willpower, Connie Durant never gave up. Gage admired her tenacity and fairness in the field and looked forward to meeting her. Over the years, she'd earned great respect, and he'd heard she was up for the Regional Director role.

Martin entered, followed by what Gage assumed was either the Deputy RSO or an ARSO—an Assistant Regional Secu-rity Officer. The men stood and shook hands as Martin made introductions, and the rest of his staff filed into the briefing space. Finally, Martin kicked off the meeting. The initial intel, centered around Pearl Bandara and her daughter, proved to be sobering, and Gage leaned forward. "Where are they now?"

"Back in the States. The human rights commission has

launched an investigation, and the overwhelming evidence of her ex-husband's past atrocities is in safe hands. Except Rajin Bandara has disappeared and has a vast network which is promoting his propaganda and dissent."

"Vast as in?" Gage asked.

"As in communities that will fight for him—why do you think we can't find the bastard. He's charming, persuasive, and focused on building his Robin Hood persona. Vast as in a suspected private army of thousands. His cohorts claim that he is hiding because the Americans are spreading lies and fabricating the evidence, and he's 'afraid for his life.' We've underestimated his loyal following, which now includes radicals willing to go to war to protect their benevolent leader. They've made threats against the ambassador."

Gannon waved a pen. "Ambassador Durant has her own MSD team in place—Team Three—they arrived a few days ago."

"Correct." Martin picked up a remote control as the projector flickered to life. "But her daughter, Chantal Durant, is a concern. They've named Chantal as a target. She's of particular focus due to her relationship with Pearl."

"In what way?" Gage rubbed his fingers along his forehead as he zeroed in on the details of his mission.

"They're good friends and have worked together in Colombo at the Confianca Recovery Center. Chantal is a chiropractor who volunteers her services and works with the disabled—war victims and the likes. Pearl Bandara is—was—a prime investor in the center."

"How does this relate to Miss Durant's safety?" Gage asked.

"Pearl contacted Chantal for help the night she 'disappeared.' It's become clear that Rajin wants to find his daughter and 'traitorous' ex-wife and knows about Chantal's involvement in helping Pearl. On two occasions, shady characters have swung by the recovery center looking for Chantal."

"Why doesn't she remain at the embassy until this dies down? Or she could fly back to the States?" Jason steepled his hands before cracking his knuckles.

"It's complicated. She won't leave the ambassador's side. They're both involved in raising funds for mine clearance and amputees. Chantal refuses to back down or accept help."

"Don't you have a local police escort?"

"Yes. Except we're not sure if the local guards are trustworthy, and implying that they aren't or removing the detail, could cause political repercussions. We've already swapped out her local detail. Rajin is—was—the Minister of Law and Order and owns the police—has police chiefs and officers on his payroll."

The communicated intel had Gage worrying his bottom lip. They'd be tiptoeing through a mafia minefield in a perfect storm. He didn't want to fuck with local law enforcement, but if they interfered with Chantal Durant—his assigned principal...

His head began to pound, and Gage asked the million-dollar question. "What happened to warrant an MSD detail for the daughter?"

Martin pressed the remote, and a choppy video appeared, which looked to be from a cellphone in a market.

"This was filmed by a British tourist in the vicinity. Two days ago, during her lunch break, Chantal, along with a fellow volunteer, visited a local market. The local officers assigned to her protective detail conveniently disappeared as two men accosted the girls. We've had the guards fired and investigated. Both women fought back. Chantal and her friend both know the basics of self-defense."

Gage watched as a hooded man tried to strong-arm the ambassador's daughter. The bruiser twisted Chantal's arm as she kicked at his knee. She hit the mark. The second man appeared to shove her blonde friend away, who punched out with what seemed to be a brutal uppercut—Gage couldn't tell as the shaky image bobbed from side to side. Their attackers lost time and locals leaped to the women's defense. Both bastards broke past the crowd and made a run for it.

"Have they been identified or caught?" Lucius asked.

Gage glanced over at the MSD agent who asked the question. Lucius Jones was the quietest member on Team Five. A tall black man built like Hercules. His talent—aside from being a deadly agent in the field—was language and dialect.

All the team members spoke a variety of languages, which was par for the course as a DSS or MSD agent, but Lucius had a real knack for learning quickly in the field and won over the locals on most assignments.

"Not yet. Facial recognition on the little we have isn't working, but we'll persist."

Someone knocked on the door, and a young woman entered, followed by the ambassador. The team jerked to their feet as the ambassador greeted the room and introduced her assistant and her Chief of Staff. Gage knew that Ambassador Durant's embassy team rivaled some of the best on the planet. Connie Durant replaced section chiefs with foreign service veterans. Slowly pulling some of the best talent from various embassies around the world took skill.

The ambassador took a seat, adjusting her black jacket as everyone resettled. Gage noticed that she favored her left side ever so slightly, and he thought back to what he knew of her history. Before he could continue his musings, she pinned him with a direct glare.

"Mr. Hendrix. I specifically requested Team Five, as I've heard good things about your actions in the field. I've also heard that you occasionally take risks, and so far, they've paid off. Tell me that I'm making the right decision when it comes to my daughter's safety."

"Yes, Madam Ambassador. We'll do everything we can to protect Chantal Durant. But my advice is that she should be heading across the globe to the States until this blows over."

The ambassador smiled. "The Durants are built of sterner stuff, and I admire Chantal's determination and commitment to the cause. I've spoken with her, and she will remain by my side while we negotiate these troubled waters. The Bandara investigation is a temporary situation. Once the authorities capture Rajin and he answers for his crimes, life will return to normal."

"Madam—"

"We're dealing with a cornered coward, and the political repercussions of his actions are containable. Chantal's new local protection detail will remain in place and work alongside your team. If they step out of line, you're running the show."

"Will she be a cooperative principal?"

"Chantal will listen. At the moment, she's angry and scared for Pearl and her child. They worked closely together for almost a year."

Gage flipped through the intel on an iPad. "In two weeks, there's a two-day trip scheduled to Hatton. That's hill country, right? Amongst the tea plantations?"

"Yes. There will be a delegation from the U.S. Department of State's Office of Weapons Removal and Abatement. We've planned the exo-kinetic and mine clearance symposium. That's non-negotiable. Chantal has worked in tandem with our embassy to bring awareness to both projects."

"Which are?" Gannon asked.

"Working with amputees and participating in de-mining efforts. There are still regions in Sri Lanka covered in land-mines. And these hidden dangers injure civilians every year. Along with Martin's department, Team Five will prep for the event. I won't stop working with communities and performing as ambassador unless I have no other choice."

Gage closed the open e-file. "We'll start with surveillance. I want to follow your daughter and her assigned local team and note their patterns. Usually, this takes a couple of weeks. I'll probably need three days, which gives a starting point in identifying weak areas and individuals in her first layer of protection, while at the same time, keeping an eye on Miss Durant."

"Should I let Chantal know that we're watching her detail?"

"No." Martin cut in. "Miss Durant will be added to the loop when Gage's team has made their assessment. The Colombo police bodyguards are decently trained, and I hand-picked them myself and added an additional detail."

They continued with the briefing, breaking down the logistics and expectations. Martin handed over a file on Chantal Durant.

Gage tuned out the room chatter as he flipped through the thin file, pausing on a couple of photographs of Chantal. Placing the driver's license aside, he picked up the second photo of her dressed in a summer dress. She sat in a hammock chair and smiled at the camera.

Her straight brown hair cut into a bob cut, sat an inch above her shoulders, and added to an understated beauty. Deep dimples creased her cheeks. Despite her upturned mouth, her large brown eyes held a darkness that Gage had rarely seen on a civilian's face. There was something in the way she sat—a discomfort and uncertainty which seemed out of place in the beach setting.

Gage looked up and met the ambassador's direct gaze.

"She's the spitting image of her father." Her lips twisted, and she glanced at the photo in his hand.

Aside from high cheekbones and her chin, Chantal looked nothing like her mother.

"We'll keep her safe."

The ambassador nodded. The meeting turned to the Local Guard Program and local resources. When the meeting finally wrapped, the men headed out to grab lunch. The heated air bounced off the street, and Gage's neck immediately dampened with perspiration.

"I hope the mother/daughter dynamic isn't going to complicate this mission."

Gage turned to Lucius, surprised that he'd picked up on the same anomalies. "I need more intel—a rundown on our principal. I'll speak to Martin." Gage stayed away from complexity—both in life and on the job. And had a feeling that they may have stumbled across Pandora's Box.

4

———————

C hantal couldn't shake the feeling of being watched as she climbed into the back of the suburban. It had been a long day, and her feet ached. Thanks to skipping lunch and only having an apple for breakfast, her stomach protested. Exhaustion ate away at her mood, but she forced a smile and greeted her local bodyguards.

The workday wasn't over, and as soon as she got home, she'd change out of her jeans into her sweats. Pulling out a thick customized planner, Chantal scribbled an observation from her last appointment and chose a colored sticker from the back as a reminder for a follow-up.

Consistency and self-discipline were both key when offering quality chiropractic services. Only she was in charge of what filled her treatment space and took up her valuable time. Lives were made-up of pattern and routine, and she refused to spend her days on insignificant habits.

Kirk, the DS Agent in Charge—referred to in diplomatic circles as the AIC—closed her door before climbing in the front. Like on all protection details, he sat adjacent to the driver, and she sat in the passenger seat directly behind him.

The AIC was the only American diplomat on the detail—standard protocol. His job was to manage every aspect of the protective security operation. Her local guards took orders from the AIC.

As they pulled off, Kirk twisted around and shot her a smile. Chantal rolled her eyes as she placed the sticker beside the patient's name. "Kirk the Flirt" was competent at his job but a skirt chaser. And not her kind of skirt chaser. He thought he was smooth and funny. Women thought differently. Ignoring her American colleague, Chantal engaged with the local lead guard who sat behind the wheel. Over the past week, she'd gotten to know Dishan, and it gave her an excuse to practice her Sinhalese while asking after his wife's pregnancy.

Chantal switched to using some of the local language. "Dishan, how was Priya's vaidyavaraya visit? What did the doctor say? How is the baby?"

"Kicking like a footballer and due any day." The big man grinned.

"You want a…" Chantal paused to think of the word as she packed her planner in the laptop bag. "Bolaya—ball— kicker? I thought you wanted a cricket player." Leaning forward, she poked Dishan in the arm as he slowed down a narrow lane.

"My kid will be the best cricket player in all of Sri Lanka!"

"Of course." Chantal laughed. "What does Priya want?"

"A computer nerd… so he can make plenty of money for his mama."

Glancing through the windshield, Chantal's smile froze as a black van drove into their path, blocking the road. Two bikes pulled up on either side of the suburban. The men wore all black, their faces masked by helmets.

Slamming on the brakes, Dishan yelled at her to get down as her guards jostled to draw their weapons. Someone shoved her to the floor, and Chantal strained her neck to see what was happening. The thought of being trapped and ambushed in a side street had her heart pounding and her hands gripping the back of the front seat.

Glancing up, she saw a biker pull away. And they were moving again, almost too fast as Dishan punched the accelerator, speeding through the suburbs.

"Where's the black van?" Chantal yelled as Dishan rounded a corner, and her head slammed into a guard's shin. "How did we get past the van?"

"We didn't!" Kirk replied, his voice tense. "It reversed out of our path."

"Are they following us?" The glimpse of huge trees lining the roadway indicated that they'd entered the Cinnamon Gardens. The exclusive suburb housed numerous embassies, high commissions, the Prime Minister's Office, the town hall, and museums.

"Not that we can see. Stay down. It may have been nothing."

Chantal complied. Only once they were in the safety of the Jefferson House—aka, the ambassador's massive home—did she rise shakily from the floor. Her black t-shirt stuck to a damp back, and she straightened the soft fabric before letting out a relieved breath as she watched the entry gates close behind them.

The mansion held sheltering strength, and Chantal loved the historic residence. Built in 1914, it was once the home of the judge of the Supreme Court of Ceylon. The United States bought the house in 1948. Surrounded by lush trees and sweeping lawns, the stately white mansion had an understated grace that warmed her heart.

Dishan helped her from the car. The driveway gates swung back open and his grip tightened. The sound of motorbikes had her turning. To her horror, two familiar bikes rolled down the private lane, followed by the black van.

Dishan pulled her behind the suburban and reached for his side arm.

"They're MSD. Take your hands off your weapons." Martin walked down the steps as the unknowns pulled alongside her detail.

"What the hell is going on?" Kirk stood to his full height as Martin crossed his arms.

"Let's head inside for a debrief."

"This is ridiculous and—"

"Now, Kirk. That's not a request."

Chantal couldn't take her eyes off her would-be attackers. The bikers shed their helmets as four other men climbed from the van. They all looked hardened and competent—almost brutal. Were these the men guarding her mother? Team Three? Chantal had heard that an MSD team had flown out to Sri Lanka to protect her mom, although Chantal hadn't had a chance to meet them—over the last week, her mother's late schedule kept her at the embassy till after dark.

Chantal had heard all about MSD. Within the DS world, they were the "meat pounders," who left delicate diplomacy to the rest of DS. MSD agents were brawny, heavy hitters that swept in at the last minute to rescue or annihilate.

One of the men pinned her with a piercing stare—like a glowing blade digging deep. Unlike the cold, hard look of his comrades, his narrowed gaze sparked along her skin like an inferno. Chantal's chest contracted, and she looked away.

What the hell was going on? Anger replaced fear as she pocketed her trembling hands.

Her face grew warmer with each step, and by the time she crossed over a heavy Persian carpet and entered the meeting room through an ornate glass and wooden door, Chantal was ready for a fight. Kirk beat her to it.

"Can you explain why MSD agents decided to fucking ambush us on the way back to the embassy? Or should this be a conversation for the ambassador? Her daughter almost got caught in the crossfire."

"That wouldn't have happened." The agent with the feral, copper-colored gaze smiled at Chantal. "Team Leader, Gage Hendrix for Team Five."

Team Five? Another MSD team? Her mother already had plenty of protection. Ignoring his inviting energy, Chantal folded her arms. Gage Hendrix retreated and took a seat in front of the antique-lead windows, which looked out onto lush gardens. He rolled his shoulders—his muscled shoulders that matched sinewy arms and a GI Joe head. His easygoing arrogance mirrored the rest of his team, all who found amusement in Kirk's discomfort.

"Let's talk this out." Martin pulled out an ornate chair. Chantal shook her head—too wired and needing to walk off residual adrenaline. Dishan also remained standing and took his place beside her in a gesture of silent support.

The MSD team leader spoke, his honeyed eyes flaring as he addressed her security detail. "You took the exact route as the day before. Three days in the same week."

Kirk sneered and leaned forward. "Not every day—"

Dishan spoke up. "Thanks to closures in the city due to roadworks, I alternated between two routes. But Agent Hendrix is right—that is no excuse."

"Dishan…" Chantal frowned, and he placed a hand on her arm.

"I made a mistake—one that could have cost your life."

"And you chose not to use a variable time system. Miss Durant leaves the center at the same time every day?" A sizeable blond agent, built like a Boabab tree, asked.

"I do not."

"You did this week."

Chantal cut in, "If you're here to train personnel then—"

"Not here to train… we're joining your detail." The fierce

team leader stood and walked to her side, extending his hand while pinning her with that gleaming stare. "And I know you're on the defensive, but our goal is to keep you safe."

~

Gage didn't like her pallor and knew the stunt they'd pulled probably shook her up some. Good. She needed to be a receptive survivor—on top of her game. Her perfume drifted, and he wondered at the familiar notes, picking up a woodsy scent with a creamy coconut vibe. Why did it smell so addictive?

Finally, she took his hand. His rough fingers gripped her cool palm, and he felt a tremble. He was the cause. Squashing a sliver of guilt, he smiled reassuringly. A firm grip from a put-together beauty with incredible skin and glossy hair and Gage tried to find a flaw in her armor.

And there it was—all in the eyes. She'd never be a good poker player—those large, chocolate-brown eyes held galaxies worth of intel. He released his grip and stepped back. Folding her arms, she backed up against the wall, looking paler than before.

"That stunt could've ended badly," Kirk pushed, and Lucius snorted.

"It took fifteen seconds for us to make our point and retreat." Lucius scratched his arm. "We watched you for a few days and knew you weren't tactically ready to unleash a defense. What happened to your surveillance and detection skills, Kirk?"

Gage knew of the agent's reputation in diplomatic circles. Kirk was a good agent but easily distracted. They'd now seen this first-hand.

"I'm reassigning you, Kirk," Martin said, and they engaged in a back and forth. The AIC threw out one justification after another, his face flushed in frustration. There were plenty of

DS agents to take his place. The man had no excuse. He'd been neglecting his principal—playing with his phone and disappearing to the market instead of sticking by Miss Durant's side. Gage had already submitted his report on the agent's performance to Martin. His next task was to get to know Chantal Durant's local bodyguards and create a working relationship. Naturally, they were now defensive; an easy challenge to overcome.

Gage hadn't yet returned to his seat, and when the ambassador's daughter swayed and pitched sideways, he lunged to catch her.

"Chantal!" Martin jerked to his feet as Gage guided her to the nearest chair. Her face held no color, and her body shook as she dropped her head between her knees.

"I'm fine…" She weakly raised a hand, which Gage caught.

"This is Kohen—the medic on the team."

Kohen took her wrist from Gage to check her vitals.

"Did you skip lunch again?" A local guard—Dishan Farook —crouched down beside her. "You're pushing yourself too hard. You have to take breaks."

Gage frowned, knowing she spent a lot of her time in the center. But, from what he'd noted, she arrived around 0800 and left at 1700—a typical workday. Gage asked Gannon to locate the kitchen to grab a sugary drink and a snack from the fridge.

"How much sleep did you get?" Martin asked.

Her shoulders rose and fell.

"Chantal?"

"Three hours. It was a rough night."

"You can't operate on three hours."

"I've worked on less."

Okay—now Gage felt thoroughly confused. From what he'd understood, she was a chiropractor that only saw her

patients during the day. She spent her nights at the ambassador's residence. So why wasn't she sleeping?

"You need at least five." Martin moved closer. "I'll talk to
her."

She raised her head and grabbed Martin's wrist. "No.
Please don't. Mom always comes first."

"Can you fill me in?" Gage addressed the RSO as Gannon
handed Chantal a Fanta Orange and a banana. Reluctantly
removing his hand off her shoulder, Gage followed Martin out
into the entrance hall.

"Is she working at night? Is there a second job—"

"She looks after her mother." Martin must've seen the
confusion on Gage's face. "Did you read the file I sent you?"

"I planned to look over it tonight."

"It has all the answers."

"Wait—she looks after the ambassador? I don't understand."

"Ambassador Durant lives with chronic pain and can't
sleep at night. Chantal works with her mother's extensive nerve
damage in the early evening hours through massage. That's her
essential role and the reason she became a chiropractor and
medical massage therapist. That, including PTSD, are why
some nights are worse than others. Some nights the ambassador can't sleep and wants her daughter by her side."

"PTSD from what?"

Kohen joined them. "She's improved, but I'd still like to
take her to the embassy clinic."

Martin nodded. Chantal appeared behind the medic, the
half-eaten peeled banana in her hand. "I'm feeling better—I'm
heading for my cottage." She stepped past the men with her
laptop bag, and walked to the rear of the mansion.

"God, she's stubborn." Martin shook his head.

"I'll watch over her." Gage backed down the passage. "I'll
be back in ten for the rest of the briefing."

Gage's pulse picked up as he approached the attractive female who now descended onto a lawn. The CMR—Chief of Mission Residence—was a beautiful estate. Gage hadn't had a chance to take in the grand surroundings, which now sat in the darkening night.

"Can I take your bag?"

"Nope."

"Are you sure you're okay?"

Nodding her head, Chantal popped the last of the banana in her mouth. Gage trailed after her along a pebbled path to a small building that sat near an elegantly lit pool, picking up her calm scent fanning out on a warm breeze.

He'd never got tongue-tied around a woman but couldn't think what to say. Instead, he tried not to breathe in her familiar fragrance. He was here to do a job—Get up to speed and keep the ambassador's daughter safe.

"Hendrix. That's your last name?"

"Yes, ma'am."

"Gage Hendrix?"

"At your service."

"I know how to find my cottage…"

"Yes, ma'am."

She paused and turned. "So, you can run back to your badass team."

"If you faint and spend the evening under some bush, your mother will fire my badass team."

She shot him a narrow-eyed glare. "Doubtful. My health isn't your concern."

"The next time two men attack you in a market, I'll need you to be fit and able enough to follow instructions."

"That was nothing—hooligans harassing a couple of women. It happens."

"You believe that? Then why did they leave bruises?" Gage

raised his brow at the fading yellowed finger marks on her upper arm.

Chantal covered the discoloration with her other hand. "Don't you have somewhere to be? A CrossFit class, perhaps? Am I keeping you from drinking napalm and eating nails with your buddies?"

He tried not to smile. "I only drink napalm in the morning... and nails give me reflux. I prefer snacking on drill bits."

"Har-dee-har. Funny man." After folding her arms, she shoved her hands in her back pockets.

He made her nervous. Interesting. Gage knew that MSD agents could be an intimidating lot—their alpha energy and tactical intensity was hard to miss in ordinarily sedate diplomatic circles. MSD teams rolled in to deal with violence and chaos and didn't always play nice.

He also acknowledged the spark of attraction. It was the first time he'd felt the pull in the field, and it didn't mean he would act on the chemistry. Gage would strive to do the opposite.

Besides, they came from different planets, and Gage was pretty sure he'd see her entitlement at some point. Miss Durant was born into money. He'd heard that her mother owned five properties in both Europe and the States.

Gage rented a crappy apartment in Virginia and hadn't figured out where he belonged. Real estate was the last thing on his mind. Doing his job right—that's all that mattered.

The earthy night air felt close and smelled like the tropical flora that surrounded them.

"How often do you exercise anyway? I'm sure you guys have a heavy routine."

"We do. When not on duty—by your side—I work out twice a day, in the morning and evening."

"I need to shower." She stepped onto a verandah filled with

plants. Their white ceramic pots perfectly arranged in size and in a neat line.

"Are these yours?" He fingered a chili plant and recognized a few of the herbs.

"Oui, ils sont mes plantes. I enjoy gardening, although I don't technically have a yard—I make do. It motivates me to cook more of the local foods."

Gage noted the French interjection which didn't align with her standard American accent.

"You like Sri Lankan cuisine?"

"Some—many dishes. I enjoy curries and seafood." She pulled a set of keys from the front pocket of her computer bag. The dangling key tag read, "Edit Your Life!"

"Me too... although I've only just arrived, so I haven't had a chance to sample much."

"Well... thanks for your concern and unneeded guidance. Have a good night, Agent Hendrix."

"Gage... It's easier to call me Gage." Why did he say that? *Jesus.*

She didn't say anything, just unlocked her door.

"What time are you heading out tomorrow?"

"Seven-thirty. I want to be in my office by eight."

Gage stepped back on to the path as she closed the door. The talk of curry had him craving a solid meal. After the rest of their meeting, a workout session and dinner in Colombo with the guys sounded perfect. Three days of close surveillance would switch over in the morning to their new role as body-guards. They still had work to do before they could rest for the night.

Later that evening, Gage and Gannon returned to their brightly painted hotel room. Gage shifted aside a basket of fruit and sat at the small wooden table before powering up his laptop. It only took him a minute to access the file Martin had sent. Yawning, he began to scroll through the history before pausing. Gage read over every detail before leaning closer.

Gannon emerged from the bathroom in a pair of board shorts and pulled open the fridge. "My shoulders are killing me. Those lateral plank walks and Hindu push-ups are insane."

Gage rolled a sore neck. "Yeah, well. Jet lag is no longer an excuse. Exercise your ass off, or you're off the team."

"Cranky much? What's up, man?"

"Did you know about the assassination twelve years ago?"

"The what?"

"I knew the ambassador was a widow… that her husband had been murdered, but I've never paid much attention to diplomatic gossip."

"Bud, what are you talking about?" Gannon pulled out a chair and handed over a water.

"Where were we, twelve years ago? My first deployment meant that I was growing testicular fortitude in the Ghan."

"Me too." Gannon chuckled. "For those first couple of years, I lived and breathed sand, sun, and gunpowder."

In Afghanistan, Gage had been doing the same—he hadn't paid much attention to developing news in the States. Glancing up from the screen, he elaborated, "A sniper shot her parents— in front of Chantal. Her father died instantly."

"You mean, in front of 'Miss Durant.'"

Gage waved a hand. "That's what I meant. The ambassador sustained a shoulder and back injury. Two of their bodyguards died protecting Chant—Miss Durant and her mother."

"The shooter tried to take out the whole family. Damn. But wait—Ambassador Durant wasn't an ambassador at the time?"

"Nope. She'd resigned as a desk officer and was about to take an assignment as a Deputy Economic Counselor—only just getting her diplomatic feet wet." Gage scrolled down. "Her husband was a business tycoon. A freaking billionaire. Yet she chose to be a career member of the foreign service and refused to use his influence to get ahead."

"Did they catch the sniper?"

"Yeah. Otto Kivela—a Finnish assassin. It was a paid hit—they never found his client. He died three days after the arrest."

"Suicide?"

"No. Cancer."

"That's odd."

Gage frowned as he read through the information that Martin compiled. "Not common knowledge, but the ambassador has extensive and irreparable nerve damage from the shooting."

"She seems fine to me."

"Look carefully; she favors her left arm. She's had three nerve grafts." Gunshot wounds were a common cause of traumatic nerve injury. A high-velocity bullet from a sniper's rifle would create a massive amount of shock waves and cavitation effects—kinetic energy could be a bitch.

"Damn. And I'm guessing that her daughter helps her to manage the pain—the ambassador's caregiver."

Gage continued sifting through the new intel. His neck itched as he tried to piece together the history. He didn't like loose ends—which tended to fray and snag up a mission.

"Let's get some shut-eye." Gannon slapped Gage on the back. "This assignment has drama written all over it—in a bright red sharpie. From politics to family calamities, and we'll need to be on top of our game."

Heart pounding, Chantal fought against her damp sheets and sat up. The oppressive darkness had her reaching for her bedside lamp and she huffed out a shaky breath, scanning the empty room. She was safe in her secure cottage in Sri Lanka. Not in Colorado. Her trembling fingers drifted down to an old scar and Chantal fought the urge to cry. When would the nightmares end?

Her tears wouldn't change the past—bring back her father or take away her pain. Shoving aside the heartache, Chantal swung her feet to the floor, checked her phone and headed to the bathroom. Four in the morning—an earlier start than normal.

After splashing her face, she headed to the kitchen and poured a glass of milk. When last had she cleaned the pot cupboard? And her spice rack needed rearranging. Knowing she wouldn't go back to sleep, Chantal hunkered down and flipped open the cupboard door, eyeing the neatly stacked pots and pans. Perhaps she could arrange them by function instead of size.

Sitting her ass down, Chantal pulled out a saucepan and got to work. Her thoughts turned to her new MSD team. She hoped they didn't restrict her work movements and didn't get in her way at the treatment center. She now had way too much security. Not that feeling safe was a bad thing—especially looking back on her past. And MSD agents looked like hardened warriors who could slaughter an army. But still...

She worried over her detail's safety. Two good men had died sheltering her family and she'd never forget their faces. Chantal hadn't known them well and yet they'd thrown themselves into the line of fire, sacrificing their lives for their wealthy clients. Without a doubt, she knew that Agent Hendrix would do the same—die for his principal. The thought terrified Chantal.

Gage Hendrix wasn't the biggest man on his team, but he was definitely the most capable-looking. Tall and solid with a cocky confidence that almost seemed annoying. His valorous energy swirled like a restless snake and those light, bronzed eyes sliced into a person's soul. Chantal wondered if he had a wife or a girlfriend. Kids? He looked like he'd be a great father.

Her heart clenched and she placed a pan on the floor. Children weren't in Chantal's future and that complicated the hell out of her dating life. Should she even bother meeting men? Did she have time for dating? The clinic kept her busy and her patients came first.

A Swiss diplomat had shown interest and it might be nice to explore her options. All work and no play made for a dull existence. Granted, her dedication to the clinic would never falter, but she could carve out a little more time for her personal life. Which could be a challenge with a dozen guards trailing her every move.

Mind made-up, Chantal threw herself back into cleaning. A busy morning lay ahead.

5

Jona collapsed onto the sand and watched the sun rise. This early hour was perfect for a three-mile run. Aside from a few fishermen, the beach lay quiet—a solitary start to the day. Wiping a sweaty brow, Jona acknowledged failure by waiting too long to take out the mother and daughter. It had been twelve years, and Jona had completed fifty-two kills and never failed. Except once… while Papa watched.

Standing frozen on the sideline like a procrastinating fucker, waiting to complete this first mission. Why the delay? Because emotions fogged up this unfinished assignment, and Jona couldn't fail a second time. Between contracts, Jona had stalked the ambassador's daughter, aware that an assassin should never get too close to their target. Years had passed without action.

Chantal Durant had everything in life, and Jona actually liked the spoilt bitch. Chantal had her choice of men—falling over themselves to be with her. Yet, the prissy princess ignored the assholes and acted like Mother Teresa.

Jona would love to take the mother and daughter together in one glorious shooting spree—but that wouldn't happen.

They rarely traveled together—living separate lives. And the ambassador was well protected.

Who to kill first? That was the conundrum. After all these years, Jona didn't expect payment. This personal vendetta was a promise made to a dying father. Perhaps that contributed to Jona's hesitation.

Regardless, the time had come. Aside from killing with a rifle, there were many fun ways to commit murder, and Jona spent over a decade honing those skills with no footprint. That was the mark of a true assassin—never leaving a trace. But Jona wanted that strikethrough—to see the ambassador's brains exploding in a glorious scarlet celebration.

Timing was everything, and now that Chantal was a political target, it made Jona's job challenging but also a whole lot easier.

A local family ran past to the shoreline and before they got to the water, the concerned mother grabbed a toddler's hand before swinging the kid up in an embrace. That must be nice—to grow up with a mother who cares.

Shaking off bitterness, Jona glanced down the beach at the distant hotel which housed the embassy MSD teams. Soon it was time for breakfast and Jona craved grilled tomatoes with sweet chili eggs. Not quite done with the strict morning exercise routine, Jona stood. A swim was a refreshing way to start the day on a beautiful island.

Gage surveyed the parking lot as his men exited the suburban. Obviously feeling hedged in by her generous security detail, Chantal pulled out her keys as they approached the front doors.

"It's already eight-thirty," Chantal huffed.

They'd arrived later than expected this morning thanks to a

last-minute meeting with Martin and Wyatt, her new Agent in Charge.

"You don't have to all come in with me." Chantal glanced over her shoulder as she unlocked the door to the Confianca Recovery Center.

"Get used to it—and we're searching the premises first." Lucius took point, and her local detail, along with Team Five spread out while Gage remained by Chantal's side.

"Are you going to follow me into the changing rooms? Because I'm swapping into my scrubs."

"Let me check them out," Gage replied.

"The rooms or the scrubs? For the love of God."

"Rooms." He grinned. "Wait out here." He made her bristle—Gage didn't give a damn. He cleared the men's and the women's space and waved her in before stepping out.

There wasn't much luxury to the center. Customer-facing areas had received the most attention—painted in cheerful colors, and humble cotton curtains decorated the box-like windows. Aside from those few warm touches, it seemed adequately adapted to perform function. In contrast, the back rooms reserved for staff looked gray and economical.

He opened a closet and peeked inside at the neatly stacked supplies.

"Gage, would you like a tour? I'll explain what we do." Chantal stepped back into the hall, looking cute in scrubs. At least one of them felt comfortable—Gage was now geared up in battle rattle which included a combat helmet, body armor, and weaponry.

He watched as she re-fastened a hairpin. She'd also used his first name, and he wasn't sure how he felt about hearing it on her lips. Her softening of the second "g" felt inviting. No-one pronounced his name that way—if anything, they emphasized the "J" sound in "GAYJ."

"Well? I have five minutes before my first appointment."

"Um. Sure, ma'am."

She took off down the passage, and he easily kept up.

"Chantal—if you're going to shadow my every move, call me Chantal. I'm not technically a diplomat and hate anyone standing on ceremony. Tell the rest of your team."

"Is that an order?" Gage chuckled at her bossy bustle.

"It cuts down on the crap, and I suspect you're all about effortless exchanges."

He frowned but realized she was correct. Communication in the field needed to be to the point. Gage would accept her reasoning.

"We'll need to exchange numbers—in case we get separated in an emergency. Same goes with the rest of the team."

"Sure. This is my office. I share it with a Sri Lankan chiropractor who is currently up north. He'll meet us at the symposium next week. We have a waiting room and two examination—"

"Up north as in?" He glanced around the neat space which housed two desks. One held typical work clutter, and the other sat bare, with only a vase and a picture frame decorating the polished surface.

"As in Jaffna. He's treating old war injuries in the Tamal region."

"Will you be traveling there at all?" Gage instinctively knew which desk was hers and walked over to the neat desk with a framed photo. Her parents stood with her on a beach. Chantal looked so vibrant as a teenager, and her eyes held light and innocence.

"No, but I have in the past. It's one of the reasons why we opened this facility. Sri Lanka's civil war ended years ago, but many victims suffered permanent injuries from the conflict. We treat soldiers from both sides... victims of extremist attacks... civilians with extensive damage. Government soldiers receive assistant packages, but there aren't existing programs to help civilians or former Tamil Tigers. We're looking at around twenty thousand injuries in Tamil regions and forty thousand in total who are left maimed by fighting or bombings."

"Tamil Tigers?" Gage frowned. "They were a guerilla organization, notorious for carrying out suicide bombings and recruiting child soldiers."

"True. But nothing in this world is black and white. Tamil Tigers strong-armed villagers into joining the cause through terror campaigns. Many soldiers unwillingly fought with fear of repercussions. Families lives were threatened. Brainwashing was used on the young and by the end of the war, the organization was a corrupt extremist mess. In the beginning, the Tigers fought for Tamil independence, but in the end, the Tamil Tigers became desperate and thousands of soldiers deserted the cause. They escaped and tried to save their families from being massacred by both the government and the Tigers."

She headed back up the passage, and Gage followed. "This is our massage facility, where we work with injured muscles and nerve damage. We have three volunteer therapists."

"They don't get paid?"

"Not by patients. None of us want our patient's money. The Confianca Charity pays the staff a small salary—enough for living expenses." Chantal straightened a folded blanket. "Most patients are desperately poor, and the Confianca Recovery Center offers free care. Some have traveled long distances, and in those cases, we provide lodging and food while treating their injuries. The building next door is ours."

"That's impressive."

"It's hard work. Somedays, we have a line of patients that extend around the block. Especially in the wet season when their prosthetics rub blisters and the damp conditions aggravate arthritis."

"You work with amputees?"

"They make up the majority of our patients. Let me show you our prosthetics room and rehabilitation space." Chantal led him to the next room filled with exercise equipment and shelves packed with prosthetics of all shapes and sizes. "Sadly, many victims purchase their prosthetics, which means that they are wearing cheaply made limbs which cause endless complications—both from a chiropractic and dermatological perspective."

Gage's admiration grew for the conscientious woman who now picked up an artificial limb. The morning light reflecting through the hazy window softened her pretty features and highlighted a delicate collar bone. Despite her slight build, she looked fit—Gage guessed it had everything to do with the physical challenges of being a chiropractor.

"This is a decent transtibial prosthesis which replaces a leg below the knee—we're trying to build up a supply as this is the most common amputation due to landmines. Sorry—I could talk about this for hours."

"No—it's interesting—tremendously educational. Your passion is inspiring."

She looked down, with a sudden blush to her cheeks. Gage couldn't look away and waited till she met his stare. The static moment stunned his soul—crackling in the air. Her eyes flared with the same heat that warmed his blood.

"Your nine o'clock is here."

A tall blonde woman poked her head in the door, pulling Gage from the heady trance.

"And where do all these gladiators come from?" The girl grinned.

Chantal waved in her work colleague. "This is Gage. Alexis is my right-hand 'Wonder Woman.' She's been here for four months and turned this place on its head, covering while some local comrades have been away in the field."

"It wasn't just me—we had a great team—the three muske-teers. I miss Pearl."

"Me too."

"You're another American?" Gage smiled. The rest of the staff at the center were Sri Lankans—aside from these two women. "Where are you from?"

"Cali. But I like to see myself as a global pilgrim. I'm thinking of joining the Peace Corps."

"A noble choice."

"Alexis is acting modestly. She literally climbs mountains." Chantal smiled and for the first time, her dimples appeared—which should come with a warning. Sweeter than sugar and a strike to the heart.

"In my spare time." Alexis shrugged and leaned against the door.

"She climbed Everest! And Kilimanjaro."

Gage wasn't paying much attention—his focus was all on that pretty mouth. Fucking dimples.

"I didn't climb Everest." Alexis rolled her eyes at Chantal. "I reached Camp Three, and we had to descend due to bad weather."

"Still a huge accomplishment," Gage affirmed, mentally shaking off his stupor.

"Enough chit-chat." Chantal tried to herd them out the door. "I have work to do. Gage, don't sit on my head. In the examina-tion rooms, it's just my patients and me, and their privacy is essential. My local protection detail understands that rule."

"I'm not comfortable with the arrangement." He followed her to the reception area, where she knelt and pulled a pen and planner from her laptop bag. Gage could apply pressure—a trained technique where he pushed the client into performing in a certain way. With regards to her safety, of course. "And I'm not your local detail."

"I'm allowing you free rein, but my patient's comfort and privacy come first."

"You're 'allowing' me free rein?" Gage quirked a brow.

"Have you seen my patients? Most of them are elderly or frail. You can vet them in the waiting room. Please don't be obvious. Some of them have traveled for days to get here."

"Fine." Gage conceded. "If anyone looks suspect, one of us will be in attendance."

Still unhappy with their compromise, Gage stepped back and allowed her to go about her business. Instead, his team got to work on assessing security in the sizable facility. By mid-morning, the place was pumping. The line of patients spilled onto the street, and Gage decided to step in. Almost every patient was missing a limb, and all looked starved and exhausted.

He pulled Alexis aside. "What can I do?"

"You could hand out water and sandwiches. They're in the kitchen."

"Done."

"I can help." Gannon sauntered over, and Gage recognized his friend's stupid grin. Oh, boy.

Leaning on the desk, Alexis played with her hair. "You could help me stock the fridge."

"I want you on the street." Gage threw out the order, ignoring Alexis's frown.

Heading for the kitchen, he inwardly groaned as Gannon caught up.

"I just patrolled the block."

"And you'll do it again."

"Why are you so pissed."

"Because we're here to do a job. Play Romeo on your own time. Not on MSD time."

"I wasn't bootie-chasing."

"Good, cos Martin just fired Kirk—the asshole—for not focusing on the job."

"Copy that, sir." Gannon turned and strode for the exit, and Gage forced himself to relax. His teammate looked pissed, and Gage didn't blame him. Gannon was a damn good agent, and drawing a comparison to Kirk's behavior may have been a harsh move.

Truthfully, Gage was the one feeling attraction in the field —for his goddamn principal. Wasn't going to happen.

After a couple of hours, the line began to lessen. The only air con units were in the waiting room and the examination rooms—the rest of the facility baked in the mid-day sun. Chantal worked under these conditions? No wonder she'd nearly passed out that previous evening. Between the cloying heat, lack of sleep and food, he was surprised she hadn't hit the deck like a felled tree.

"We're waiting for a consignment of wheelchairs, but there is a delay." Chantal made her last adjustment and moved the right leg, gently feeling around the lady's severed joint. "How many prosthetics have you worn?"

"About ten."

"Twelve," her husband corrected. "They all cause her pain, and I'm tired of seeing my wife in such agony. She can barely walk."

"Can you stand again?" Chantal helped the fragile woman stand on her good leg, conversing in English with the multi-lingual couple who resided in Colombo. "How does that feel?"

"A little better. I feel relief in my back."

"Good. I want you to rest while we adjust the prosthetic. I'll also need to work on your back for the next two months."

"Thank you, doctor."

"Don't cry, dear. Let's fit a temporary limb until your next visit."

Once they'd left, Chantal went to her office and reached for her voice recorder. "54-year-old female. Victim of the Easter Sunday Bombings. Physical evaluation revealed asymmetrical leg length, restricted lumbopelvic motion. The working diagnosis is sacroiliac joint dysfunction, with lumbar facet syndrome secondary to a leg length inequality causing an alteration in gait. Intervention requires chiropractic management, including manipulative therapy to the lumbar spine and pelvis. In addition, the center's prosthetist will shorten her prosthetic device. Additionally, a wheelchair has been requested."

Gage appeared in the doorway and waited for her to pack away her recorder. She took her time, first wrapping it in a protective cloth—the device cost over two thousand dollars. Although Chantal could afford luxury equipment, it didn't mean she'd be careless with her money.

"Don't you have a recorder app on your phone?"

"Not as reliable. What do you need?" She powered up her laptop and reached for her monitor wipes.

"You—in the break room—ASAP."

"I'm busy."

"It's two o'clock, and you haven't eaten a thing. Lunch is up."

"I—"

"Remember what I said about having a healthy principal?"

"Fine." Chantal switched—grumbling in another language to herself as she followed him out of her office.

"You said 'bateau.' Are you speaking French?" Gage asked.

"Yeah."

"I also speak a little," Gage confessed. "I'm not well-versed."

"I'm definitely fluent," she replied. "Although I've grown

up in the States, I'm half-French. My father was... nevermind."

Gage suddenly turned, and she walked straight into his chest. He eased back and held her arms. "I'm sorry about your father. I've read about your history and—"

"And he was the best of men. The greatest daddy in the world, but it happened a long time ago. I think and talk about him often."

"I'm glad." Gage squeezed her arms. "I lost my mother when I was a kid—and she was the perfect mom."

"Gage—"

Dropping his hands, he turned on his heel. "Your curry is getting cold, and I can't promise that a team member won't claim it."

Chantal had never seen so many bodies crammed into one room. Bodies filled with testosterone. Alexis stood in the corner, chatting with Gannon, and Chantal recognized her friend's flirtatious stance. Alexis liked the strapping agent. Gage cleared a path to a table and sat Chantal down like she was a kid.

"Eat. Dishan says this is your favorite." Gage placed a steaming bowl under her nose, and Chantal grinned in surprise.

"Dishan! Is this from your aunt's restaurant?"

"Yes, ma'am. Agent Hendrix asked me to recommend a lunch you couldn't resist."

Gage joined her at the table and dug into an identical bowl. He sat back and closed his eyes. "Holy shit. This is heaven."

"I'm a regular at his aunt's place. Totally yummy." Chantal poked her fork into the wet rice and polished her bowl as she listened to the easy camaraderie between the teams. The rest of the center's staff wandered in and joined the lunch party.

A young MSD agent with thick brown hair sat down beside her and peered into his bowl, looking hesitant.

"The curry is good. Try it."

After cautiously tasting the rice, he smiled. "I like it."

"What's your name again?"

"Jason, ma'am."

"Please don't call me ma'am. I'm your age."

"You're older than Jase." Gage concentrated on eating. "He's only twenty-five. Youngest MSD agent on the planet."

"I may be the youngest, but I ain't the newest on Team Five. That's Kohen."

Chantal glanced at the medic, who sat in a corner. His surly attitude didn't gel with the rest of the agents. She wondered how Kohen got along with his new team leader.

"You're from Colorado," Jason confirmed.

Chantal smiled and wiped her mouth with a paper napkin. "So are you? I recognize your accent."

"Whereabouts?" he asked.

"Castle Pines," she answered.

"Wow. That's super fancy. I'm from Lincoln Park."

"I visited Lincoln Park often and loved the arts district."

"I painted a street mural there once," Jason said proudly. They chatted about his passion for art.

Gage's enthusiasm for curry drew Chantal's attention. He tore off a piece of flatbread, ignoring the crumbs scattering around his bowl as he laughed with Dishan in a debate of Rugby versus American Football.

In one short day, Gage not only had begun to win her over, but he'd done the same with her local guards and the clinic's staff. The guy was dangerous and deceptively easy-going.

She'd heard from Martin that Gage's MSD team had an excellent reputation, and she could see why. Their leader seemed fair and direct. Yeah—Gage Hendrix was an ignitable stick of dynamite that she should best avoid. After all, he was a diplomatic agent, which meant he'd soon be racing to his next assignment.

After lunch, she stepped into the rehabilitation center and observed the prosthetic training in progress. Her heart squeezed as she watched a group of children familiarize themselves with their new limbs and the training equipment. They varied in ages, from four to twelve years old, and Chantal had worked with all of them over the past months. Some of their parents and relatives sat on the far side and Chantal waved hello.

Most of the kids were victims of landmines. And one had been caught in an extremist attack. All of them were eager to discover their abilities in their new world. Their dedication warmed her heart—a significant contrast to their broken spirits when they'd first visited the center.

Chantal chose a seat as the local therapist interacted with the kids.

"Can I join you?" Alexis sat beside Chantal and smiled. "They've come a long way."

"They have."

"What's wrong?"

"I'm a little tired today."

"It's more than that—I can tell."

"I miss Pearl and little Aysha." Chantal worried her lip as she watched a tyke fall and jump back up. "Do you ever think about having kids?"

"Not anytime soon. My biological clock is broken." Alexis glanced at Chantal. "Are you getting broody?"

How did Chantal answer? It wasn't a secret—just a sad story not worth sharing. "It doesn't matter. We're surrounded by children who need all the love we can give."

"This job. When I first volunteered, I had no idea how rewarding it could be."

Chantal glanced at her friend. "You're doing awesome work."

"Speaking of awesome... we're surrounded by hunky gods. You gotta admit—your mom's vocation has its perks."

Chantal laughed. "Those agents are here for a reason."

"Maybe two reasons? I like the big guy—Gannon. He looks like he bench-presses trucks. Maybe he could bench press me."

"Alexis!"

"What? Their chief is also a hottie."

"He's called a 'Team Leader.'" Chantal gritted her teeth.

"A cute team leader. I like his eyes."

Standing, Chantal forced a smile. "I need to get back to my patients. Calm those hormones and tidy the reception desk. There are files everywhere."

"Don't exaggerate." Alexis kicked her leg. "A couple of extra binders. You're such a control freak."

Chantal hated that term, even though she might agree. Her ordered existence was her fortress and now more than ever, she needed to remain focused. Especially with an explosive agent shadowing her every move.

6

Gage watched Wyatt—the new AIC—open the car door for Chantal, and as she climbed out, he glanced over at his team, who were eager to head to the embassy to stow away equipment and weapons. The sun had already set, and they'd locked up late due to a last-minute patient with ulcerations from his prosthetic.

"Wait here." Gage knew it was wrong, but even though they were in the safe confines of the Jefferson House, he chose to walk Chantal back to her cottage. He headed to her side, and she shot him an odd look.

"Are you going home?" he asked.

"Yeah. Clean-up time."

"I'll walk you. Let me take your bag. It looks heavy."

She laughed nervously. "You don't have to. I'm perfectly capable."

"Still, I want to."

She handed it over, and he mock-groaned. "What's in this thing, bricks?"

Chantal laughed. "My planner is the culprit."

"Is your planner a person? Like a little old lady living at the bottom of this massive satchel? Your not-so-virtual assistant."

"Stop." A giggle escaped. Dimple jackpot… Gage internally fist-pumped.

"I'm serious. It's that heavy. I'm picturing the confined biddy, ready with a pen and paper in hand in case you need to rattle off orders."

"Is that what you think I do—rattle off orders?"

"For sure."

"Pot calling the kettle black." She nudged his arm.

"I don't rattle." He stroked a hand across her bag. "I roll out requests with a powerful and smooth voice."

They both laughed as they slowly wandered across the sweeping lawn.

"Powerful and smooth? Huh? Are you sure you're still talking about your voice?"

Surprised at her insinuation, Gage felt his cheeks warm, and Chantal's grin widened.

"You didn't expect that comeback, did ya?"

He changed the subject, reversing out of dangerous waters. "Is it like that every day? The center—that chaotic?"

"Most days. We're also trying to prep for that symposium."

"How long have you volunteered?"

"For the Sri Lankan charity? About a year and a half. Before that, the State Department assigned mom to Mali—a riskier deployment. I ran a side massage business for embassy staff."

"Do you ever give yourself a break? Act like a tourist?"

"Sometimes—usually when I first arrive in a country. And then I challenge myself to learn languages and their culture and to make a difference."

"What about dating?" Gage wondered if she had a boyfriend back home—or in Sri Lanka.

"I'm too busy, but I'm actually—"

"You've never dated at all while traveling?" He should talk. Gage stayed away from complications while deployed. And after moving to Virginia, he rarely went out except with his teammates. A few casual flings back in the States was all he had time for, so why was he so interested in his principal's love life?

"I had a boyfriend in high school."

"Not in college?"

Chantal's forehead creased. "I focused on my studies. When my mom became ambassador, I traveled with her to Algeria." Her frown deepened. "The first year was tough. Then I met someone."

"Sounds serious."

"It was more of an infatuation in the beginning. I loved his long hair and thick beard with that hippie vibe—a real cool cat. He was from Paris, so it made it easier. We spoke French, and I felt at ease—my grandparents live in Paris, and I grew up speaking French with my father. So…"

"Did he wear 'Jesus sandals'?"

Chantal punched him in the arm and giggled. "Be nice."

"Did he?"

"Okay, yes. And maybe a sarong—but not all the time."

Gage laughed. "Why didn't it work out? The sandals?"

Her smile dropped, and Chantal shook her head. "We had different paths to travel. And I removed my rose-colored glasses. Infatuation turned to frustration. He had no concept of time. He'd always be late for our dates. Once or twice, we'd be at dinner, and he'd wander off with his friends or explore the city. I'd be stuck finding my way back to the embassy."

"Wait…he'd leave you alone on the streets of Algiers? At night? What the hell?"

"Yip. I never told my mother. She would've skewered him alive."

"Her and me both! I would've hung him up by his sandals and whipped his ass."

"I handled it and dumped the bum. Haven't dated since."

"Good… you may have questionable taste in men."

"You're probably right." Chantal laughed. "That's why I stay away from charming, diplomatic dudes."

"Ouch."

"I have a lunch date tomorrow."

Irritation stirred, and Gage clenched his jaw. "We're hearing about this now? Do you have a name?"

"Fredrik Blomberg. Martin has already vetted the man. Fredrik works for the Swedish Consulate."

"I thought you said you stayed away from foreign service?"

"Anyone who works for my mother."

"And you know 'Fredrik' how?" Gage stiffly took the lead, picking up his pace as they neared the cottage.

"I don't know him. I met him at the Marine Ball last month. He swung by the center a few times. Fredrik is persistent."

"What does he do?"

"I think he's an administrative assistant."

"I'm sure you'll have a lovely time." Gage pulled up short when he spotted a shadowy figure sitting on Chantal's porch.

"I'm not having a lovely time." The recognizable voice had Gage relaxing—to a point.

"Madam Ambassador."

"Mum. What are you doing here?"

"Waiting patiently for my daughter." The ambassador spat the words as she rose. "Where have you been?"

"We closed up later than usual. I'm sorry."

Gage frowned at Chantal's meek reply and how she almost withered in her mother's presence.

"I don't ask for the world—daylight hours are yours. But, when I retire for the evening, I need my daughter to earn her keep."

What the hell?

"I know, and I apologize. I didn't watch the time and—"

Ambassador Durant stepped off the dark porch. Her mouth looked pinched, and she cradled her arm. "I'll be waiting. I still have reports to write."

"Yes, ma'am." Chantal nodded as her mother slid past.

The ambassador paused and turned to Gage. "Why are you not with your team?"

"Madam Ambassador, I was seeing your daughter safely home."

"She's home, have a good evening, Mr. Hendrix."

"Remember, we have an earlier start tomorrow," Gage confirmed with Chantal. Her security teams would be going over security procedures and scenarios with their principal, ensuring they were all on the same page.

All forgotten except her mother's "orders," Chantal rushed for the door. Gage could feel her panic as she fumbled for her keys and pushed her way inside. He doubted Chantal would rest. Instead, she'd race to the ambassador's side. Did she ever relax in her mother's presence, or take time for herself? Curling his hands into fists, Gage retreated into the night. They'd have another busy day tomorrow, including her damn lunch date.

7

C hantal escorted the elderly gentleman out of the treatment room and directed him to the exit. Happy with the spinal adjustment, he pressed his palms together and bowed. Chantal did the same.

"He's here!" Alexis called from down the passage. "Sunil is outside."

"You saw Sunny?" Chantal turned to the excited blonde, her spirits rising.

"He's waiting in line. He has to be in pain to turn up now."

"Is his sister with him?"

Alexis shook her head as they both headed for the front door. Wyatt and Dishan fell in from behind once they saw where the women were heading. Chantal pushed open the doors and followed the line of patrons alongside the building. She hated that patients had to wait for treatment and wished that they had additional staff. Although, the center had more therapists than ever before—there was still such a great need.

"Whoa!" Gage moved to her side. "Where are you going?"

"Not far." Chantal turned her back on the large operator

and scanned the line, hoping Sunny hadn't pulled another disappearing act.

Alexis nudged and pointed near the door, at a skinny kid leaning against the wall. Damn, the fourteen-year-old had lost weight since they'd last seen him. Last she'd heard, the kid worked in a sweatshop as a sewing machine operator, earning only a hundred dollars a month.

"You're exposed out here." Gage touched her arm and Chantal tamped down on irritation.

"Leave me alone—I'm doing my job." Feeling claustrophobic, Chantal stepped away from her generous security detail. Sunny had spotted them, and looked like he'd bolt. Damn, Chantal couldn't lose the teenager again.

"Dishan, send your team inside," She ordered.

"The hell he will." Gage bit out the words.

"You're getting in my way—I need to talk to a patient. Thanks to PTSD, he's not comfortable around guns and soldiers. I need you to back off."

"Not gonna happen." Gage widened his stance as two of his MSD teammates walked over. "I'm anchored to your side."

Wyatt agreed and her local team scanned their surroundings.

"Anchor your cocky ass ten feet away. You're getting on my last nerve." Chantal shoved past and pasted on a reassuring smile as she approached Sunny. He'd pushed off the wall and now watched her entourage like they were vipers about to strike. She'd love to shepherd him inside, but the rest of the patients would protest if he jumped the line.

"Sunny, it's good to see you. Is the prosthesis giving you problems?"

He didn't answer, just watched Gage's team behind her.

"Where's your sister today?"

"Safe. With a friend."

"Good."

Sunny pointed at his leg. "Doctor, I need more of the…" He searched for the right word.

"Chafe ointment? Do you have blisters?"

Sunny nodded. "I can't wait long. I need to get back."

Chantal knew he'd traveled a long way, but needed to talk to him in her office. There were seven patients ahead of Sunny and Chantal hoped that he'd stay.

"Chantal. A moment?" Gage moved into her line of sight and Sunny tensed.

Goddammit.

"I'll see you in a minute." She smiled at the wary kid and stepped away.

Gage's body heat felt intimate as his arm brushed hers. "I've noted two suspicious vehicles doing drive-bys. We're not comfortable with you milling around on the street."

"And I'm not comfortable with your interference." Chantal marched back to the reception area. "I've been waiting for months to see that child. He's an orphan who's trying to take care of his little sister. A church bombing killed his parents and took his leg when he was just seven."

"Your safety comes first." Gage pushed open the door and allowed her through.

"My patients come first." Chantal headed for the desk and grabbed the next file.

"Look, all I'm asking—"

Reaching her limit, Chantal swung around to face her tough nemesis. "Don't interfere with my job. I won't ignore a patient for the sake of security and if you're concerned about cagey vehicles in the vicinity, then work harder. That's your mission, not mine." He stood too close and she had to look up to glare into his harsh face.

A muscle ticked in his jaw. "There's a difference between loitering on the street and being minimally exposed when we walk you to a vehicle. We briefed you this morning on what to expect and how to be a cooperating principal."

Gage was correct. They'd even run through scenarios if the clinic were attacked.

"Let me make this clear." He pinned her with a flat stare. "Your clinic is under surveillance by unknown targets. We've spotted a cell of informants—a large cell. What would we prefer if we're attacked?"

Chantal rolled her eyes and looked away.

"What do we prefer?"

"A defensible space." She ground out between tight lips.

"Is that busy street an ideal location for a showdown?"

Chantal shook her head.

"I'd love to have a happy principal all of the time, but that doesn't always equate to a safe principal."

"What if I gave you a thirty-minute heads-up next time I exit the building?"

Gage grinned. "Not ideal, but sure. You can ask…"

"And you'd say no."

He shrugged and stepped back. "Carry on… you have that lunch date to worry about."

Shooting him a glare, Chantal headed for a treatment room. Gage took up too much space—both in her clinic and in her head. What an arrogant jackass… with that confident swagger. Acting all tough in his MSD gear which looked to be heavy.

The bullet-proof vest alone looked like it weighed a ton. Chantal wondered when last he'd had a spinal adjustment. It helped that he was in peak physical condition. Shoving aside thoughts of MSD agents, Chantal focused on her next patient, hoping to soon see Sunny and to make a difference in his young life.

∾

Chantal didn't have much time. After his therapy session, Sunny slid into the seat and looked around the office. Alexis sat nearby and offered him a reassuring smile.

"Thank you, Miss Chantal. My leg feels better." He clutched the jar of lotion on his lap as he stretched out his sore thigh. The amputation was just above the knee and Chantal hated seeing those blisters from the prosthetic rub. He needed a better artificial limb.

He needed everything she hoped she could give him. His worn clothes looked gray and hung off his thin frame. A bruised cheek spoke of a rough life on the streets. He mentioned recently finding accommodation in a hostel, but worried about his sister's safety.

"You look tired, Sunny. How many hours do you work?"

He shrugged a thin shoulder. "Too many. I won't go back to that orphanage. They tried to take my sister away—split us up. I can provide—I'm planning to send Roshani to school next year."

"Good. How about this year?"

Sunny frowned.

"We're looking for a caretaker for the clinic—someone to learn from the ground up. We're including accommodation—we have living quarters at the back."

"Okay…" Sunny shook his head in confusion.

"Sunny, I'm offering you the job. But there are conditions."

He straightened his back, looking wary.

"Your sister will go to school. You will attend online classes. You will only see to the clinic's needs once your classes and homework are complete."

"I… I have no idea about computers." His eyes darted about the room.

"That's okay. Alexis will teach you and we'll send you on a course."

"How much?" Sunny's chin jutted forward and Chantal's

heart broke. He expected a low-ball offer—a similar salary to the pitiful hundred dollars he currently earned.

"Two thousand dollars to start."

His eyes widened. "Per year?"

"Per month. Two thousand per month."

Paling beneath Chantal's gaze, Sunny looked shellshocked.

"Yes." Alexis smiled. "As long as you attend classes. I help with the running of the center and will teach you everything you need to know."

"I know nothing about being a... a caretaker."

"That's okay. I'm confident in your abilities. Say yes."

"Ah. Yes, Doctor...Okay. Yes." He licked his lips and sat back.

Chantal pointed to a calendar. "Call me Chantal, and you'll start next week. In the meantime, I'd like you to fetch your sister and get settled in your new rooms. I'll leave a welcome package on the bed."

That package would include new clothes for the pair. A new laptop for Sunny and shoes and toiletries. The fridge in the center's kitchen was fully stocked.

"Who... who are the men walking around?" He looked back at the door nervously. "I can't accept the job if they could hurt Roshani."

Bless him—he'd sacrifice the job to shield his sister.

"They are here to protect me. There are bad people trying to hurt me."

"I'll protect you!" Sunny stood and stuck out his chest. "They'll fight me first."

Chantal smiled at his voracity. "That's not your job, honey. Your job is to learn and grow and help your sister. And to take care of the closed clinic when we are away and helping patients. Can you do that?"

"Yes. I will never rest."

Both women laughed, and Chantal corrected him. "You

will definitely rest. This isn't a sweat shop. You never have to work those hours again. Come, Alexis will show you around and give you a key."

Chantal walked with them out into the hall and introduced Sunny to the other staff as they headed to the connecting accommodation. His eyes sparkled with excitement and she wanted to hug the kid. She glanced at her watch—only fifteen minutes until her date.

"Chantal. A word?" Gage approached from behind and she excused herself and joined him down the passage.

"Yes, I know—we're leaving."

"Fuck the date. I wanna know why you hired someone without consulting your teams."

"Excuse me? Listen, buddy. I don't need your attitude—I have my own!"

"Which may need an adjustment. You never said you were hiring the teenager. We haven't performed a background check —for all I know, he's a card-carrying mercenary. You've just provided the perfect opening."

Her temper flared. "And you're an ass! I'll hire whoever I want and if you don't like it, there's the door."

"Agent Hendrix has a point." Wyatt joined the discussion. "We're not saying you can't hire him—but we need a heads up."

"I got the go-ahead from the charity. I'm not kicking that kid back to the streets."

Wyatt raised his hands. "We're not saying that, it's just—"

"You're all pushing the wrong buttons today. Get your boulder asses out of the way."

Gage followed her to the changing room and Chantal turned to glare. "What?"

"Your soft heart could get you killed."

His quiet words got on her last nerve. "Take a hike. Thanks to all your complaining, I'm late."

8

F redrik raised his brows at the two large men at the adjacent table. "Do they have to sit on top of us?"

Chantal wondered the same thing and forced a smile. Gage insisted on practically sitting by her side and watched Fredrik like he was the Unabomber. Unlike Chantal, her date didn't seem fazed and flashed a white grin.

Fredrik certainly didn't lack in confidence and wore a well put together suit, which made her feel underdressed in a white t-shirt and jeans. In her defense, she'd added a black blazer, gold earrings, and applied careful make-up that morning.

They sat in a fancy Indian restaurant—Chantal had hoped for a casual lunch at a beach café, needing to get back to work. She wondered how Sunny had settled in and took a slow breath to slow her racing heart.

The agent beside her flustered her composure which rarely happened. Getting used to her large protective detail was proving to be a big challenge. Perhaps Gage was right—she needed to communicate with her details. They were there to keep her alive and that morning, she'd made their jobs more difficult. But she'd never regret hiring Sunny. The deed felt good.

Usually, her therapy provided temporary relief from physical pain. Now she helped in a different capacity—providing a future for two kids who had nowhere to go.

Chantal ordered a lentil soup—a Dal Makhni, as her date decided on ordering multiple dishes from the menu. She'd never escape.

"How's your mother? The last time I saw her was at the ball."

"Busy." Chantal lined up her cutlery on the neatly folded napkin, hoping to restore order to her distracted mind.

"She made an appearance at that trade fair—for the women's entrepreneurship program."

"Sure." Chantal changed the subject, bringing them back to "first date" material. "Fredrik, how long have you been in Sri Lanka?"

The tall Swede warmed up to the question and leaned forward. She studied his beautiful features—perfect in all its proportions and tried not to compare those features to Gage's unforgettable face. Both handsome men and yet complete opposites.

Fredrik may be all smooth lines and baby-soft skin, but he lacked the rugged looks of a man who'd lived on the edge. She refused to look at the MSD team leader sitting at the next table. His presence shattered her concentration—he infuriated, yet drew her in at the same time. Like a bothersome magnet.

"Seven months. And you?" Fredrik asked.

What had she asked? "Sorry—I zoned out for a second. Work stuff."

Fredrik's nostril's flared. "I said, seven months. Before that, I was in Budapest."

"I apologize. And you grew up in Sweden?"

"For most of my childhood. My father lived in Finland.

Thanks to my parent's divorce, I traveled between both countries. My mother is all about her glamorous life in Stockholm, and we have nothing in common."

"That's tough."

"I like traveling. It was an acceptable arrangement. That's why I chose this job. You're the same—I can see the wanderlust in your eyes."

Oh, she had lust... of the passionate variety. Inappropriate thoughts for an agent with a fiery gaze, and at that very moment, she could feel Gage's stare tracing over her face.

This date was a mistake. Yet, Chantal knew her complicated feelings for the MSD soldier could never go anywhere. She wasn't about to break her own rule, which was there for a reason. Besides, she was his principal, and he'd only ever acted like a professional in her presence. A professional prick at times... Her one-sided attraction would get her heart crushed under his capable boot.

Gage stood and pulled out his buzzing phone. God, the man was annoyingly tall. His strong jaw flexed beneath a five-o-clock shadow as he glanced at the screen. Answering the phone, Gage walked away.

"You seem distracted. Would you prefer to reschedule?"

Chantal's gaze shot back to Fredrik. "I'm rude. I never got much sleep last night."

"Why?"

"I was with my mom."

"That bad-ass U.S. Ambassador reminds me of my mother."

Chantal frowned. "In what way?"

"Both are perfectionists and always disapproving. I bet your mother is a street angel—house devil. Right? As sweet as honey to those who matter in her upscale world, and not so nice behind closed doors."

Chantal's neck heated. "You don't get to talk about my mother that way."

Fredrik raised his hands apologetically. "I know what it's like to live in a parent's shadow. Just saying."

"You know nothing about my life." Realizing she wouldn't be sharing any intimate details anytime soon with the man at the table, Chantal picked up her handbag. Fredrik seemed nice enough at the Marine Ball—handsome in his tux. Now, his appeal evaporated, revealing a presumptive arrogance. "As a U.S. Ambassador, my mother has worked tirelessly for the good of Sri Lanka, and I'm betting if she were a male ambassador, you wouldn't be examining her personality traits. She can be whoever she damn well wants to be."

"I didn't mean any disrespect."

The problem with having a distinguished diplomat as a parent was that sometimes, it was all about that famous relative —how they might further one's career. Fredrik, constantly mentioning her mother on a first date was a huge red flag in Chantal's world, and she felt defensive given her complicated relationship with her mother, but Chantal didn't give a damn.

"Enjoy your Butter Chicken."

"Wait, Chantal." Fredrik reached out, and Jason stood.

"Date is over, buddy."

Gage hung up and headed their way as she rose.

"Everything okay?" he asked.

She offered him a polite smile. "Fine. Can we head to a beach bar to grab takeout?"

His large hand cupped her back, and her spine tingled. "We can't. We're heading back to your residence."

"I have patients—"

"Which will have to wait. We're walking fast."

Chantal obeyed the command. She knew enough about Mobile Security to listen to their orders, and they hurried across the road as the rest of her generous local and MSD teams converged from all angles. The men were on high alert.

Gage stuck close but stepped back when Wyatt—the Agent in Charge—guided her into the backseat. The rest of her local bodyguards climbed in as Gage hurried to the MSD vehicle. Standard protocol meant that Team Five would follow her armored suburban. Wyatt was in charge of the overall command and close protection of the "principal"—which was her frustrated ass.

Chantal didn't know what was happening, and at that moment, she wanted Gage by her side. Realizing she instinctively trusted him, Chantal twisted in her seat and watched his van pull out into traffic behind her.

"Dishan, what happened?" Chantal asked, ignoring the comms chatter.

This time her local friend sat beside her, the only one not on the radio.

"Relax. We're taking precautions. There's been a tip-off—protestors loyal to Mr. Bandara plan to march to the embassy and your center."

"I have to warn the staff!"

"Already done, Miss Durant. Your assistant, Alexis, has closed up early." Wyatt gave her a thumbs up from the front passenger seat, and Chantal turned back to resettle.

"I need to call her and check on Sunny."

"Seatbelt, ma'am."

Complying with Dishan's request, Chantal held on as they raced back to U.S. soil. She despised Rajin's corrupted soul. She'd seen one of the tapes—how he'd beaten helpless prisoners with a steel pipe before slicing them with a knife.

And Chantal hated that he hunted her dear friend. Pearl and Aysha's safety was a constant worry, and the bastard wouldn't give up on finding his ex-wife. If he thought Chantal was a soft target, he was wrong. Even if she knew where Pearl ended up, she'd never give up the location of her friend.

Gage never took his eyes off the lead vehicle as Lucius negotiated traffic. His men were armed and keyed up, ready to roll into action. The developing intel troubled Gage. Not only could he be dealing with a possibly violent mob descending on the embassy, but they could be facing an armed crowd.

Martin had called with news of two trucks stopped by police near the embassy, carrying AK-47s and machetes. How many unaccounted caches were smuggled into Colombo?

"At least 'Chanel Five' cooperated. Walked her ass to the transport." Kohen clicked a knuckle.

Gage stared straight ahead. "What the hell does that mean? Quit sipping on your haterade."

"She's thrown tantrums all day—doing whatever the fuck she wants."

"Dude!" Gannon warned.

Twisting to face the asshole, Gage pinned Kohen with a deadly stare. "At least her heart is in the right place, fucker. Unlike you, she saved a couple of lives today."

"That's harsh, man. I'm just saying—"

"Call her 'Chanel Five' again and I'll sack your ass."

The other agents exchanged loaded glances as Gage turned back. Lucius whistled a tune and Gage bit back a smile. A song called "Haterade."

What he'd learned was that their principal took after her mother in many ways. Chantal had a stubborn streak a mile wide, and a quick temper to match. And she wasn't afraid to go head-to-head with an MSD team to fight for a cause. However, she needed to work on her communication skills and adjust to her new normal. Safety protocols existed for a reason.

As they neared the Cinnamon Gardens, his men grew quiet and scanned the busy streets for threats.

Gannon spoke through comms. "Four o'clock. Say cheese."

A suspect in a blue sarong and white shirt took a photo as they drove by. Thanks to his team's scouting efforts, Gage recognized the individual they'd marked as a potential Rajin Bandara cohort. One of at least thirty spies who hung around the embassy neighborhood.

The two-vehicle motorcade cleared the gates without incident, and Gage barely waited for the van to come to a complete stop before he exited, but paused in surprise as the ambassador walked over to Wyatt.

"Is Chantal okay?" she asked.

"Fine, Ambassador Durant."

She returned his smile and greeted her daughter with a nod. "I'm sorry you closed early. Will this interfere with the symposium roll-out from your end?"

That was why she'd walked out to greet her daughter?

"Nope. We've already sent the majority of our supplies to Hatton. I'm short a couple of massage beds, but we can make a plan." Chantal smiled proudly.

"Yeah, well. You have a bunch of new-age volunteers working for you. I'm expecting your best."

"Madam Ambassador, would attending this event be wise?" Gage had to ask.

Pinning him with a scornful glare, the ambassador replied, "I issue at least one security alert a month due to unrest. Like you, I have a job to do. If the political climate worsens, I'll revise our plans. If I needed your advice, I'd ask. Thankfully, I take advice from a Deputy Chief of Mission and an RSO. Who knew?"

Damn. Gage felt his balls shrivel. Gannon sniggered, and Gage shot him a withering stare. The ambassador turned away to talk to Wyatt.

"The Anaconda got you good. Crushed you, real tight."

"Shut up, Jase."

The ambassador was wrong and should listen to the instincts of the men on the ground. And fresh eyes saw trouble simmering down narrow alleys and on passing faces. Her dismissal disappointed Gage and could expose her daughter to unseen dangers.

9

T hat evening, Chantal saw to her mom. After massaging the tight muscles behind her mother's scapula, and shoulder, Chantal walked to the quiet kitchen and made herself a jelly sandwich. After pouring a glass of milk, she walked over to her small residence.

Chantal needed privacy and when they'd first moved into the Jefferson House, she'd been pleased to see the small cottage tucked at the back of the yard. Choosing the quaint lodgings over an elaborate bedroom in the main house, was first met with resistance from her mother. But, as much as Chantal loved helping her mother out, at twenty-eight years old, she needed her own space.

Many nights, her mom turned clingy, especially when the nightmares came. She'd call and wake Chantal, asking her to come to her room. Chantal would then doze in a chair as her mother either paced restlessly or rambled on about politics.

As she walked past the pool, Chantal glanced at the inviting water, and decided to eat her sandwich in the cool evening air. All day, she was closeted indoors in stifling heat. Sri Lanka was all about the outdoors.

After removing her sneakers and placing them neatly on the grass, Chantal sat by the edge of the pool, lowered her plate and glass, and rolled up her jeans. Dipping her feet into the tepid water felt satisfying, and she kicked them in small circles, before picking up her half eaten sandwich.

"Pool party?" Gage stepped around the side of the house, and Chantal raised her brows in surprise. He'd shed his body armor and wore a black Henley shirt with tactical pants.

"For one."

"How about, for two? I promise... I'll behave. No splashing."

"What are you doing here?"

"Your mother asked if two MSD agents could remain behind. Gannon is patrolling the house. I'm on a break. The rest of the team are back at the hotel."

"Stay? Why?"

"There's unrest near the embassy. It could roll this way."

"You'll sleep here?"

"We'll take turns. We have a bed in the 'west wing.' Gannon is on first shift."

"You're taking a risk." Chantal nodded in the direction of the gate. "Our local police guards might take offense."

"That's why only two of us stayed back. I'll keep a low profile. Wouldn't want them to feel inadequate..."

"Your sarcasm is showing." American diplomats and their families were guests on the small island. Stepping out of line and onto the boots of local protection could lead to political tensions. But her mother had given the order and would deal with potential repercussions.

Gage sat beside her and removed his boots. "It's late, and they haven't noticed the two missing MSD agents. Not yet. All of the guards are currently down by the front of the property. We'll roll out early in the morning. I don't trust some of the men—some could be on Rajin's payroll."

"Dishan isn't."

"You don't know that—but he seems like a solid fellow with a clean track record. As do the rest of the guards on your detail." Gage tossed his boots to the side.

"You vetted them?"

"Of course. My team works beside them. I don't want dead teammates or a dead principal."

"Gee, thanks."

"Why do you think I wanted to vet the kid? Everyone in your proximity is a possible danger. The water is nice."

Chantal watched his tanned feet floating beside hers. Well-shaped with noble-looking toes. Could toes look noble? His did.

"She may not show it, but your mother cares and wants you protected by the best."

"I know. She can be difficult. The pain wears her down."

"And she takes it out on you." He picked up a twig and leaned down to rescue a moth.

"Sometimes."

Gage shot her a wry look.

"Okay… much of the time." Chantal smiled. "After a bad night, I escape from her den, and meditate."

"You meditate?" Gage lowered the winged insect onto a slated edge.

"Yes, do you?"

"Maybe." He splashed her leg with his hand.

A giggle escaped. "I can't picture you meditating."

"Why not?"

"Because you're a restless panther."

"Does Taekwondo count?"

Chantal poked him in a huge bicep. "Tai chi, maybe."

"Are you eating the rest of that sandwich?"

"Uh. No."

Gage leaned around her front, and she sucked in a breath.

His broad chest pressed into her shoulder and his arm grazed her front.

"God, you smell good. Sorry. I shouldn't have—"

"Thanks."

Gage snagged the plate and withdrew. He'd smelled good too. Way too fine.

Chantal crossed her legs and looked up at the clear night. "Did you know that the planetarium and the observatory are in this neighborhood?"

"It's my job to know that… every building within a five-mile radius."

Rolling her eyes, Chantal leaned back on her elbows and smiled at the sky. "Show-off. Lyrid will be peaking next week. It's best viewed in the early hours of the morning."

"What's Lyrid?"

"One of the oldest meteor showers. It runs for about ten days and comes from the constellation of Lyra and is the remains of a comet."

"So, you'll be out here? At what? Three am?"

"More like four. And I won't be here at its peak—I'll be inland. Symposium, remember?"

"You like the stars."

"We might not see them in a while—heavy rains are predicted. It's been a late monsoon season. What's your passion —aside from guns and ammo?"

"Way to stereotype." Gage leaned back on his elbows and grinned. "Lately—I like lemurs."

Chantal sniggered. "What? You're a fan of the National Geographic channel?"

"About five months ago, I rescued a baby lemur in Mada-gascar." Gage turned his head, and Chantal stared into his twinkling eyes. "It had been hit by a car. We saw this rangy, little fluff ball lying in the road and we stopped. I scooped it up, and we rushed Monty—we named the critter—to a nearby vet."

"We…as in?"

"The team. Deployed to Madagascar for two months."

An image formed of six tough guys rallying around one tiny lemur. Talk about a strike to the heart.

"Did Monty survive?"

"Yeah. Barely, but she—Monty turned out to be a female—pulled through. They took her to a nearby sanctuary. I've been obsessed with lemurs ever since."

"That's the sweetest. You guys are a bunch of softies." Chantal couldn't resist jabbing him in the side.

"Stop." He tried to grab her finger and she went in for a second strike.

"Like a big teddy bear."

"Don't poke the bear!"

"Like this?"

"Woman!" In one smooth move, Gage grabbed her wrist and flipped her over his chest and onto her back.

"Was that a 'Taekwondo' move?" she asked breathlessly.

"Perhaps."

His intense stare had her wanting to look away, but she maintained eye contact.

"There are those eyes again."

What was wrong with her eyes? They weren't anything special—brown in color. Good vision—did their job.

His mouth sat too close, and Chantal reached up to trace his carved lips. Everything about Gage felt hard—like granite. Yet, he handled her like glass.

"Chants, don't." He didn't pull away.

"One quick taste."

"Once won't be enough." His eyes blazed, reflecting her hunger. "You're my principal and if I kiss you... I'm inviting chaos."

"I miss chaos. All I do is work."

A thumb stroked the side of her breast through her t-shirt, and her breath quickened.

"Don't look at me like that." His voice sounded raw. "It's not worth the risk."

"We're alone. Look."

"Fuck." Gage crushed his lips to hers, and Chantal took full advantage. Gripping his neck, she pulled him close and traced his lips with her tongue. He responded, devouring and feasting on her eager mouth. One of them—both of them—groaned. His hand fisted in her hair, holding her in place. He lit her brain on fire, obliterating all reason.

Nothing else mattered. Chantal wanted more. Instead, he slowed the kiss, eventually withdrawing. And as their breath mingled, he released her hair and traced a thumb over her temple.

"We broke the rules. Shit—it was worth it."

"But it can't happen again?"

Closing his eyes, Gage shook his head. "I can't fail you. Or my team. Or your mother."

"Because it always comes down to her." Chantal shoved him aside and got to her feet.

"It comes down to you. Your safety is why I'm here."

"Spare me the bodyguard speech. It was a kiss. No biggie. I'll see you in the morning."

"Chants—"

"Don't call me that." She widened her stride, heading for her door. A rock bit into her heel and she realized she'd abandoned her sneakers. "Especially not in front of your team. You protect me, and I'll protect your reputation. I won't go all 'googly-eyed' in the 'field.'" She unlocked her door. "Our secret is safe."

"Wait—"

"Bonne Nuit." Closing the door on the sexy MSD operator

felt gratifying. And Chantal threw back her shoulders and marched to her bedroom. Time for a shower. Her chin still tingled from his stubble, and Chantal swiped at her mouth.

Claustrophobia swarmed as she paused to sit on her bed. This was her world—trailing behind her mother across the globe. Losing out living a normal life where she could go on normal dates and hang with her girlfriends. Have a place she'd call home.

When last had she had a home? Chantal couldn't remember. Why couldn't she step out from beneath her mother's shadow—walk away and find her normality?

She knew why. Guilt. Deep down, she knew it was all her fault. She'd killed her father and maimed her mother. She'd pay for her selfishness. Sentenced to a nomadic life. When would penance to her only relative be enough? She'd swapped freedom for atonement. That sacrifice included forgetting about Gage and that ground-shaking kiss.

10

The rain drummed against the rehab center's windows, indicating that the southwest monsoon hadn't yet finished its five-month deluge. Chantal stepped around Alexis, who swiped at a dirty patch with a balding mop. They'd need a new supply after the long rainy season.

The muddy parking lot caused issues. Dishan and some of her loitering guards helped to replace an elderly patient's flat tire in the sludge. Lucius and Kohen escorted a drunk panhandler out of the center, and his shouts grew faint as they walked him down the street.

Pausing to straighten a picture frame on the wall, Chantal scanned the packed waiting room. Forgetting about Gage turned out to be an impossible challenge, especially when he knelt to play with a toddler in the corner. The warrior's shoulder flexed as he reached back to ensure that his weapon sat out of reach, and Chantal paused to stare at his amiable expression as he handed the girl a packet of gummies.

God, Gage was good with people—good with kids. Way better than the rest of his team and could probably outperform Chantal when it came to connecting with patients. Although she loved her work, she still kept a professional distance. If she were honest, her reasons for separation included self-preservation.

Engaging in Arabic, Gage laughed with the kid's father as the older man relaxed into their conversation. Turning serious, the man showed Gage his scarred arm and dysfunctional right hand.

Chantal knew the new patient's history. His old injury was a result of a xenophobic attack. Muslims were a minority in Sri Lanka—only nine percent practiced Islam. Anti-Muslim sentiments came on the heels of anti-Tamil attitudes.

Not all of the majority population felt this way about the minorities, but rising religious tensions played a massive role in Sri Lanka's past, present, and possible future. Large-scale violence on Sri Lankan streets was an ever-present possibility.

"Are you going to gape at him all day? Or take the next patient?"

Chantal jumped to attention. "Next patient... yes."

Grinning, Alexis handed over a file. "We have a SMOS." A "SMOS" meant a standard manipulation of the spine.

"New patient. Bram Miller. He's an American who's feeling stiff and needs an adjustment while on vacation."

"And he waited in that long line?"

"No. Mr. Miller came in ten minutes ago. Says he has a train to catch and asked us to squeeze him in. A local told him you're the best."

"We can't have him pushing in front of other patients."

"We can, when he writes a generous donation check. He's in room one."

"That is an exception." Chantal grinned.

She headed for the treatment room, passing Gannon, who paced the hallway.

"If you're bored, Gage is handing out candy in the front. You can join him."

"Yes, ma'am." Winking, the massive agent mock-saluted as she stepped through the doors to greet her patient.

A physically-fit-looking man sat on the chiropractic table. The severe lines of his face made her pause. Close-seated eyes framed a warped nose—which looked like it had been punched apart too many times. A scar ran across his jaw, and it flexed as she entered the intimate space. He looked to be in his early fifties.

"Morning, Mr. Miller."

"Howdy." He growled the word.

Chantal chose the nearest stool. His gaze had her focusing on his file instead.

"Can you describe exactly how you feel?"

Pale blue eyes ran over her face with an unsettling intensity. "Feel fine. Reckon, I need some cracking."

Picking up on his strong accent, Chantal asked, "Are you from Texas? I visited Houston about eight years ago."

"I'm from all over." He ran a hand through greasy black hair. "Can we get this done?"

Forcing a smile, Chantal stood and directed him to lie on his stomach. She made a few adjustments and then, ignoring his stale body odor, asked him to turn on his side for a direct thrust technique.

He turned, and striking out like a viper, he grabbed her wrist and covered her mouth with a meaty palm. Her heart thumped as Chantal tried to wriggle free of the vicious hold. He wrapped his legs around her thighs in a vice-like grip. Like a python crushing a tiny mouse, and all she could do was squeak in alarm.

"You're sweeter than a baby's breath, aren't ya."

The whispering kiss to her neck had her whimpering. As he squeezed his bruising grip on her mouth, pressure increased, and her pulse throbbed behind her eyes in time with her frantic heart.

"Fucking gorgeous."

Would he rape her in the room? The first chance she got, Chantal would scream and fight the asshole with everything she had. Her local detail and six MSD agents patrolled the center. She needed just one to hear her cry for help.

"Relax, sweetheart. You're to stay quiet. If you don't, innocent people will die. I have a team ready… parked down the block—high-powered rifles, ready to execute patients and decorate your clinic with pretty bullet holes. And I'll blow out your sweet brains before your fancy-ass soldiers come through that door. Do you want that?"

Sweat trickled down her neck.

"Do you fucking want that?"

Chantal shook her head.

"I'll ask you a few questions. Answer them, and no-one dies. Are we clear?"

She nodded.

"I ain't right in the head, honey. I don't mind dying on the job. Get me?"

Swallowing past her dry throat, Chantal jerked her head.

He slowly released his hand from her sore mouth and twisted her to face him. "I don't have time for a lengthy interrogation. But, one day, I'd love to use my knives on you."

Oxygen flooded her lungs, and she tried not to hyperventilate.

"Where's the USB?"

"The… what?"

"Don't play games. That bitch who stole the cassettes, also walked away with a flash drive. Where is it?"

"I… I have no idea." And Chantal didn't. The only evidence Pearl had handed over at the embassy was the camcorder cassettes.

"You know what's on the drive, don't you?" A hand wrapped around her neck and began to squeeze.

"I don't... please."

Chantal kicked out in a panic. Fingers tightening, he flipped her onto the table. Gasping for breath, she clawed at his hand.

"I expected more from Henri's daughter. C'mon, fight me."

Eye's widening, Chantal tried to claw at his face as he squeezed. The flat, cruel face of a monster would be the last thing she'd see. Her vision blurred, and her head pounded. Chantal's tears trickled into her hair.

"Relax, kitten." The bastard released his grip, and she rolled onto the floor. "Not your fault that you had a sorry excuse for a father."

His baffling words punched through her terror and her fight for oxygen.

Kneeling, he traced her ear. "Your daddy was a nasty man. We were partners once. Why do you think an assassin spectacularly shot him on your school steps? The dickhead's ten-gallon mouth earned him a bullet to the head."

Jabbing her elbow back, Chantal caught him in the chest. Falling forward, she kicked out and clocked him in the jaw.

Opening her mouth, she screamed. Nothing happened.

"Gage." Chantal tried to shout his name as she scrabbled towards her equipment shelf in the corner and grabbed the nearest makeshift weapon—a steel activator. The room swayed, and she collapsed to the floor.

"Rajin needs answers. If you don't have the USB, call Pearl. If the information on that drive is leaked—you'll take the fall."

The door opened and closed, and Chantal twisted to face the table. Her entire body shook as she pointed the activator at the empty room. Minutes passed as paralyzing horror spread through her like icy tentacles.

Move, Chantal. Get help.

Muscles twitched, and she forced herself to move. Would

he still shoot up the building? Chantal tried to stand. Her legs wouldn't work. Wasting time, Chantal crawled for the door, calling Gage's name in a whispered cry.

Reaching up, she pulled the handle and spilled into the hallway. And there was Gage, talking with Alexis.... his back to her. That broad, shielding back. Alexis greeted Sunny as he walked by.

He was the first to see her and shouted her name. "Miss Chantal! Miss Chantal!"

Gage turned, his dawning horror reflecting Chantal's own shattered confusion. As if in slow motion, he ran and skidded to his knees. His form clouded in a swimming haze. Warm hands cupped her face.

"What happened, Chants? What the fuck!"

"Patient... Miller... Quick." The words came out on a croak.

Gage spoke through comms as Alexis knelt and stroked Chantal's arm. She immediately jerked away.

"Easy." Alexis eased onto her haunches. "Miller? The American patient?"

Lucius ran up.

Chantal forced words out past her aching throat. "Working... for Rajin. Team with guns... going to hurt patients. Get them to safety."

"Understood." Gage stood and swung her into his arms. "Lucius?"

"On it, sir."

"Hospital. Now!" Gage shouted, hurrying down the passage. His fiery eyes flashed as they traced over her throbbing neck.

"No. I'm... okay."

"You can barely talk." He growled the words from gritted teeth.

"There's an emergency care two blocks away," Alexis

volunteered as she ran up from behind. Agents and guards converged from all sides as they rushed for a side door. In a daze, Chantal realized that they'd rehearsed a retreat, and she couldn't stop the rolling protocol—even if she had the strength.

Resting her head on Gage's solid vest, Chantal concentrated on breathing through the shock. Her throat throbbed, but it didn't feel damaged enough to warrant high care, but she could be wrong.

"Put her in the back." Wyatt opened the door, and Gage tucked her close and climbed in. Kohen—the MSD medic slid in beside them.

"Gage, you're here for support, which means MSD falls back. You can't ride with us." Wyatt ordered Gage to climb out. "Your medic can stay."

"I'm not leaving her."

Chantal didn't want anyone else near and gripped the strap of Gage's ballistic vest. She hated all the armor and wanted to feel his broad chest. His arms tightened in a possessive hold.

"This isn't your detail. The local—"

"They fucked up just as we did," Gage shouted the words.

"He's right." Dishan climbed in the driver's seat. "A wolf slipped through our defenses and got to the principal. Gage can stay. The rest of my men will follow."

"We're wasting time. Close the damn door, Wyatt. Let's go."

Nostril's flaring, Wyatt did as asked, but Chantal couldn't relax her hold. The scent of her attacker clung to her skin, and she could taste his odor—feel his hands squeezing. Shuddering and reaching out, she grasped Gage's fingers. His hand wrapped around hers in a reassuring grasp.

"You're safe," he whispered. "Where do you hurt?"

"Neck."

"I'm so sorry. I'm so goddamn sorry."

So was Chantal—that monster could have easily killed her. Continued strangling instead of letting go. Even with her self-defense training, he'd overpowered her with ease. She'd traveled the globe, thinking she was invincible. Not invincible—foolish. Feeling weak and scared, Chantal allowed her tears to fall.

11

This was the worst day of his career. The first time that a principal under his watch had gotten hurt. Gage didn't care about the implications of his vocational fuck-up. All that mattered was Chantal—an individual who he cared for. An innocent woman cornered by a savage hireling.

When he'd turned and seen her on the ground, shattered and hurt...

Gage wiped a hand over his face as he pieced together what happened. He sat by Chantal's side in a sectioned off area of the emergency room. She wouldn't let go of his hand and knowing it might get him into trouble, he still held on. He'd removed his helmet and ran his other hand through his hair.

At some point, he'd need to let go and step back. Slip back into an MSD team leader mode. But she wouldn't allow anyone else near her. And damn, if he didn't feel as possessive as all hell. Gage should shut down this mounting attraction, which could only lead to the dismantling of her heart and his career.

They'd given her a light sedative, and although she'd calmed down, Chantal fought the urge to sleep.

While they were alone for a minute, he stroked the back of her hand with his thumb. She hadn't said much since arriving at the hospital—just described her assailant and whispered that he'd interrogated and strangled her for information.

And her mother hadn't yet arrived. Depending on how long Chantal remained at the hospital, the ambassador might choose to meet them at her residence.

Still, Gage couldn't fathom a reason for not rushing to your daughter's side after such a traumatic encounter.

"Merci—Thank you." Chantal licked her swollen lips. Her voice sounded raspy, and it looked painful to talk. The red finger marks on her neck darkened as the bruising began to form, and Gage tamped down his rage.

"Don't say thank you. I've done nothing. My team failed, and you paid the price."

"I tried to call your name... After he... I couldn't speak."

"Jesus, Chants."

"Knew you would kill him."

"I would've. A hundred times over. He won't get away—DSS will track him down."

Glassy eyes still reflected her shock as she rolled to face him. "Bram Miller—probably not his real name."

"No, honey. It doesn't mean we won't find him. Now, rest that voice."

Brow creasing, she squeezed his hand. "He says he... he knew my father. Worked with him."

"The shithead said that?"

"Said they were... partners." Face crumpling, Chantal shook her head. "My father would never—"

"You need to rest. We'll deal with unanswered questions once you've recovered." However, it wasn't likely that Gage would remain by her side. Chantal would most likely fly to the States under the protection of hired help.

"I should've insisted on being in the treatment rooms. A tango slipped past my team. How did I let that happen?" Gage rubbed his forehead, analyzing the morning routine.

"Knew who you were… the flat tire and the beggar."

Chantal was right. Rajin's hired help planned and executed the infiltration, providing enough distraction to allow one man to slip through. No-one had known about a missing flash drive. Whatever was on that device was worth going head-to-head with an MSD team. They'd all underestimated the threat.

"Ambassador Durant has arrived." Gannon stuck his head past the curtain, and Gage stood.

She'd arrived two hours after her daughter's attack. Gage hoped that whatever took precedence was worth the delay. Not wanting to let go, he exchanged a last lingering glance with the damaged woman curled on her side.

His nonperformance when it counted had added distress to her already haunted gaze. Shame warmed his skin. Unaware, she released his hand and smiled shakily. "Get back to your team. Thank you for your protection when I needed it most." Her voice cracked on the last word, and she winced.

"Ice and rest. Listen to the doc." Gage reluctantly stepped back and placed his helmet back on.

"Chantal?" The curtain whipped open, and the ambassador approached with a scowl. "I was on a conference call with the White House when I got the news. Let me see that neck."

Chantal twisted to her back, flinching reflectively when her mother traced her jaw. She'd reacted that way with the doctor and even the nurses. But not with Gage. He gritted his teeth and looked away as he fastened his helmet strap.

"How did this happen?" The ambassador turned on the two MSD agents in the room.

Gage wouldn't make excuses. He deserved an ass whipping, and Chantal's' entire detail earned a dressing-down.

"A hostile pretended to be a patient, and we dropped the ball. I take full responsibility for the assault."

"Good. I'm holding you to that."

"It's not his fault…" Chantal sat up.

"Chantal." Gage shook his head.

"You'll address her as Miss Durant. Is that clear?"

"Yes, Madam Ambassador."

"I asked for privacy in treat… treatment rooms."

"Stop talking." Gage clenched his fists. "You heard what the doc said."

"You put me in this situation." Chantal grabbed her mother's jacket. "Where's the flash drive?"

"The what?" The ambassador turned back to her daughter.

"Is whatever is on that thing, worth… worth my life? That monster wanted Rajin's flash drive." Chantal's face flushed, and her chest heaved. Gage stepped forward.

"We don't have a flash drive."

"Don't lie to me." The shouted words came out as a whisper. Her eyes filled. "Don't leave me… out of the loop. It's my life!"

"I'm not. Sweetie. It's okay." Her mother grasped her wrist, and Chantal drew back.

"Don't. She doesn't want to be touched." Gage's muscles locked, and he craved to pull the ambassador away from her traumatized daughter.

"What about Daddy?"

"What?"

"Knew him. He knew him." Chantal pointed a trembling finger at her mother. "He knew."

"You're not making any sense."

"Madam Ambassador, your daughter should rest her throat." The doctor stepped around the curtain.

"Want to go home." Chantal swung her legs over the side, and Gage sidled closer.

"In about an hour. The IV should do its job." They'd treated the inflammation with an Ibuprofen drip. "For pain, you can take over-the-counter meds—Advil or Tylenol."

"Let's go, man." Gannon grasped Gage's arm. "She's good —with family. Team Three are providing support for the drive back to the Jefferson House."

Gage nodded, knowing after today, Team Five would take a backseat until they knew their fate. They'd either stick with the detail, be reassigned, or sent back to Virginia for the debrief. This could be the last time he'd see Chantal—hurting and angry.

He took a moment to take in every last detail—her glistening earthy brown eyes, her soft, slightly downturned mouth, and that one solitary freckle below her left eye. Chantal's entire focus was on her mother, and she didn't see him walk away— forcing one foot in front of the other.

Gage hated the smell of hospitals, which reminded him of another tragic day—when he'd seen his mother for the last time. The hollow feeling in his gut expanded, and Gage shook off his friend's hand on his shoulder. It was time for a debriefing, the first of many. His heart rate ratcheted as he left the room. Every step in the opposite direction bolstered his failure.

"Son, a word?"

Gage gritted his teeth and swung to face Martin. "I'll save you some time. Her assault happened on my watch, and I take full responsibility."

"You're not the only one who'll be raked over the coals." Martin clamped a hand on Gage's shoulder. "You look like shit."

97

LOUISE DAWN

"I let her down. She relied on me for protection and…" Gage covered his mouth and shook his head.

"We all did. Can I remind you that it's impossible to guard a principal while also allowing for freedom and movement—you know it's a compromise." Martin squeezed his arm. "Take some deep breaths."

Gage did as instructed. His insides shook with unspent adrenaline.

"The ambassador wants the local details and Team Three on duty tonight. You can return to the hotel. If we need you, we'll call."

Fuck—the dismissal felt like a reprimand and Gage gritted his teeth.

"The poor girl can't catch a break."

"What do you mean? Chantal?" Gage asked.

"Let's sit." Martin walked over to an empty corner of a long waiting room. Gage chose a seat beside his mentor and waited for the older man to speak.

"You're already too involved—with her."

"Sir, listen—"

"You don't know what she's lived through."

"You're talking about the assassination—"

"And her college years. The first year of college to be exact."

Gage frowned at the opposite wall, thinking back on what he'd read about the younger Chantal.

"Her file mentioned a confrontation," Martin stretched out his legs. "but details weren't included."

"At the University of Colorado." Gage recalled a brief mention of a mugging and assumed the thief had made off with Chantal's purse. The word 'assault' conjured up dark alternatives.

"Yeah. Just a couple of years after her father had died. Chantal started her studies with a broken spirit. Still, she persevered and split her time between her mother's recovery and her classes."

Gage folded his arms, not liking the image of Chantal in a bad mental space—seeing her parents sliced apart by an assassin, losing a father, and piecing together a shattered existence. Gage's traumatic childhood had sent him spiraling in a similar downward plunge. If it weren't for the man next to him…

"One night, after a late class, Chantal walked to her vehicle." Martin leaned forward and clasped his hands. "A masked thug with a knife ambushed her in the lot—demanded her purse and phone."

Gage swung his gaze back to Martin, bracing himself for what came next.

"He stabbed Chantal."

"Fuck!"

"Yeah. The angel didn't know what hit her. Luckily, the college football team who'd just finished practice, heard her scream. The bastard ran, but it was too late."

"How bad?" Gage's fisted hands craved vengeance.

"He knifed her in the stomach, and she almost died. But she's tough like her mother and went on to make a full recovery, catching up with her missed studies."

Gage swore softly. "Did they catch the fucker?"

"No—and Connie left no stone unturned. She even hired a team of private investigators. The assailant was a ghost. After her father's death and the attack, the trusting kid became an afflicted and rebellious girl."

"Her rebellious phase? Is that when she dated the French dude—with the sandals?"

"Correct—about four months after graduation. Chantal fell in love with the ass, and after the break-up, she turned into a tame shadow. That's her story to tell. My point is, you shouldn't get too close. After today, your team will likely leave Sri Lanka. It's time to say goodbye before it gets too messy."

"Why should it get messy?"

"I'm trying to protect you, son." Martin stood, and Gage sensed he wasn't getting the full story. "If the ambassador thinks you're interested in her daughter—in the principal— she'll nail your balls to the wall. That's a career-ender."

"Great talk… pops."

"Gage, don't—I'm trying to help."

"Good night, Martin. Sir. I'm big and ugly enough to take care of myself." Gage wanted to hit something. Instead, he headed for the stairs. Martin was right. They should never be at a hospital—not with an injured principal. And why couldn't he stop thinking about her as more than a job?

Jona walked by the waiting room and smiled at Gage's raised voice. Team Five had been kicked to the curb and the men looked pissed. The sun had dropped from the sky by the time Jona stepped out onto the rough pavement.

Rajin Bandara had made his move. An aggressive and risky move that should make the daughter's killing a little easier. Easier did not necessarily mean quicker. Twelve years was a long time to stew over a job, and Jona wanted the satisfaction of a personal and drawn-out kill. Would that happen?

Anger from that fucked-up day slowly turned to bitterness. Cheated out of the right goodbye with Papa, had Jona blaming the targets. It should have been a glorious win, and Jona should have had the guts to go to the killing grounds alone. It was all about timing and drawing out their demise.

Never again would Jona fail on the job. A partnership would result in the required carnage necessary for payback. Rajin hid from the world, but Jona knew where to find his dirty minion—the one who'd attacked Chantal.

For the right price, Jona would have an army of hired help.

Working as an assassin paid off over the years. Untouched millions sat in Jona's Swiss bank account. Enough to buy loyalties and topple diplomats.

Entering a humble rental just blocks from the embassy, Jona headed for the kitchen and opened a cupboard, reaching for the whiskey. This was the Sri Lankan safehouse that Jona had used over the years when in-country. A night off meant that Jona could drown out the memories in this solitary safe place.

Not all the kills were easy. Sometimes lightly tainted targets had to die—riffraff who'd strayed mildly from the path. Those were the times when Jona killed quickly. Eliminating established and corrupt scumbags? A different story. Jona enjoyed drawing out their agony—making the evil assholes beg for their filthy lives.

The last kill involved a mafia kingpin who owed money to the wrong people. He also bought young girls for his hidden harem. Slicing up the flabby turkey had felt satisfying—one less perverted deviant in the world. Papa said never to get emotionally involved—you did the job, came home, and left the baggage at the door. Jona wasn't built that way. If the target deserved to hurt, they'd feel every last sliver of pain.

Chantal is an innocent.

Jona pushed the uncomfortable thought away along with past actions.

This mission wasn't about the target; it was about mending the past's wrongs—a broken promise to a great man. Memories of their hunts rose to the surface... waiting for hours in the bitter cold for a passing elk.

"Aim for a strikethrough."

"Yes, Papa."

"Don't be scared. You're a good shot. We'll eat well this year. Look... there's a herd beyond those trees."

"My arm is itchy. Can't I scratch it?"

"And scare the elk? If you miss, you know the consequences."

A night alone in the wilderness. Papa threatened to return to their cabin and leave a seven-year-old Jona alone in the forest. He'd done it before and would do it again. That was the punishment for missing the target.

A sound outside the window had Jona pushing off the counter and reaching for a weapon. A thorough perimeter check revealed a stray dog, rifling through garbage cans. Jona went back inside and grabbed leftovers from the fridge. After feeding the starving animal, Jona locked the doors and pulled out a laptop. Time to go hunting. The killing would soon begin.

Rajin didn't exactly suffer in exile. The out-of-the-way, fortified villa had been a wise investment—purchased from war spoils. And he paid the price—hiding like a scared hare. Rajin eased himself into the chlorinated infinity pool and pushed off from the side.

That damn flash drive would get them all killed—or flogged and, at the very least, arrested. He'd underestimated his bitch of an ex-wife. He'd rarely trusted, but over the years, he'd fallen for the classic beauty and her infinite love for him and their daughter.

Rajin had tried to remain faithful and succeeded for the first years of their marriage. But, the more he'd traveled, the less he'd thought about Pearl. And there was temptation everywhere—fresh blood for a shark who couldn't ignore his true nature.

When Pearl had found out about his affairs, and her anger had settled, they'd decided on a strained friendship. He'd still wanted her in his life. Pearl was a good mother and forgave him for bad behavior for the sake of Aysha.

Doggy paddling to the side, Rajin paused to catch his breath. He missed his daughter with every cell in his body. Running away with his heart and soul was an unforgivable act, and Pearl would pay dearly for her deceit.

Rajin's burner phone buzzed on the pool chair, and he waved his hand at a servant. The man immediately scrambled to bring the phone and towel over to Rajin's outstretched hand.

"And? Does she know where it is?" Rajin asked.

"I don't think so. But the chiropractic bitch will find it if we don't locate the drive first."

"You're sure about that?"

"I drove the message home—with my bare hands." Harris chuckled. "She has a real pretty neck."

"You'll be strung up by the neck if you don't complete the mission. Are we working the American angle?"

"I have a Stateside team on the ground who'll find Pearl and force her to give up the location of the drive. We're covered on all fronts."

"Tell them not to be gentle. I want my daughter back."

"Yes, sir."

"In the meantime, find out what her friend knows. My intel indicates Pearl went first to the rehab center and spoke with the ambassador's daughter. The next stop was the embassy before leaving Sri Lanka."

Harris's voice rose. "Harassing the daughter is one thing... you want me to go after the ambassador? Then you'll pay me a higher fee. That's a million-dollar contract. I'll need resources. We can burn the whole fucking place down."

"Hold off. If the U.S. government had the drive, we'd know by now. And it would be too late for damage control. I don't think the ambassador received that juicy titbit."

"So, it's down to your ex-wife or her therapist friend."

"Both will die. One had better produce the goods," Rajin stated.

"That drive? I'm guessing at the content. Twenty-three months ago…"

"I don't pay you to be nosy. Do your damn job." Rajin ended the call and handed the phone back to his man, who knew what to do, immediately destroying the device. The lackey broke open a new box and turned on the new burner. Rajin waited impatiently. When it was ready, he dialed the one number he'd vowed never to call. No-one answered. He tried again. Finally, a voice sounded at the end of the line.

Rajin swallowed past his dry throat. "Mr. President. We have a problem."

12

"You can't squat inside like a caged animal. Come with us to the beach—night swimming." Kohen tapped Gage on the back. "By the way, you look like shit."

He felt like shit. Gage ignored the medic and focused on the screen. Shifting the laptop away from the prick, he scanned the article looking for seeds of intel on Chantal's father. By all accounts, the man had been a generous philanthropist who'd raced around the globe helping disadvantaged communities. Henri Durant made his money as a shipping magnate, not a whisper of controversy surrounding his livelihood or charity pursuits.

Gage stretched. The dining chair felt as uncomfortable as all hell. "Where did I put that photo of the asshole?"

"You mean on this bird's nest you've weaved?" Gannon shifted a pile of papers, and Gage scowled.

"I know where everything is—back up."

"You've had your ass glued to this chair for two days. At least take a damn shower." Gannon produced the photo of the target—the mercenary who'd attacked Chantal.

It wasn't much to go on—a blurred image from a camera

across from the center, but still, Gage scoured the internet and reached out to informants to see if he could find the missing link. The Confianca Recovery Center needed better surveillance equipment—a error Gage would rectify.

"Look, bud. Digging around in our principal's past is not our job. And she might not even be our assignment anymore." Lucius grabbed a protein bar from a cupboard and jabbed it at his team leader.

Leaning his elbows on the table, Gage ran his hands over his cropped hair. "I can't ignore this—ignore her. Fuck!"

"Talk to me." Gannon sat down and pinned Gage with a hard stare.

"I screwed up. Chantal matters, and if we get reassigned…"

"Matters because she's the one principal we couldn't protect, or matters because you're attracted to her?"

Gannon always asked the hard questions.

"I don't know. I like her attitude. I've always been able to separate work from play."

"Except this isn't play." Lucius grinned. "I've seen how you are back home. You don't let the chicks get too close. Now? You ain't playing."

"Oh, he wants to play," Kohen added. "Chantal Durant is one hot piece of ass."

Gage stood and got in the dick's face. "Apologize."

"Whoa. Dude. I'm just saying."

"Bold words for a man who's about to get laid out." Gage shoved Kohen back.

"You want to work in this team, learn some respect." Gannon backed his team leader. "You're talking about our principal—an unselfish individual who's earned the highest regard."

"Whatever. You all can screw off." Kohen grabbed a beach towel and stormed out of the room.

"I don't know about that guy." Lucius shot Gage a worried look. "Doesn't hang with us after hours, even exercises on his own at five in the fucking morning. He ain't vibing with the team."

"None of us are vibing as a team. If we were, we wouldn't have an injured principal." Gage stood. "I'm taking that shower. Get some sleep, boys, and stop screwing around on the beach. If you want to exercise, hit the gym."

Gage found privacy in the bedroom, changed out of his clothes, and blasted the hot water. His mind kept latching onto Chantal's college trauma. He'd called in a favor to access the police records only to discover that the case was sealed.

First, an assassin tries to wipe out her family, and two years later, an assailant knifes Chantal on her campus? And the bastard was never found.

Saying that Chantal had herculean grit was an understatement. You'd never guess from her composed commitment to others what she'd endured. And, for the third time, she reeled after a vicious attack—Gage's fault. Twenty minutes later, Gage stepped out of the shower. His phone buzzed on the bathroom counter, and he frowned at the number. Answering, he ran the damp towel over his chest.

"Chants?"

"Gage."

He immediately picked up on her distress, and his stomach bottomed out. She'd been recovering at the Jefferson House, surrounded by state of the art security. "What's wrong? Are you safe?"

"Fine… I just…" Her voice sounded stronger than when they'd last spoke.

"Talk." Placing her on speaker, Gage grabbed a pair of cargo pants, imagining all sorts of dire scenarios.

"I can't sleep. I see his face and…"

Gage fell back on the bed, his pants halfway up his legs.

Relief had him releasing a slow breath. "PTSD. You're battling PTSD."

"I need to talk to someone. Are you free to chat?"

"Where are you? In the main house or your cottage?"

"Cottage, but we can speak on the phone."

Swearing inwardly, Gage winced at what he was about to do. He was losing his damn mind. "No—I'll be there in fifteen."

After getting dressed, indecision over his insane promise had him pacing the room. *Stay strong and stay away. She'll complicate the hell out of your world.*

Gage didn't care. Chantal needed him. He'd talk her down from her anxiety attack and stay with her until she fell asleep. An hour tops. Maybe two. He'd be back by one. Who did she really have by her side in Sri Lanka? Her mother was a cold fish. Chantal could call Alexis, but although they worked together, they weren't exactly besties.

Gage couldn't deny his connection with Chantal. It couldn't go past tonight. They'd go their separate ways, and he'd appreciate the time he'd spent with her. Yeah, this was what he needed. Closure. A chance to say an actual goodbye.

Why had she called Gage? She could do this on her own—power through and place the incident behind her. And allowing him to come over could complicate his assignment even more. Chantal paced the modest lounge. She loved the relaxed vibe of the cottage. Sparsely furnished, but the bed and the sofa set were comfortable—the two luxuries that counted. Her nomadic lifestyle kept her from gathering junk, and Chantal firmly believed that a home was a living space and not a storage unit.

Checking the time on her phone for the tenth time wasn't

helping her nerves. And the lack of sleep over the past couple of nights contributed to her hyped state of mind. Should she have changed out of her lounge clothes? Chantal glanced in the mirror at her pale yellow, off-the-shoulder, baggy sweatshirt worn with gray leggings. Sexy or casual? Casual sexy? Was that a thing?

The loud knock had her jolting before stumbling over to answer.

Breathe. It's Gage. You're fine.

After opening the door, Chantal forgot to breathe. His solid build took up most of her brightly lit porch. Thanks to the humidity and soft rain, his t-shirt clung to a chiseled frame. No armor, just warm skin. Chantal resisted the urge to reach out. Her gaze traveled up to his face and froze. Set in a harsh grimace, his expression savage, Gage looked ready to go to war.

"Your neck."

"I know… it looks worse than it feels. Come in."

Chantal stepped aside, yet he didn't budge.

"I can see every fucking finger mark."

"Fun times." She focused on the pitter-patter of drops bouncing off the gutters.

"Jesus, Chants. This isn't a joke."

"Believe me, I know." Chantal walked to the small kitchen and picked up her glass of wine.

Finally, he closed the door and followed her to the dimly lit space. The lamp next to the sofa glowed in the small room, lending a comforting feel.

"I poured you a glass. Hope you like white. Did you have trouble at the gate?"

"No. Dishan was one of the guys on duty, and I think he knows."

"Knows what?" Nervously swiping a thumb over the moisture on her glass, Chantal avoided his gaze.

"That I can't stay away."

Looking up at Gage's guarded expression, she tried to think of what to say. Was that the truth?

"So… you're not sleeping." He carried his glass to the sofa. "Let's sit."

"Uh…"

"I know what it's like to experience contact violence—close quarter combat for the first time. And over the subsequent years, I've experienced some haunting shit. Fighting for your life with your bare hands—your mind is consumed with the need to survive."

"The thing is…" Gathering her courage, Chantal circled the single chair and chose to sit beside him on the longer lounge sofa. "I'm angry at myself."

"Why?"

"Because. I don't know; I should have fought harder. I kicked the hell out of the hooligan at the market. How did I get into such a vulnerable position… with a monster's hands… his hands wrapped around my neck?"

"Your assailant is more than likely hired muscle—a well-trained mercenary who's dealt with larger prey in the past. He planned the attack and anticipated your panic and your defensive moves."

Curling into the large cushions, Chantal tucked in her legs. "He purposely strangled me so that I wouldn't cause a disturbance—so that I wouldn't scream. Right?"

"Yeah, Chants. He knew what he was doing." Gage's eyes kept straying to her bruised throat.

"Next time, I'll be ready."

A frown creased his forehead. "There isn't going to be a next time. Martin mentioned your flight back to the States."

"Yeah—no. I'm now staying. I have a symposium to finish."

"Are you insane!"

"I'm not running away when I could be helping so many patients. This event has taken months to plan. One asshole mercenary isn't going to stop me from making a difference. We're understaffed as it is, and I'm one of three chiropractors."

"That's dangerous and foolish." Gage shifted closer.

"My mother isn't the only battle-ax in this war. The clinic needs funding, and Sri Lanka needs the mine clearance donations, so we don't have any more accidents. Amongst the inland patients, I'm seeing three children while I'm there—three kids who had their limbs blown away in separate incidences thanks to old landmines. Kids living in spinal agony. Their growing bodies need newly fitted prosthetics. And there are so many more youngsters out there, living with missing limbs."

"I get that, but Chants, if you die while securing funding…"

"There will be so much security at the symposium, and it's out of the city. And if your team is—"

"My team may be sent away. We fucked up."

"No. Gage! I want you by my side." Chantal placed a hand on his chest, and he covered her fingers with his own.

"It's not up to you, or me, or even your mother."

"It's never up to me." Her mouth twisted. "I'm sick of fate. One moment, I'm standing with my parents on one of the best days of my life, and the next, I'm covered in my parents' blood and lying beside a limousine."

"Chants…"

"I re-lived that moment for years, in my nightmares—seeing Daddy's lifeless body lying on the concrete—his blood dripping down the steps. I couldn't stop screaming. And when mom fell…"

Gage pulled her to his chest and she continued to talk. Aside from therapists, Chantal had never spoken about those dark days to anyone. "I hated that man—the assassin who ripped apart my family. Hated him and imagined killing him over and over. Instead, I watched my mother suffer for years. Endless surgeries and night terrors."

"That's why you became a chiropractor."

Chantal pulled back. "If I could help my mom in some small way. It wasn't a choice. I don't regret my decision which has led me to help others."

They sat in silence, and he stared at her mouth before looking away. "I heard about what happened at your college—the assault."

That wasn't what she wanted to hear, and Chantal tried to think of what to say. Heat traveled up her neck, and she tugged her hand away.

Gage held on and pulled it back to his chest. "That on top of losing your father…"

"I'm assuming Martin told you? What did he say?"

"Just that your attacker stabbed you on the campus."

Judging by Gage's expression and words, he didn't know of the complications from her injury.

"Not something I'm ready to talk about." She rubbed her thumb on his shirt. "I have a scar."

"Never be ashamed of scars. You survived, and you're insanely courageous." Gage's eye's simmered with warmth.

All an act that didn't include the broken parts of her soul. Gage had no idea.

He must've picked up on her misery. "What's wrong?"

Ignoring his concern, she asked the hard question. "When will you know?"

"Hopefully, in the next twelve hours."

"And if it's a no, then you'll be sent away."

"Yes, ma'am. I'm almost sure I'll be leaving."

"So… this could be the last time I see you?"

"Chants." His eyes blazed, and he fell silent.

She could feel his heart pounding beneath her palm. Had

she ever seen anything more perfect than his rugged face? Those toasty eyes always looked like they'd devour her whole. Pulse-pounding, she rubbed a thumb over his shirt and watched Gage audibly swallow.

"I should go," he croaked.

"And I might never see you again."

"We can't."

"It's just us… and the rain." Feeling bold, she shifted closer.

His hand released hers and traced over her temple. "You're perfect, but I don't think touching you would be wise, especially after…"

"Tais-toi, et embrasse-moi."

"Did you tell me to shut-up?" His tantalizing lips sat close.

"Oui, chéri. I told you to shut up and kiss me."

"That's an order I can't ignore." Gage swept in, and she sighed into his mouth. Easing her back gently, he settled, careful not to place all his weight on her. Relaxing into the moment, Chantal took her time enjoying his taste and his touch.

Goosebumps broke at his hot mouth on her earlobe. Lips shifted back to her mouth and then to her shoulder, Gage bit and sucked, moving down to her collarbone before dragging down her sweatshirt and licking her cleavage. Her chest rose, inviting his touch, and he slipped fingers beneath her shirt, tracing her bare stomach. His hand moved higher, and he groaned.

"No bra? Chants…"

Raising her arms, she smiled at his agonized expression. Without hesitation, Gage pulled the shirt over her head, and she kept her arms raised as he took in his fill.

Closing her eyes, Chantal felt him touch the scar on her pelvis. The two-inch knife injury sat low, below her bellybutton. Not terribly wide or unsightly as her mother had paid for the best plastic surgeons in the States.

Gage's lips feathered over the old injury, and his tenderness made her eyes burn. And then he stopped. Eyes snapping open, Chantal frowned. His gaze had drifted upward to her neck.

"Don't."

"Seeing those marks makes me ill. I wasn't around to prevent the attack on your campus—but your neck?"

"There's only two of us in this room. And I'm not inviting misplaced guilt to the party."

Flexing his jaw, Gage glanced away. Chantal waited as he grappled with his mental demons.

"I need you tonight. Your hands and your mouth."

He turned back and kissed her breast with great care, and she reached up to stroke his hair. His warm tongue circled her tightening peak, and when he sucked hard, delicious warmth spread throughout her body. When he blew over her nipple, her back arched towards his lips. Gage paid equal attention to both breasts before lifting Chantal and carrying her to the bedroom.

He laid her on the edge of her bed and pulled off his t-shirt. He unclipped a holstered handgun and placed it on the bedside table. Sitting up, she stared at his perfect chest and ripped stomach. The guy did eat nails for breakfast. No-one looked that cut without sticking to a brutal regimen. Did he lift sumo wrestlers in his spare time? The MSD spartan workout for possible armageddon scenarios?

"You're grinning like a Cheshire Cat."

"I am. Let me guess… brutal burpees, ice baths, and twelve hours in the boxing ring?"

Winking, Gage stepped between her legs. "Bingo." He traced the top of her pants. "Are you sure you want my tongue between your legs?"

"Well…when you ask me like that." Chantal laughed. "Yes, please."

Peeling off her pants and underwear in one swift move, Gage dropped her clothes and stepped back.

"What are you doing?"

"Taking in the incredibly gorgeous woman lying in front of me. Get comfortable."

Chantal scooted to the middle of her white sheets and lay back. Starting with her ankle, Gage slowly worked his way up her leg, kissing and nibbling. When he reached the top of her thigh, he bit down and sucked. Chantal bucked at the erotic sensation. Hands cupping her ass, he moved to her center, pausing before blowing gently on her damp heat.

"Gage…"

"I love the way you say my name. It gets me hard every time."

His hot mouth covered her, and she fisted the sheets. Using his tongue and teeth and fingers, he drove her upwards with an unrelenting skill that had her toes curling as he stroked deep.

Blazing eyes watched her every expression, and when Chantal met his gaze, he rolled his thumb across her clit, demanding her release. Obeying his command, she split apart, as wave after wave of pleasure rippled outwards, and she screamed his name. Softening his strokes, Gage brought her back down, and Chantal sighed in contentment. Standing, he loosened his pants, and she smiled.

Something buzzed. Once… twice. Gage swore as he pulled out his phone.

"What's wrong?" Chantal raised her head.

"It's Martin. I'd better get this." He turned away as Chantal sat up and pulled a sheet over her shoulders.

"Sir?… Are you sure… it's a risk… no, I understand." Gage squeezed the back of his neck and muscles rippled across

his back. "What time... yes, sir. I won't let you down."
Hanging up, he stared at the wall.

"Everything okay?"

"This was a mistake."

"Excuse me?"

"You're still the principal. This is a mistake."

"I'm a human with feelings. Screw that."

"Chants." He turned, and she ignored his agonized expression.

"Which is it? Chants or Miss Durant? Make up your mind."

"You don't understand. Team Five isn't reassigned—you're still my responsibility, and I let my emotions dictate—"

"Your dick's next move? Did your 'emotions' tell you to stroke me to orgasm? Let's blame those pesky emotions." Rolling off the bed, Chantal walked over to her silk robe hanging off the door.

"I didn't think I'd see you again."

"Oh! So this was the bon voyage special?"

"Stop! Jesus. You're taking this the wrong way. I can't protect you if I'm not thinking clearly."

"And that's my fault." Fastening her robe a little too tightly around her waist, Chantal bent to pick up her clothes.

"I didn't say that." Getting the hint, he reached for his gun and clipped it back on his waist.

"I'm tired of this. Of living a limited existence where diplomatic workers won't come near the ambassadors' daughter. Do you know how long it's been since I've trusted? Pearl was my closest confidante in this crazy-ass existence.

I refuse to be isolated, and guess what, I don't need your pity. I won't live on the sidelines—not anymore. After the symposium, I'm going to go out into the world to find love and develop friendships without having to ask permission. Without having to beg for scraps of my time. My time!" It felt good to toss his t-shirt at his chest.

"Honey—"

"This was fun. I'm sure I'll see you on Monday." Chantal marched to her front door. "Heads-up, it will be a busy day. Try to keep up."

"I don't want to leave like this."

Staring past his shoulder, Chantal shrugged. Tears burned, and she willed them away. "You got what you wanted—getting back to a professional relationship with your principal."

Gage reached out, and she stepped back.

"Good night, Agent Hendrix."

"We'll talk when you've calmed down."

He'd have to wait a long time because she'd woken to the fact that she had choices. Next time, she'd choose a man who'd take her out on dates… bring her flowers… kiss her on her front step. Diplomatic agents be damned.

13

Did the rain ever stop? It was supposed to be partly cloudy today. The gray clouds reflected Gage's mood as he watched Wyatt lead Chantal from the car to the printing house. She'd been right about hitting the ground running. They'd traveled the length and breadth of Colombo as she'd gathered supplies for the upcoming symposium while methodically ticking off a to-do list in her unwieldy planner.

Not only had she fought at the docks with customs over duty payments for wheelchairs entering the country, but she'd bought blankets, loaded up food packages from a food bank, and picked up medical supplies from a wholesaler.

Throughout the day, she'd completely ignored Gage and stuck by Alexis's side. Chantal laughed and giggled with her friend—even flirted with a medical rep. Tamping down on his irritation, Gage and his team trailed behind as her local guards helped her haul supplies to the car.

Like the MSD team, her protection detail was on high alert. He'd fucked up so many times on the op. First, on the job and then in the bedroom. Gage hated that he'd hurt her when he'd backed off, but it was the right decision. Both for the sake of her safety and the sake of his career. So why did he feel like he'd blow apart at any moment?

Gannon joined Gage as they crossed the busy road, speeding up to avoid a moped. "Have fire ants crawled up your butt?"

"What are you talking about?" Gage brushed at his damp neck.

"You're all twitchy."

"I'm doing my job."

"If you combined that with fifty cups of coffee. Is it the rain? Is it the pretty girl ignoring your grouchy ass?"

"It's your annoying voice whining in my ear." Gage zoned in on two men hanging outside the printers. Exchanging money for cigarettes, they didn't seem to notice the security detail brushing past.

"She's looking adorable in her little rain boots."

"Shut up, asshole."

Chantal did look cute in designer rubber boots that matched a black flared dress and a leather jacket. At the docks, she'd purposely splashed through a puddle on her way to the customs office. Gage had tried not to smile. At least someone enjoyed the rain, and it was nice to see spontaneity in that rigid demeanor.

Dishan and Gannon walked to the back office with Chantal to retrieve boxes of marketing materials and tablecloths. Gage chose to remain in the front of the store as the rest of Team Five kept an eye on their surroundings. He watched Alexis as she fiddled with the promotional items on display. She'd pulled her thick blonde hair into a high pony, which served to highlight her cat-like eyes and pouty mouth.

"What was the fight about?"

Gage raised his brows.

"Whatever you did, pissed Chantal off." Picking up a mug, Alexis shot him an amused glance.

Folding his arms, Gage leaned against the window and scanned the street as Wyatt and a local guard stood in front of the window. His neck prickled. They were being watched, and Gage could feel it in his bones.

"The big, brooding bruiser attitude doesn't fly with me." Placing the mug back down, Alexis sauntered his way, and he stiffened. A finger traced his tactical vest, and she leaned in to whisper in his ear. "Stay away from Chantal. Her soft heart isn't meant for an alpha gorilla like you."

Narrowing his eyes, Gage opened his mouth to reply.

"Am I interrupting?" Chantal carried out a box, and Gage felt his cheeks flush.

Shoving away from the blonde, he opened the door. "Can I carry that to the car?"

"No, Agent Hendrix." Chantal shot him a nasty glare. "Wouldn't want you distracted on the job."

"Chants—"

"Hold the door open for Dishan and Gannon—they're carrying the heavy stuff." She almost ran to the suburban, and Gage took a deep breath, wanting to explode.

"Oops. My bad." Alexis smiled and stepped into the rain.

Gage waited for the rest of the detail to file out of the shop and followed from behind. Alexis was either overprotective of her friend or enjoyed playing games. Her ambush had taken Gage by surprise. And her words cut deep, highlighting the fact that he and Chantal came from different backgrounds.

He'd lived a rough life after his mom died and he'd chosen to hone himself into a killing machine. Of course, he served the greater purpose of keeping diplomats and civilians safe, but Gage had nothing to offer a partner. Zero balance and Chantal craved stability.

The convoy headed to the Jefferson House as Chantal decided to store the equipment and supplies in her cottage's spare room. As they entered the upscale embassy neighborhood, Wyatt communicated via comms. "Miss Durant wants to stop at Cargills."

"Copy that. The grocery store?" Irritation stirred, and Gage rubbed his neck. "That's not a planned stop."

"Yeah, I know. She wants to buy additional food supplies for her patients in Hatton. The clinic will send the provisions on a separate truck."

Shit. Gage couldn't deny her request. The free clinic she'd set up would cater to the poorest of the poor.

"Fine. Let's make it fast." Spotting the billboard for "Cargill's Food City," Gage briefed his team on the unscheduled detour.

Cars filled the parking spots in the small lot, and the MSD van pulled into a side lane. Separated by a small wall, his team moved fast to rejoin her detail and chose to stick close to his principal, regardless of her prickly attitude.

The cramped store held a mix of western and local supplies, and Chantal and Alexis decided to split up the grocery list, both grabbing a shopping cart. Chantal stopped at the bottled waters, and when Gage moved in to help, she stopped him.

"I've got this."

"Yes, ma'am." He stepped back and folded his hands, trying not to grin at her muttered French profanities.

Thanks to the rain, her usually straight bob-cut had morphed into soft waves, and Gage ached to run a hand through the silky strands. Instead, he squeezed his fisted hands and scanned their surroundings—a local family... a squabbling couple... and damn.

"Chantal!"

Gage swore softly as a turd walked their way.

"Fredrik?" Chantal straightened and took a small step towards Gage.

With a mental fist pump, Gage slid closer and waited for

the Swedish diplomat to approach.

"What are you doing here?"

Fredrik raised his shopping basket. "Buying snacks for the office. Listen… about the other day… I don't know what went wrong, but I'd like another chance."

"Um… I don't think—"

"I heard about what happened—the attack at your center."

Chantal's hand subconsciously drifted to her neck, and Gage gritted his teeth.

"Did they catch the bastard?"

"I'd rather not talk about it."

"Sure. You look pretty." Fredrik's megawatt smile could light up a city, and Gage envisioned ways to wipe away that smarmy grin.

"Do you need help with those waters?" Fredrik put down his basket.

"Sure. Why not?" Chantal shot Gage a grin, and he narrowed his eyes.

"So about that second date…"

The man was persistent.

"I'm busy with the symposium, and I've decided not to date—at least for the moment."

Another mental fist pump. Gage took pleasure in watching Fredrik's face fall.

"I would think your protective detail would help with these waters—like this big lad." Fredrik nodded at Gage while hoisting a pack into the cart.

"We have to conserve our energy." Gage smiled. "For good killings and all."

"Really?" Fredrik shrugged. "I thought you just stood around all day looking pretty—flexing those ridiculous muscles."

Fucking prick.

"You want some? Ridiculous muscle? You're a little on the

skinny side."

"Gage! Stop." Chantal pursed her lips as she re-arranged the water pallets in the cart.

"Gage…" Fredrik paused and cocked his head. "You call your security detail by their first names?"

"You have a problem with that?" Gage's blood heated. Jason moved down the aisle like a panther, joining his team leader.

"I guess I know why she isn't dating—screwing her MSD team is way more fun."

Chantal's mouth fell open around the same time as Gage moved in for annihilation.

"What did you just fucking say?"

Fredrik stumbled as Gage backed the ass-hat into a shelf. "I was joking. It was a joke."

"You want to disrespect the lady—with two protection details breathing down your neck. We should stand by and listen to filth drop from your crappy mouth. Is that it?"

"I didn't. You seemed interested in our conversation and—"

"And her personal life is your fucking business?" Gage got real close.

"If you touch me—I'll report you. I'm… I'm with the Swedish consulate. Dare to touch me."

"Gage. He's not worth your job. I'll deal with him." Chantal's soft words fell on deaf ears.

"Insult her again, and my fists will do the talking. Pick up your basket, pay for your shitty items, and get the fuck outta here." Gage still loomed in the bastard's face, and Fredrik had to slide sideways out of the line of fire.

Everyone turned and watched the diplomat retrieve his groceries and rush for the check-out counter.

"Are you okay?" Wyatt asked Chantal as Jason raised his brows at Gage.

"I'm fine. And still have a list of items to buy. Can you grab the bread for me?" The AIC nodded and shot Gage a curious glance before moving off.

"Jase, give us a moment." Gage waited until his agent left the aisle and turned to Chantal. "I may have overreacted, but I couldn't let him disrespect you."

"I was never in any danger from his words. I'd known on our date that Fredrik's charm was a cover for his unpleasant disposition."

"Good. Because you deserve better."

"I do." Folding her arms, Chantal stepped close and raised her face to his. "I believe in editing my life frequently. I'm in charge of what and who takes up my time and space."

Turning, she gripped her cart and headed up the aisle. Why did that feel like a well-aimed arrow? Damn. Gage still sat firmly in the doghouse.

After helping her mother off the table, Chantal stepped back as her mom gingerly stretched her arm.

"How does it feel?"

"Good. Better. You're a miracle worker; you have the magic touch."

"It's a learned skill and nothing to do with miracles." Chantal folded a towel as her mother slipped a cardigan over her vest and walked to the sofa in the bedroom corner.

"It's late. Join me for a drink."

"I'm tired—it's been a long day gathering remaining supplies for the symposium." Chantal suppressed a yawn.

Shrugging, the ambassador uncorked the brandy decanter and poured out a splash of golden liquid. Chantal took in a slow breath, gathering courage.

"I mean it when I say that anyone else could step into my

shoes."

"You're my daughter and have my best interests at heart. You'll continue with my therapy." Connie took a small sip and sat.

"Does this arrangement serve my best interests?"

"What do you mean? I'm your mother."

"And in a few years, I'll be thirty. I'm tired of this life."

"You're tired." The ambassador laughed. "You're tired? Are you also in pain 24/7 without relief? Does the pounding agony eat into your sanity? Do you lie in bed, trying to imagine a world without pain?"

"Mom, perhaps you should also be reconsidering your path? Is this what you want? To work yourself to the bone for diplomatic infamy?"

"I serve a higher purpose. I fight for peace, and I will never have that serenity in my own life, but I can secure it for others through diplomacy."

"And that's your journey—your chosen path. It's not mine. I don't even know what I want from life."

"Chantal, stop whining."

"As much as I love helping communities, I became a chiropractor and a medical masseur to help you—to ease your pain over the years. But my future is uncertain. I might open a practice or choose a different field like prosthetics. I want to take a break and consider my future."

"You're not going anywhere, so sideline your existential crisis. I need you, and besides, you're not safe."

"You're wealthy enough to afford a full-time specialist. Once Rajin no longer poses a threat, I'm taking a sabbatical. I can recommend—"

"You're going to abandon your mother."

"That's not my intention."

"What do you want? Because if it's a happy family, we lost that a long time ago. If it's a future family…"

"I can't believe you just said that." Heart hurting, Chantal stepped way back from the woman who'd raised her.

"Walk away, and I'll disown you."

"Are you kidding?"

"What would your father say? If he knew you were leaving me."

"Yes… what would he say? Because I'm wondering if my happy childhood was an illusion. Who was my father?"

"How dare you!" Connie's hand shook and the brandy spilled. "You were Henri's entire world!"

"And I got him killed. Why do you think I've remained by your side for all these years? Thanks to my selfish tantrum that night, you got hurt, and daddy died. I wanted him to attend my play and I nagged him for months. He knew it was a risk and I pushed him to step away from a secure home environment. I should've known it was dangerous—that week, he'd hired more guards."

"No, Chantal—"

"Don't touch me. Don't! I hated seeing your pain. I love you! But you owe me my freedom."

"And you're all I have left."

"Then don't push me away! I'll always be your daughter."

"Let's talk about your future together."

"No, Mom. I need air." Swinging open the door, Chantal raced down the stairs and through the old home. The warm rain felt good against her skin, and instead of rushing for her cottage, Chantal found the nearest bench under the green canopy of a palm.

Large drops of water fell from the leaves and snaked over her arms. Raising her feet to the bench, Chantal wrapped her arms around her legs and stared out into the wet night. Her thoughts rolled back in time, settling on that fateful day in Colorado when a hit-man shot her innocent world to smithereens.

14

Hands in pockets, Jona entered the dark pub, glancing over at the big screen's cricket game. A crowd watched a replay of the one-day international match. Veering past the snooker tables, Jona zoned in on a quiet booth held by one lone occupant. Jona slid into the opposite seat, and the man straightened.

"'Cheers.' Really? You chose a bar called 'Cheers.'"

"They have good food. British pie." Beady eyes took in Jona's hoodie as the thug forked at a piece of pastry and chicken before swiping at the gravy on the plate. Harris shoveled the food into a hungry mouth, glancing up nervously at Jona's lethal stare.

"What's your fucking problem?" he asked.

"Imagining the different ways I could kill you. It's a game."

"You're crazier than I am."

"Damn right. And I've racked up more bodies at half your age. Never forget that."

"You're getting too big for yur britches, and one day, life is gonna teach you a lesson." Pushing aside his plate, Harris took a long swig of beer.

"It ain't gonna be you. Besides, you owe me this meeting." Jona leaned forward. "I have your balls in a vice-like grip."

"Then talk. Time is expensive."

"The daughter doesn't know the location of the flash drive. Squeezing her for information is futile."

"Oh, I squeezed all right." Harris grinned. "Watching her pretty face turn red as I held her down, that gave me a solid hard-on."

Jona forced a smile, trying not to show obvious distaste. Harris was an unprofessional bastard who gave killing a lousy name. But, over the years, they'd occasionally worked together. As a former contact of Jona's father, Harris knew way too much about Jona's past and had spent time at the Kivela cabin.

Harris spoke Finnish, Russian and Chinese—the bastard had an affinity for language and had contacts all over the globe. For some reason, Harris trusted in Jona. That misplaced loyalty stemmed from his relationship with Otto. Sentimental asshole.

When the time was right, Jona would eliminate the sick prick. For now, Jona would need to stroke a deadly ego. Harris wouldn't be the first assassin that Jona had killed—or client, especially for the Durant women.

The stupid hired dick who'd stabbed Chantal on her campus had met Jona's wrath. Chantal was Jona's mark. No-one else would claim the kill. And Jona had made that clear with the client after he'd sent another killer after the teenager. When the wealthy fucker had refused to back down, he'd died a grisly death. No client—no contract.

Harris looked around and leaned in. "Three people know the whereabouts of the drive. Pearl, the ambassador, and her bitch of a daughter. If the ambassador has the USB evidence, she hasn't given it up. If she had, Sri Lanka would be in a state of anarchy. And my contacts in Washington haven't heard a whisper."

Jona wondered what that flash drive held. "She still might have it tucked away in a drawer."

"An excellent tool for blackmail although the ambassador doesn't seem like an extortionist. And her fuckable daughter may be innocent. If Pearl slid it her way, she might not even be aware."

"The other alternative is that Pearl still has the drive."

Harris nodded and yawned. Rubbing his stomach, he grinned. "I think we've found the bitch—I sent a team to her location."

Jona ran a finger over a knot on the wooden table, curious about his plans. Silence always drew Harris into the conversation.

"I told Rajin that thanks to the value of the drive, why not eliminate all the threats?"

"What do you mean?" Jona asked.

"If the daughter or the mother has the flash drive, it will be either on their person or back at their residence. We should take care of the problem swiftly. The more you stand in shit, the more it spreads. I have a man on the inside who'll search the residence while a surprise attack takes care of the women."

"An attack will bring way too much heat down on Rajin's head," Jona spoke softly. "Killing a U.S. Ambassador in a brazen attack? Fuck, no."

"Sometimes brawn is preferred." Harris grinned.

"Harris, what's on that drive?"

"None of your damn business."

"You and I go back for fifteen years. Let me help you. I can't do that without intel."

"You're dangerous. And I've known Rajin for longer than that."

"I am dangerous."

Harris dropped his hands to his lap, straightening his burly frame.

LOUISE DAWN

Jona needed his cooperation—at least for now. "I'll kill the mother and daughter, and I'll find a way to blame it on Rajin. If we work together…"

"No. I'm bringing you into Rajin's fold, and we'll deflect the blame. There are plenty of emerging extremist regimes that don't particularly care for the United States. Rajin is a useful ally—use him to get your revenge."

"Until he gets caught." Jona turned thoughtful. "You want to blame it on Islamic extremists. Not a bad idea. What's on the drive? More torture?"

"Rajin likes inflicting pain." Harris leaned his elbows on the table and lowered his voice to a whisper. "So does the President of Sri Lanka."

Jona's brows shot up. "They partnered up?"

"Two years ago. The night went badly. I got rid of the bodies."

"And Rajin secretly filmed the murders?" The pub suddenly felt warm, and Jona reached for Harris's beer, taking a large sip.

"Yeah. The president was unaware."

"Who died?"

"Do you remember that British reporter that went missing, along with his crew? He was working on a story—corruption at the highest level in the Sri Lankan government. Including lewd sex acts by the commander in chief. I destroyed his research and all channels linked to the investigation."

"By channels, you mean…"

"The whores who gave evidence. I'm an excellent cleaner."

Jona nodded. "That was always your forte."

Harris's confession didn't sit well with Jona. Slaughtering innocent women for a corrupt despot's political career shouldn't happen. Growing tired of the depravity bathing a reclusive conscience, Jona stood. Perhaps working alone was the better path.

"Wait. Let's talk some more and figure out a plan. I'll call Rajin."

"Fine. Call this number. Burner phone." A folded note hit the table. Jona said goodbye in Finnish, "Moikka."

And without waiting for a response, Jona headed for the exit. The dartboard on the wall proved to be a temptation. Pausing, Jona picked up a dart with a gloved hand and aimed. The projectile found its mark.

"Nice shot!" The bartender smiled. "Bulls-eye."

"I call it a strikethrough." Jona nodded at the cheerful man. The poor guy had no idea that the deadliest killer on the planet played darts in his establishment.

"I always say, you miss a hundred percent of the shots you don't take."

The barkeeper's words grated and Jona forced a smile. A hundred percent sounded about right.

They'd leave in the morning, and Gage still wasn't happy with the arrangement. He'd follow orders, but not before he laid some concerns to rest.

The whole situation bothered him, and Gage knew it related to Chantal's past. More specifically, her father's history. The guy was too clean for a self-made billionaire. What skeletons lurked in his closet? Running an empire that large would mean coloring outside the lines. The question that nagged was, how far out of the lines had Henri Durant ventured?

Gage greeted a familiar DS agent as he wound his way past to Martin's office. He was hoping to speak with the RSO as a friend and not as an agent. Depending on Martin's mood, this might go south instead of north. Gage knocked before entering, finding the RSO at his desk.

"We have that meeting in ten, so make this quick."

Gage nodded at the abrupt greeting and sat.

"I know about your budding relationship with Chantal. If you're here to chat about your "inappropriate" feelings on the job, I'm not interested. You're screwing up this assignment."

"I'm here about the job."

Martin cocked his head and folded his arms. "What are you doing, son?"

Gage hated when Martin called him that. It made him feel like the same kid who needed rescuing all those years ago.

"I thought you didn't want to talk about Chantal?" Gage countered.

"I never pinned you as a skirt chaser who'd muddy the waters with a principal."

"Jeez. You're going for the jugular. I… I care. More than I should. Do you honestly think I'd risk my career for a quick roll between the sheets?"

"I don't know what to think. What do you need?"

Gage tightened his grip on the folder he held. "I don't have enough intel on Henri Durant."

"He died twelve years ago. How does this relate to your duties?"

"The thug who attacked Chantal claimed that he'd worked for—with—Henri."

"And he could be talking smack."

"And if he isn't?" Gage asked.

Martin rubbed a hand over his mouth.

"He insinuated that Otto killed Chantal's father for a reason—for shady practices."

"I still don't see the point. If Henri was dirty, that was over a decade ago."

Gage pushed. "If we can uncover the link, we can find the mercenary and his cell. I need a face and a name."

"We all know who's behind Chantal's attack. Rajin is the man with the painted target on his back."

"Why was only Otto Kivela's rifle recovered at the assassination site?" Gage asked. "He admitted to the killing and immediately confessed to his history, but only the weapon was found—no field glasses or sniper tools. Where was the range finder?"

"Otto may not have used one."

"Bullshit. He used one in all his long-range kills."

Martin rubbed his eyes. "True. The FBI already mentioned a possible partner in crime."

"Yet, they never caught that individual."

"You think it was Chantal's attacker?" Martin crossed his arms and frowned.

"Could be." Gage paced the room. "Her philanthropist father is dirty. I feel it."

"That fact will break her heart."

"If it is true, do you think the ambassador was aware of her husband's activities?"

"Don't sully Connie with your speculation. It's not your job."

"Yeah? I hate rolling around on a chessboard without seeing all the damn pieces. I'm not going to act like an ignorant bullet catcher. That's not how I roll."

"Fine. I'll dig around and see what I can find. Watch your back. I think we should be scrapping the symposium, but we've run the program by all the fucking chiefs, and the U.S. is throwing a lot of money at the de-mining efforts. Since 2002 we've provided 60 million dollars to clear explosive hazards in Sri Lanka, which cleared one out of nine districts. The ambassador is determined to follow through with her pet project. Speaking of the itinerary, are you ready for the final briefing?"

"Yes, sir. I've come prepared. Moving from an urban environment to a rural setting has taken work. My team is waiting down the hall." The trip to Hatton would mean worse communications and zero emergency service response. Colombo might be congested, but at least they had the right tools for easy comms.

"Well, then let's get this tank rolling."

15

Hatton, Sri Lanka.

Getting out of the city was what Chantal needed. She paused to take in the lush surroundings as she climbed from the armored suburban on stiff legs. Surrounded by the hills of the Sri Lankan tea country, Chantal found relief in the cooler air. First the three-hour inland trip from Colombo to Kandy, and then the forty-mile trip to Hatton, which sat at an elevation exceeding 4000 feet. The perfect climate for growing the finest tea in the world.

Mixed feelings over the location for the symposium had Chantal turning her back on the lavish plantation bungalow. To tourists, the tea fields provided a perfect getaway, set amongst green vistas, and waterfalls. Their every whim was taken care of, in luxurious rooms, between visiting tea estates and tasting herbal beverages.

Many visitors ignored the colonial air permeating the region or the reality for the female workers picking tea for ten-hour days—a back-breaking existence for a $4-a-day liveli-hood. For that pitiful salary, the Tamil women risked stepping on snakes, facing off with leopards, or being swept away in a mudslide. Yet, as broken as the industry seemed, the planta-tions throughout Sri Lanka still provided work for thousands of families.

Wyatt led Chantal inside, and she resisted the urge to glance back at the MSD team exiting their vehicle. They paused at the reception desk, and Wyatt whistled as he scanned the sweeping lawns overlooking the valley. "Damn beautiful."

Chantal adjusted her scarf to cover the yellowed bruises. "I've never been past Kandy. This place is freaking insane."

Dishan stood quietly beside her as they waited in the long check-in line. Chantal turned to face him. "You shouldn't be here… if your wife goes into labor."

"All our parents are there, and this is my job."

"I know, but—"

"Stop worrying. We're here for a few nights, and then I'll be home."

Gage walked over and stood beside her local friend. His direct stare had her looking away before fiddling with her purse. Those devilish eyes would lure her over to the dark side.

"Let's talk about landslides and leopards."

Chantal looked at Dishan like he'd lost his mind.

"Landslides are an increasing danger during monsoon season, thanks to export crops replacing forests. We see catastrophic mudslides every year. So, keep alert, and if the staff tells us to evacuate, we move."

"I've heard about the dangers," Chantal acknowledged Dishan's concern.

"And leopard is a rare sighting," Dishan continued. "But there have been some attacks on tea pickers this year. Don't go wandering off."

"You wouldn't allow that anyway. Unless I decide to

explore a trail… a solitary hike sounds incredible." Laughing at their sudden agitation, Chantal turned back to the reception desk. "Relax, boys. It's so easy to get you worked up."

"And the Americans have arrived." Fredrik sauntered over to the desk dressed in a fitted sports coat and preppy-looking scarf.

Gage visibly stiffened. Getting a handle on Fredrik's arrogance, Chantal raised her brow.

"You aren't on the guest list. Why are you here?"

"Your mother invited Ambassador Lindberg. He decided to come at the last minute and I'm assisting. And we're joined by a couple of fellow Swede investors."

Chantal would never say no to investors who could potentially donate to the cause. "And you're staying here." Now she had to deal with a human peacock parading across the lawns.

"Of course." Fredrik winked. "Do you have your room number yet?"

"Come to her room, and we'll share more than words," Gage spoke loudly and to the point.

"Easy, big guy. I mind my own business—just came to the reception to book a massage in my room." Twisting to face her, the handsome Swede grinned. "I hear you're good with your hands."

Good God, the man, had a death wish, and Chantal hurriedly stepped between Gage and Fredrik. "You're right. I have strong hands—brutal at times. I use them to pop, twist, and wrench appendages." Chantal's gaze drifted down. "Are you looking for an adjustment?"

Almost jumping back, Fredrik chuckled nervously.

"After you're done, I'll adjust his attitude," Gage added, amusement tinged his statement.

Grinning, Chantal winked. "Not a bad idea. Partners in crime."

"Both comedians." Fredrik sneered. "Very funny."

"Good afternoon, ma'am. How many rooms have you booked?"

"Eight." Ignoring Fredrik, Chantal turned to sort out the accommodations. Her mother would cover her protection detail expenses, and Chantal felt grateful that they'd all share the same lodge. The symposium took place at a different estate a few miles down the road. That gave Chantal the option to escape the lavish parties in the evenings and return to her hotel.

"There will be a mix of luxury rooms, garden suites, and master suites." The receptionist sorted out the keys as Chantal watched Gage keep an eye on Fredrik while he booked a massage with a concierge.

Then, Gage trailed Fredrik to the door. His vital power drew her in like a magnet, and she hated the attraction she held for the agent. Even in a crowded room, she felt Gage's powerful presence.

"You took your sweet time!" Alexis walked across the elegant lobby and threaded her arm in Chantal's. "I've already checked in and run over to the other estate. That place is buzzing with activity. Come, I'll walk you to your room."

"I still need to go over my notes for the panel discussion and run through my presentation before dinner."

"You have plenty of time. Have a little fun. Let's do wine and lie by the pool?"

It wasn't going to happen. Chantal's brain buzzed with checklists and prep work for the following day. The women waited while Dishan and his team cleared her room. A light fragrance of jasmine drifted on the air, and a peafowl's call rolled over the lawns.

Once inside, Chantal paused to look around the affluent "colonial" space. Antique-style furnishings matched the wooden recliners scattered on a wide porch that sat beyond the glass doors.

"Can we talk?"

Chantal swung around to face Alexis, who helped herself to a glass of champagne.

"About what?"

"About that awkward moment at the printer when I tested your hunky boyfriend's resolve."

"He's not my boyfriend, and I'm not interested in silly games. What I want is to get past these crazy threats, and then I'm going on vacation."

"Vacation?" Alexis raised her brows. "Impulsive... that's not you."

"It is now. I need time to think about my future—how I can help best."

"What about your patients?"

"There'll be a new chiropractor joining the team who's recently graduated from the chiropractic college in Colombo. She's a strong addition. I won't be gone for long."

"Where will you go?" Alexis handed Chantal a glass, which she refused.

"I'm not sure yet. I haven't had an actual vacation away from my mother in years. When I'm ready, I'll organize a physical therapist for her care. What about you?"

Alexis looked taken aback. "What do you mean?"

"Are you planning to work at the center for the rest of the year? Or go back home?" Chantal walked over to the glass doors and pulled them apart, allowing in the fresh breeze.

"Home doesn't hold any appeal... I will continue exploring Sri Lanka and I'll possibly travel up to India. You should join me."

India sounded tempting, and Chantal smiled. "You're as directionless as I am."

"I'm aware of who I am." Alexis placed her glass on a cabinet.

That made one of them.

"Knock, knock." Gage's voice had Chantal twisting towards the front door. "I rescued your pretty Mac before it disappeared—you left your laptop at the front desk."

"Shit. Where's my head!" Chantal lunged towards him as he handed over her computer bag. "That has all my notes for tomorrow's presentation."

"No problem." He slipped his hands into his pockets and stepped back. "I should go."

"No! Stay."

She hadn't just blurted that.

"Uh… awkward." Alexis saluted Chantal. "Later, boss lady. I'm in 22B when you need me for setup." Chantal's team would run a treatment room, offering free adjustments during the symposium and they still needed to prepare and arrange the beds and equipment.

And, suddenly, they were alone.

"Nice room." Gage glanced around. "I hope your detail is close by."

"They're in the adjoining room."

"Good. I'm behind and opposite. We'll take shifts. If anything happens, scream. I'll come running."

"Tried that before… didn't work."

"Everything is a joke, right?" He looked pissed.

"I like to get you all fired up. Champagne?"

"Are you setting up at six?"

"Yeah," Chantal confirmed.

"Good. Gannon and Jason are already scoping out the venue, along with some of Team Three."

"Mom is arriving in the morning."

"That's why they're securing the venue." He turned to the door.

"I don't want things to be awkward between us. Let's at least be friends while working together."

Gage swiveled slowly. "I don't want to be friends. I want more. You were wise to throw me out."

"Gage—"

He came close, and she inhaled a breath, enjoying his green—almost mint, gingery cologne.

"All I can think of is taking you like a fucking barbarian. Hot. Rough. Sex. I want to do very bad things, and if we choose that path…" Gage cupped her neck and shifted closer. Time stretched as his gaze ran over her face. "Such lovely, lonely lips."

Chantal leaned towards his mouth. He had the energy of a caged beast, and she wanted to taste that wild spirit.

Abruptly pulling away, he strode for the exit. "Lock up. I'll see you at six."

Cheeks burning, her mind reeled with frustration and irritation. Damn the man! Throwing out orders like he was General Custer. But Chantal did as asked, following in his wake and bolting the latch. She should probably close the verandah doors. Muttering beneath her breath, she secured the room before sinking into an armchair.

The back of her neck still tingled from the warmth of his touch. Chantal traced her skin and smiled. Good to know that she wasn't the only one affected by this passing attraction.

16

The stuffy auditorium had Gage on edge. Both MSD teams and local forces had locked down the symposium. Gage now stood to the side of the small stage and watched the crowd, made up of VIPs, local politicians, the media, and foreign diplomats.

Chantal was the next speaker. Feeling on edge, Gage shifted his stance and focused on the packed room. Thanks to intel, he recognized many familiar faces. After flagging a few unknowns and communicating with his team, Gage watched Chantal step onto the stage.

She looked sophisticated in a navy pants suit—not overtly sexy, but it didn't need to be. A pale blue silk scarf concealed the healing marks on her throat. Gage hated that reminder— of his failure of her physical and mental protection.

He watched Chantal move across the stage. The way she walked and held herself communicated alluring confidence. Like her mother, Chantal played the intellectual card well and to her advantage.

Tearing his eyes away from the stylish beauty, Gage scanned her audience, and when he spotted Fredrik, Gage paused. The guy's fixed expression seemed sinister and out of place. Fredrik's focus was on Chantal, and the man barely breathed as his gaze ran her entire length. Stiffening, Gage moved closer to the stage while watching the creep's hands.

"My mother is here today to talk about de-mining efforts in Sri Lanka. She's personally committed to ridding this country of landmines that not only killed innocent citizens years after a war was over, but still destroys future prosperity in this great nation. Economic and agricultural expansion is limited, as many regions remain littered with unexploded ordnance including landmine fields and IEDs."

Chantal paused and glanced down at her notes. "I'm here for a different reason. When it's time for me to do my work as a chiropractic physician, it's already too late. I see the pain and trauma—the aftereffects of losing a limb. And not just a year down the line. Five, ten, thirty years later. An amputation affects the entire body and may lead to skin infections, deep vein thrombosis, muscle contractures, a damaged spine, and arthritic joints. And in children…"

Gage spotted her trembling hand—the kids affected her. It affected him as well. Seeing their brave coping abilities daily as their tiny bodies adjusted to dramatic change—heartbreaking and inspiring at the same time. Gage's attention switched between Chantal's distress and her diplomatic stalker. As she clicked through her slideshow filled with case studies, Fredrik's focus never wavered.

Chantal paused on a photo of a tiny girl who'd lost her right leg. "In children, the effects are devastating. Their tiny bodies are still growing and developing. To lose a limb at that young age, all because they'd ventured out to play with their friends in a nearby field. Civilian casualties remain high. Governments and rebel groups who use these vicious weapons have accepted that children will die due to their actions. What future does this child have when her parents cannot even afford to feed their family?" Chantal's righteous anger rang clear. "If this six-year-old survives her recovery, she is dependent on health care services and rehabilitation measures—a human right which is absent in many rural communities. There is a need for comprehensive rehabilitation, prosthesis education, and psychological support for these victims. I need your help."

Her passion filled the room and even the hardened MSD agents looked at her like she was Wonder Woman. Gage admired everything about her and had protected some incredible principals in his career. He'd follow Chantal anywhere, into battle, no hesitation.

The harder Gage ignored the undeniable attraction, the more it persisted. Could he afford to risk his livelihood and a promising career by getting involved with his principal? The question hammered around his brain, and Gage rolled his shoulders.

After her speech, the attendees filed into the lobby for lunch, and Gage kept an eye on Fredrik as the asshole headed to the snack corner.

"We're driving into the town." Chantal addressed both Gage and Dishan, looking eager to join the center's local team, who were already setting up onsite at a local hostel that offered a large assembly space. Gage knew of her afternoon plans and loved her obvious enthusiasm. Aside from requesting funding and spreading awareness, this was why Chantal helped organize the symposium—to work with the villagers and to treat the survivors of war, bombings, and mines.

"Congratulations." A Charge' d'affaires walked by and patted her on the shoulder. "It looks like the Confianca Recovery Center might get the funding it needs. I loved your pitch."

"Thank you for all your help." Smiling, Chantal shook his hand.

"Are you leaving?"

"Heading into Hatton central to see to patients."

"Well, make sure the press catches your team in action. They're gathered around your mother like honeybees on a hive."

Gage surveyed the humming lobby filled with delegates and dignitaries who still industriously networked despite the long morning. In her element, the ambassador graciously mingled with the masses. You'd never guess that she was probably in immense agony after being on her feet for seven hours.

She barely noticed her daughter leaving and hadn't said two words to Chantal all morning. Yet, they worked successfully in different capacities to solve funding issues related to landmines—both passionate advocates for the cause.

Gage knew that the Durants were wealthy and that they both contributed heavily to both causes, but the amount of funding needed to turn the region around far exceeded their scope or investment abilities. Governments needed hundreds of millions of dollars to make a dent with de-mining efforts. The constant search for investors took dedication.

Fredrik, the worm, stood beside the Swedish Ambassador —his gaze either locked on Chantal or her mother. Gage didn't like the man's pursuant vibe and the way he tracked Chantal's exit from the lobby.

"Let's go." Jason nudged Gage as he passed. "Everything okay?"

"I don't like that leech."

"He's a small tadpole in the diplomatic pool. Don't let him get to you."

"No-one 'gets to me.'" Gage huffed as they walked towards their transport. "But there's something off—unnatural—about the fucker."

"He's just pissed because Miss Durant dumped his slick ass."

"I'll speak to Martin. I want an extensive background check."

"Bro." Jason grabbed Gage's arm. "Don't go off on a tangent. Our focus needs to be on Rajin Bandara—the direct threat."

"What are you saying? That I'm distracted?"

"Maybe. I see the way you look at her. We all do."

"That's bullshit. We're all here to do a job and—"

"Yes, we are. That job is keeping Chantal Durant alive." Jason leaned in. "You're thinking with the wrong head—from the minute you laid eyes on her. If she were any other chick at the embassy or in Sri Lanka, I'd say, have fun. But she's our damn principal."

Gage swore, knowing he was already in too deep.

"We're here for you, man. I'm here if you ever need to talk." Jason squeezed his shoulder before heading up the path.

An occasional tuk-tuk passed their convoy down the mountainous pass. Clusters of children walked home from school, passing groups of female tea pickers who carried tarpaulin bags destined for the tea factory floor. Dishan had filled Gage in on the billion-dollar Ceylon industry and how the cultivation of black tea shaped the lives of every Sri Lankan.

The majority of plantation workers were ethnically Indian Tamils—first transported by the British to work on plantations —versus the Jaffna Tamils, who originated from the north of the island. Unlike other native dialects in Sri Lanka which dated back thousands of years, the tea pickers spoke a dialect called "Hill Country Tamil," which was around a hundred years old.

Gage found the origins of language fascinating. Diplomatic Security pushed for agents to learn new languages and held classes in Washington for new deployments and teams.

Chantal had already picked up on various dialects within the region. Gage had listened over the past couple of weeks as she'd tried to engage with the locals in their language. He admired her determination to learn—not only when interacting with patients but with her fellow Sri Lankan colleagues.

Pushing aside thoughts of the ambassador's daughter, Gage watched two women chatting and smiling beside the suburban as they waited for children to cross the road. The older woman rubbed a hand which looked callused and swollen.

Throughout their history, the Tamil plantation workers had endured hardships. In 1948, the Sri Lankan government classified them as "non-Sri Lankans" and had stripped them of their citizenship—retracting their voting rights in a region where families had resided in the same homes for generations. And the slave-like conditions hadn't improved their economic hardships, regardless of recently restored civil rights.

"Divide and Conquer" policies led to civil war and destruction. When would governments ever learn? A man like Rajin Bandara would escalate tensions in a still healing nation. The cruel bastard was in the presidential race for himself.

Whatever was on that missing flash drive drove Rajin to the hunt and would probably mean a catastrophic ending to his political ambitions. Except if he continued to stalk Chantal, Rajin's only concern wouldn't be his career. It would be Gage Hendrix.

Chantal looked up as Wyatt approached, taking the opportunity to stretch out her back as she helped a patient off a bed.

"You've been at this for hours. It'll get dark soon."

Dishan joined her Agent in Charge and agreed, a concern reflected in his eyes. "It's time to call it a day, after fifteen hours on your feet."

"I could help so many more." Chantal looked around the humble meeting space where they'd set up their makeshift treatment site.

"You still have tomorrow."

She did. They planned to leave in two days, and she wanted to see at least sixty more patients. She wasn't the only one hustling—the two local chiropractors who owned the center took the lead on the operation and shouldered the bulk of the work.

"Nanri." The Tamil term for thanks rolled off her tired lips, and conceding to Wyatt's request, she gathered her supplies from beside her assigned table in the curtained-off treatment room. Chantal wouldn't risk the lives of her security detail at night while traveling up the side of a mountain—not while Rajin was a viable threat. They'd leave now while it was still light.

Chantal chatted with the treatment squad before leaving, settling on the best time to start in the morning. Alexis pulled her to the side. "Can I hitch a ride back to the hotel? My car is giving me trouble, and I don't think it will make it up the hill."

"No surprise. That's the oldest Toyota Corolla I've ever seen."

"Hey! I got a deal—Ralph cost twenty dollars!"

"Ralph? You've named that rusty wagon. And you're paying the price."

"Ralph lasted months. I'm guessing the Ceylon hills are too much for the old guy."

"Talk to Wyatt. There's hardly any room in the suburban. I don't think he'll take kindly to you sitting on his lap."

"I can sit on yours… or wait. I could ask Gage to give me a lift. Balancing on those strong thighs while he cradles his big gun…"

Jealousy roared to life, and Chantal gritted her teeth.

"Relax. I'm teasing. Your slice of hot beef only has eyes for you. The way he looks at you…"

"Shut-up, Alexis." Chantal strode across the room. "He has a job to do, and so do I."

Lengthening her strides to keep up, Alexis grinned. "I'm sure he'd like to get to work between your—"

"Stop!" Face flaming, Chantal swung on her friend.

"I'm just saying. That's noble work. If he could get your toes to curl—job well done."

Chantal pressed her lips together and shook her head.

"See? I made you smile. You need to laugh more. Practice for that sabbatical vacation. Maybe Gage can get you to loosen up."

"I'm loose." Chantal waggled her shoulders.

"No. You need to find a new level of wild. Right now, you're flatlining on the crazy scale. Oh, there's Wyatt—let me work my magic."

"Alexis, you're impossible," Chantal called to her friend's retreating back.

"Climb that man-tree. A great way to relieve tension."

Feeling his gaze from across the room, Chantal glanced at the agent who'd become her daily obsession. His team spread out and began moving to the exit, ready to cover her walk to the car. Their gazes locked. The air crackled, and Chantal swallowed past a suddenly dry throat.

Alexis's naughty words bounced around in her brain.

Strong thighs… big gun.

Don't look down. Look away. Damn. Chantal surveyed Gage's entire length, lingering on his wide stride. Someone touched her shoulder, and she jolted in surprise. "Ready to go?" Dishan asked.

"Please. I need some of that cool air."

"It's warm in here."

It certainly was. Chantal grabbed her satchel and reluctantly left the school hall.

The trip back to the hotel took time as two horse carts held up traffic on narrow roads. In a tired daze, Chantal stared out of the window at the passing tea fields and valleys, and once they hit the bungalow, she showered before calling her mother to see if she needed help with her sore shoulder. It took a few tries before the ambassador answered.

"I'm busy. What do you want?"

"To see if you need any help?"

"I'm having dinner with friends. I'll take painkillers when I get in."

"Well, if you need me…"

"Hand me off to a fellow doctor. There are plenty at the bungalow."

"Mom—"

"Goodnight, Chantal. Enjoy the break."

Her mother loved to play hardball and knew that ignoring her "people-pleasing" daughter would work in her favor. Chantal wouldn't let her mother's snarky attitude ruin her night.

Glancing through her curtains, she spotted Dishan heading across the lawns to the dining quarters. Her stomach rumbled. After changing into black jeans and a striped fitted t-shirt, Chantal slipped on a pair of red pumps and grabbed her denim jacket and a purse. Her three local guards stepped up as she locked her door.

"I'm hungry."

"What about room service?"

"I need a beer. Let's go." Grinning and feeling rejuvenated after her warm shower, Chantal slipped on her jacket and headed towards the distant hum of guests enjoying their food. She waved at Lucius and Jason patrolling the lawns.

Her mouth watering, Chantal headed inside and straight

for the buffet and began loading a plate with homemade flat-bread. She slid along to the hot dishes and took in the delicious smells. Taking her time, Chantal lingered over the steaming pots.

"What are you deciding between?" Gage's deep timbre had her turning. He stood close, and the khaki t-shirt couldn't hide his carved physique. He'd also showered and smelled like mint toothpaste and woodsy citrus. He wasn't dressed like an armored Rambo and her eyes ran over his chest.

"Um... Um." Chantal focused on the question, feeling lightheaded in his presence. "The Dhal or chicken curry."

"I went with the chicken." He pointed to his bowl at a far table.

Chantal chose the same, first dishing up a generous portion of rice before adding the curry. "Where's your friend? Gannon? He's usually glued to your hip."

"He is. We've served together for a long time. We're taking shifts. Unless something comes up, I have the night off."

"Room service for the rest of the team?" Chantal spooned sliced banana onto her plate. A mango side sauce drew her attention.

"They'll be walking the property—working. Speaking of room service, you should be tucked away in your room."

"I'm not a prisoner." Chantal shot him a glare and headed for Dishan's table.

"Eat with me," Gage said.

Hesitating, Chantal looked around. It wasn't like they were acting inappropriately. They were friends—at least in her eyes. His words came back to haunt her. *I don't want to be friends. I want more... All I can think of is taking you like a fucking barbarian. Hot. Rough. Sex.*

Just dinner. With an insanely attractive man.

Unable to stop herself, Chantal followed Gage to the small table and set down her food. "Beer?"

He shook his head. "Working… remember?"

"You said you had the night off."

"And if there's a breach in security, I'll be back on point."

"Well, I need alcohol." She headed to the bar area for a brew called a Lion Stout.

Finally, she sat, and his knee brushed her thigh. He didn't shift away, and she focused on quenching her physical hunger instead of focusing on the warmth of his leg beside hers. Gage did the same, and when he leaned back to take a sip of lemonade, Chantal took a long swig of beer.

"Zut. That is good."

Gage smiled at her French.

"No, really. It's like a dark roasty mix of caramel and chocolate."

"Roasty mix? Roasty isn't a word. You mean roasted."

"It's my word—actually Mom's word. When something tastes or feels like decadent comfort." She took another sip. "Reading beside a roasty fire. My famous roasty potatoes."

"Famous huh? And how do they taste?"

"Divine!" Chantal grinned. "Mom's been making them for years—or at least she used to for the holidays. Parboiled potato which is then roasted in the oven. Served drenched in shaved parmesan and crispy bacon bits. Crunchy bites of roasty heaven."

She leaned forward. "The secret is laying the partly boiled potatoes in spitting hot oil. And then later, adding a spoon of butter. The butter—along with the oil—browns the potatoes to a rich golden shade."

His eyes sparkled in amusement. "Good to know."

Curiosity had her pushing away her plate. "Do you miss your family back home? When living out of a suitcase?"

"Nope." Gage shook his head. "I'm with my family."

Chantal frowned. "You mean the team guys?"

"They are like family—except for the new medic who's an

asshole and about to get his butt kicked. But, no. I mean Martin."

"You're related to Martin? Martin as in the RSO? I thought you were just good friends?"

"We're not technically related, but he raised my sorry ass. It's complicated."

"I've got time."

"You have a long day tomorrow. And look, the restaurant is emptying."

He spoke the truth. Besides her security detail, sitting a few tables down, they were one of the few left.

"C'mon. You know all about my crazy family secrets... a tragic past, a harsh mother, a father who I've realized is a stranger."

"Don't." Gage leaned forward and traced her fingers. "And your mother loves you in her own weird way."

Chantal half shrugged and focused on the table. "I've decided to part ways with her for a few months. I need my own space. I don't love her any less, but her control can be suffocating, and when I'm ready, I'm permanently moving out of her residence."

"When I was twelve, I saw my father kill himself."

Chantal's gaze shot to Gage, who sat stiffly, his hands folded in his lap.

"We'd fought just before... I didn't want to take out the garbage. Dad yelled, and I told him I hated him. At the time, I thought I did. He was always drunk and belligerent. Ever since my mother died, we'd both battled with the loss. She died on my tenth birthday—from cancer."

"Gage." Chantal stretched out her hand. He didn't take it; instead, his eyes glazed as he re-lived the past.

"I loved her so much... to see her take that last breath. Mom was sunshine and joy—our pillar that glued the family together."

As if shaking himself from a trance, Gage shifted and rolled his shoulders. "After losing his wife, my father went mad and forgot about his son. Aunt June—mom's sister—would come over and cook me dinner. Help with my homework. At the time, she was dating Martin, and eventually, I'd spend more and more nights at my aunt's place. Martin taught me how to play baseball, and he'd tell me about all his adventures overseas. He cared about a lost and grieving kid."

"He's a good man. I think he's in love with my mother."

"I think so too." Gage met her smile, which turned to a frown.

"What about your aunt, where is she?"

"Aunt June died in a car accident, six months after losing her sister." Gage swallowed. "That was a dark time for a kid. I'd lost everything. A month later, DSS sent Martin to Spain. Before he left, he took me for ice-cream and gave me his contact details. But, I was angry, because all the good in my life was gone. It was just good old dad and me."

"Did your father ever hurt you? Beat you?"

"No. He'd clocked out of life. I tried to engage with my father, and when that failed, I acted out. Dad didn't care about my bad grades at school or my poor choice of friends. Months passed in a depressing blur. And, then that fateful night, we had the usual argument. Except, after I took out the trash, I returned to find him, sitting on the sofa with a pistol to his head."

Eyes burning, Chantal wanted to offer comfort and wrap him in a firm hug.

"His last words were, 'Julie is waiting for me.' That's my mother's name."

Chantal swiped her hand over a cheek, feeling anger and sadness for Gage's father. He must've known what that would do to his son.

"I didn't speak for three months and was placed in foster

care. I was unaware that Martin searched for me. He wasn't family so locating a lost kid was complicated. Finally, I called Martin, and like a superhero, he swept in and pieced me back together. Put his career on hold for a boy he hardly knew." Gage's eyes grew moist. "He freaking loved me. A skinny kid who hated the world. I owe Martin everything."

Chantal nodded.

"He told me once—years after my father's death that 'bad people are sometimes just sad people—in disguise.' At the time, I felt such bitterness towards my dad, but Martin's words changed my perspective."

"How?" Chantal asked.

"To a young kid, it seemed like my dad didn't give a fuck. He didn't buy food or get off the sofa. He barely acknowledged he had a son. I saw him as a bad father. But it was the sadness—the grief—the depression that ripped apart my dad's soul. I never saw beneath his harsh shell. Martin gave me that gift—to look back and learn how to forgive. I finally understood."

Gage reached for her hand, his burning intensity locking her in place. "I never want to disappoint Martin. Never have until you came along."

She tried to pull away, and he looked over at her two guards, who walked over to the opposite side of the room to the buffet.

"I don't care what anyone thinks," Gage continued. "The need that I have for you drives away any reason. Tell me this is one-sided. I'll walk away."

"It's not," she answered quickly. "And I'm not ashamed to want you. We're not hurting anyone."

"You will get hurt when this is over. And I might be putting your life—"

"Don't be so dramatic. Are you focused on the job?"

Gage swore. "No. Yes. I'm off duty but—"

"Let's enjoy tonight, and by the morning, we can focus on other things. It might not even be all that."

"Oh, honey. We're going to shake each other apart. I can feel it."

What else would they shake apart? His career? Her heart? Body feeling heavy and warm, Chantal ignored reason and placed her napkin on the table. "Come to my verandah door."

"Are you sure about this?"

"I'll be waiting." Rising, she shot him one last look.

Gage followed Chantal and her local detail across the lawn, watching the shadows for danger. When he had clear and unseen access to the verandah, Chantal slid open the door, and he slid through. Gage held up a hand and texted Gannon.

"What are you doing?"

"Stepping up your detail. Approaching your room so easily reveals a gap in local patrols. I'll get more of my team involved —more patrolling bodies."

"Hang ten. Let me first close the curtains. Don't you share a room with Gannon?" she asked as she slipped the drapes in place, tamping down on her nerves.

"Yeah. He can draw his own conclusions." Gage walked up and ran his hands over her hips. "I like your shirt. Stripes look good on you."

"How about my bra?" Chantal grinned and pulled her t-shirt over her head.

Gage's mouth twisted into a smile. "Soft lace and even softer skin."

"Which needs your 'soft' touch."

"Nothing soft about me, honey."

She couldn't help laughing aloud, and he grinned and leaned in to bite her strap. Pulling it over her shoulder with his teeth, Gage's hand slid up her ribcage, and his thumb traced across her skin as he released her bra and nibbled a path across her breast.

Relaxing into his touch, Chantal grasped his shoulders and leaned into his warmth. Gage took his time... nuzzling... nibbling. His mouth on her skin felt heavenly and she closed her eyes as heat built. He lifted her and carried her to the bedroom.

"You also have a four-poster bed. Yours is bigger." He laid her down on the white cover and stepped to the side to fiddle with the tie to a sheer canopy curtain.

"What are you doing?"

"Embracing the decor. Lie still while I light the candles."

"Am I seeing a romantic side to a tough MSD machine?" Chantal giggled.

His voice filled with humor; Gage replied, "MSD agents always use their surroundings to their advantage."

He loosened and allowed the curtains to drop. Next, he lit the honey-scented candles and switched off the lights. The ceiling fan pushed cool air down, stirring the soft fabric encircling Chantal's private lair.

"Are you sure you want this?" Gage parted the curtain and crawled to her side.

The tingling in the pit of her stomach had her turning to face him. "Every moment. How about you?"

He settled on the pillow beside her, and his vitality pushed her to shift closer. His hand cupped her cheek as they lay nose to nose. Noticing the tiniest of scars near his temple, Chantal scanned the rest of his face for past injuries.

"Your job is dangerous."

"Not as risky as when I served in the military. Why do you ask?"

"You don't get much downtime, do you?"

"Depends. I've never needed a vacation." Grabbing her

hand in his, Gage drew her wrist to his lips. "You smell like champagne and roses."

"I want to smell like you when I wake." She loved his smell —like mint and lemongrass.

Raising his brow, Gage drew back. "Chants, is that a challenge?"

"Tonight, you get to possess me completely. And I'll do the same." Pushing him onto his back, Chantal straddled his waist and bent to kiss him.

His nearness made her head spin, and she felt his chest rise and fall as she slid up his shirt, revealing a chiseled stomach that tensed beneath her touch. Tucked away in their romantic refuge, Chantal took her time, exploring every plane and carved muscle.

"That feels good," Gage growled, the words making her smile. Chantal guessed that they'd both missed out on tactile human contact for a long time. From what she'd gathered, he was dedicated to his time overseas and rarely went back to the States. And she didn't see him as a one-night stand kind of guy who'd hook up with "randoms" around the globe.

Gage was all about establishing a relationship and building rapport with all those in his immediate environment. She'd noticed the difference the first day they'd met.

Gage always burned with curiosity and had immediately worked at establishing a connection with her local security team. He'd done the same with patients and her staff. Yeah. The man craved connection, and for the next few hours, she'd give him just that.

Now confident in her ability, Chantal leaned down and licked a nipple before sliding her mouth to his collarbone. Her hands wandered, playing, tracing over his jeans. Cupping her ass, Gage pulled her firmly against him as her lips met his. Feeling his hard length between their clothes, Chantal moaned as she rubbed against his thighs. When he groaned into her mouth, she unbuttoned his jeans and slid her hand down beneath his boxers.

"Fuck!" Tearing his mouth away, Gage took control. Flipping her to the bed and pinning her wrists to the pillows. She grinned as his gaze seared across her heaving breasts. Releasing one hand, Gage traced her cleavage. Her nipples tightened at his intimate touch—first fingers, then tongue.

Next, it was his turn to unbutton her jeans. He pulled her pants and undies down in one smooth move before shedding the last of his clothes and slipping on a condom from his back pocket.

She took a moment to take in the glorious, perfectly proportioned man spreading her legs. Gage cupped her wet heat, and she pressed into his warm hand. Still, he didn't move. Chantal held her breath as her senses heightened, feeling him roll his palm across her clit. Once. Twice. Pleasure radiated from his gentle massage, and she heard herself groan.

A finger slid into her entrance as he continued his sensual, rolling strokes. Chantal gripped the covers as he watched her face. Leaning down, Gage widened her legs with his broad waist and touched his lips to hers, kissing her with long deep strokes. Devouring his mouth, Chantal wrapped her legs around her captivating anchor and arched to meet his thrusting finger, which pressed deep, brushing and circling until she moaned his name.

A hard length replaced his hand, rolling over her damp opening.

"You sure?" Gage spoke between gritted teeth.

"Please. Yes. Oh. My God."

And then he was in. Her body stretched to accommodate his large length as he filled her completely. She could feel him everywhere. His stubble brushing against her cheek with every slow thrust. His pelvis rocking against hers. His breath in her ear.

Chantal clung to his back as a hot tide of passion carried her upward with every surge of his hips. Swearing softly, he gripped her hair in a curled fist as they found a tempo that melded them together in a race for gratification. The commanding warrior took his time, surging deep with long, languid strokes, and it felt like heaven. An explosive pleasure like she'd never felt before raged in an upward spiral.

"J'aime ca." The words escaped as she shattered beneath his sheltering strength. Pulling him close, she rode the glorious wave. Her body clenched and released, pulsating with waves of pleasure.

"Chants! Shit."

Thrusting deep, Gage swore, pinning her to the bed in a shuddering finish. Cradling her close, he rolled onto his back until she lay atop, and rested her head on his chest.

"Don't move." Firm hands ran over her back and buttocks. "You feel incredible."

"Not going anywhere." The feel of his fingertips running along her skin had Chantal melting into his embrace, and she drifted in blissful sleep, only stirring when he placed her gently on her side, slid out, and walked to the bathroom to dispose of the condom.

Once he'd returned, Gage played with her hair and rubbed a thumb over her lips. "I can't stop touching you. We've only begun, and I want to make you come again. This time I'll take my sweet time."

"Sounds intriguing." Chantal stretched, allowing him access to her sated body. "I feel like a noodle."

"You cried out in French as you came—blew me apart. I couldn't make out what you said?"

"J'aime ca—'I like this.'"

Shooting her a quizzical look, Gage traced her breast.

Smiling, she arched her back. "Like really, really liked it…"

"Like… the best sex you've ever had?"

"So far. You have your work cut out for you. We still have the rest of the night."

Eyes twinkling, he lowered his lips to hers. "Deal."

The room began to lighten, and Gage pulled Chantal closer to his side. He'd soon be back on duty and didn't want to stay past sunrise. Gage was in for a long day without barely any sleep.

He'd kept to his multiple-orgasm promise, and now Chantal slept soundly in his arms. Leaving their delicate cocoon meant facing the reality that soon they'd go their separate ways. And he didn't want to leave her while Rajin was still on the run.

Stirring and stretching, Chantal shot him a satisfied smile, and his heart clenched with unnamed emotion. "Morning, honey."

"Is it? It's still dark."

Gage reluctantly forced out the words. "It is, and pouring with rain. I have to leave soon."

"Five more minutes." Her kiss to his chest had him remaining in place. "You didn't sleep much—I mean when we weren't—"

"I checked my phone earlier. A message came through from Martin with an attachment."

Chantal raised her head.

"We're getting closer to a name. Shit. How do I say this?" Ignoring her frown, Gage let go and sat up. "Your father was in Sri Lanka during the civil war. He spent a great deal of time in Colombo, and that was the last place he'd visited before he died."

"No. Daddy never mentioned Sri Lanka." Chantal rose to

face him. "We always spoke about the places he'd visited when he returned from his travels. He'd tell me about the people he'd met—his adventures." A crease formed between her brows. "Before he died, he told me he went to France. He even spoke about visiting a stable and seeing a show jumping horse for me."

"He wasn't in France. Unfortunately, we've linked his movements to a number of war-torn regions. Your father may have operated as a war dog investor—providing illegal weapons through a dummy corporation. Martin found photographic evidence from an archive holding online. And Chants, there's a photo that you'll need to see—of your father in Colombo with a group of mercenaries." Gage reached over for his phone and clicked on the downloaded image before handing the device to Chantal.

Her breath caught as she looked at a group of men gathered in a tea field. Some carried weapons. "The monster who strangled me—he's in that photo." Fear flashed over her now pale face. "With my father. He spoke the truth—he knew my father."

"Now, we have a lead. We'll run a facial recognition search." Gage gently took the phone from her shaking hands. "You're safe. We'll find him."

"My father lied to me. About where and who he was."

"I think the assassination is linked to your attack. The pieces aren't fitting together. Not yet, but I'll get names and untangle this mess."

"Why you? It's not your job to investigate my father's death or my assault. I don't understand."

"I care about what happens to you. And you deserve the truth."

"My father was a good man."

"I've never said otherwise."

"He was… wasn't he?" Her eyes begged for reassurance

and Gage's heart broke. He knew that feeling—realizing that your father wasn't a swashbuckling hero. Just a broken dead-beat who didn't care about consequences. That wasn't fair. Grief and depression destroyed Gage's father and perhaps, if he'd sought professional help…

"Was my mother aware of the deceit?" When Chantal rubbed her forehead, Gage grasped her hand and pulled it to the covers. "I'm not sure, but it's best to wait until we know more. I'll get the answers you need."

"Is that why she took the post in Sri Lanka? To right the wrongs of her corrupted husband?"

"I can't answer that." He pulled her in for a long hug. Skin against skin. Gage stroked her back, enjoying the intimate feel of her body against his. Offering comfort to this gutsy woman fortified a connection he'd never felt before. His possession grew with every passing second. How could he protect her from past and future hurts? Physical protection wasn't enough.

"You don't need to do this."

Gage replied, without hesitation. "I want to." He pulled her in for a long kiss. "I hate leaving you. Last night was incredible."

"Special. Last night was special." She smiled against his lips.

"I love that dimpled smile." He pulled back. "I see it in your eyes."

"That's usually how a smile works." Chantal laughed.

"No." He shook his head. "Your eyes hold too many sad stories and not enough happy ones."

"Well, that's depressing. Gee thanks."

"That gazelle gaze reeled me into this bed."

"If I'm a gazelle, what does that make you? A hungry lion?"

"You have no idea."

After playfully biting her shoulder, Gage left her in their

love nest and quickly changed back into his clothes. As he turned to go, Chantal poked her head out of the curtained canopy. "Walk of shame!"

"Nothing shameful about it." Winking at her mischievous grin, he swooped in for one last kiss. "Lock up behind me. I'll see you on the other side."

"Other side of what?"

"Your verandah sliding door as I walk the grounds."

"Mmm. Breakfast with a view."

Chuckling, Gage let himself out and waited to hear her slide the lock in place. Gage walked the hotel property and checked the perimeter. He waved at Dishan and his men who stood near the pool.

Satisfied with security, Gage headed back to his room. The luxury accommodations sat unoccupied. After a quick shower, Gage walked back into the living area and nodded at Gannon, who now sat on a sofa in his MSD gear.

"Rise and shine! Where did you disappear to last night?"

"Nowhere. I went for a long walk. I was off-duty."

"A ten-hour walk, huh?"

"More like seven and I had my phone."

"You're so full of shit." Gannon stretched his hands along the back of the couch. "So? Who is it? Someone from the symposium? A tourist? Don't fucking say her name—not the ambassador's daughter."

"None of your damn business what I do on my time off."

"Bro, you didn't." Despite his casual facade, concern rolled off Gannon in waves. "That's a career-ender."

"Don't be dramatic."

"She's our principal. Even if she weren't, you'd still be playing with fire. The Chief of Mission is trusting you with her daughter's safety."

"And, like all of us, I'd sacrifice my life to protect the family."

"No. You'd sacrifice your life for Chantal Durant. I can see it in your damn eyes. You'd voluntarily get shot in the head."

"She's a good person and—"

Gannon stood. "Don't play games. Be honest about how you feel and how your decisions affect the rest of the team. You're the team leader and speaking of duty, we're prepping for roll-out in Jason and Lucius's suite. Are you coming?"

"Of course. Don't be a dick."

"I love you, man, and I don't want you committing career suicide. If this 'thing' is serious, then you need to plan ahead. How are you going to deal with the Anaconda? I doubt she wants her precious daughter dating a bullet catcher. Just saying."

And there it was—the antithetical elephant in the room. Would a diplomatic foot soldier ever have a chance with a billionaire's daughter? Gage knew of her private schooling and her prestigious childhood neighborhood, and of course, her parents had both been wealthy beyond imagination. Her mother still was.

So, what was Chantal looking for in a man? Was she passing the time while playing with her newest boy-toy? Would she eventually settle down with an IT giant or a wealthy phil-anthropist?

Gage knew he was a good judge of character and didn't see Chantal as the shallow type. Aside from her charitable nature, work ethic, and their wild attraction to each other, how much did he know about Chantal? Should it matter?

As they walked over to join the rest of Team Five, Gage internally listed insights as he trudged through the rain. She didn't get along with her overbearing mother. Chantal wanted independence. She'd dated a couple of guys in the past—both didn't sound terribly wealthy. Did she purposely avoid wealthy guys? Why—to rebel against her mother? What type of man did Ambassador Durant want for her daughter?

"See? You're already distracted." Gannon whacked the side of Gage's skull.

"What the hell?"

"You're acting like a zombie." Gannon knocked before entering, calling out to the team.

Rubbing a hand over his face, Gage refocused his energy. He couldn't shake the weird feeling that time was ticking, and they hurtled into an unchecked reality. He wouldn't drop out of sight again. His team needed their hard-nosed team leader and disappearing for hours wasn't setting the right example.

Gage had a lot to think about. His night with Chantal had altered his mental make-up—her vitality engraved on his soul. Plastering on a smile, and setting aside his infatuation, Gage walked down the passage to greet his men.

17

C hantal felt along the patient's scapula. "I'm not doing an adjustment. She needs to see a doctor and possibly have an MRI. I suspect a torn rotator cuff."

Shoulder pain was a common occurrence with many tea pickers who carried sacks every day, hoisting them over their backs as they walked.

The translator told the hunched woman sitting on the table. The lady replied, agitation apparent as she pointed at her shoulder.

"She can't afford that. Even with her husband working in Dubai."

Chantal nodded at the translator. "Of course not. She should check first with her plantation manager. They may cover the costs through insurance. If not, here's the number for a free clinic in Kandy. If she can get to that town, they'll take care of her appointments and surgery."

The lady still shook her head and babbled in Tamil.

"She can't stop working in the fields or leave her three children. She says no."

Chantal couldn't force her patient to seek care, and frustration ate at her patience. She knew that time away from the plantations meant starving families, and many of the pickers literally worked themselves to death. "Okay. If it gets worse, she'll need to go to Kandy. She could sustain extensive damage if she keeps using the arm."

After giving the patient the clinic's card, Chantal opened the curtain and thanked the translator. It was only nine in the morning, and exhaustion had her suppressing a yawn. She'd lost sleep, but it was worth it.

Scanning the assembly hall, Chantal paused on Dishan, who paced with a phone to his ear. His agitation had her leaving the private curtained space and walking over to the head security guard. He hung up as she approached. The look on his face made her pause.

"What's wrong?"

"Nothing." He forced a smile.

"Dishan."

"Priya is going into labor, and she's on the way to the hospital. Except, my father's car broke down, stranding them in the middle of nowhere. They've called for an ambulance."

"You need to leave!"

"No, ma'am. You're my first concern. We leave tomorrow."

"That's bull. Go! Your wife and baby need you."

"I can't. If I abandon my duties, I will be fired, and I need this job."

"What's going on?" Gage walked over, pinning Chantal with a concerned gaze. "By the way, your mother has arrived."

"Dishan's wife is in labor."

"Congratulations, man!"

"You don't understand—"

"Chantal!" At her mom's voice, Chantal glanced over and blew out a frustrated breath. Fredrik, along with an unfamiliar older gentleman, followed on her mother's heels.

"Chantal!"

168

"I'm busy, Madam Ambassador."

"Don't take that tone. I didn't waste my time traveling into town when I should be heading back to Colombo."

"Then why aren't you?"

Connie gritted her teeth and turned with an outstretched hand. "I'd like you to meet Mr. Hugo Elofson. He's an investor who would like to contribute to the clinic."

Chantal recognized the name as she shook the hand of the wealthy Swedish philanthropist and chairman of a medical device company. He'd personally contributed 250 million euros to worthy causes. Although Chantal and her mother had donated generous funds to the Confianca cause, a tycoon like Hugo Elofson could make a real dent in their plight.

"That's very thoughtful. Thank you." Chantal waved over the local team. "He'd need to speak to our director—"

"I'll need to see your clinic. And I'm leaving in the morning for India."

"Mr. Elofson is looking at a generous contribution. You can return to Colombo with us and show him around your center."

"Mom, no. I have patients, and…" Chantal narrowed her eyes in thought. "Wait a second. This might work. We have enough staff here in Hatton." Another therapist had joined their efforts that morning, helping to relieve the long lines.

Chantal turned to Dishan as the rest of her colleagues gathered. "You might be in time for the birth!"

"That's not on the schedule," Dishan protested.

"He's right," Gage agreed. "We haven't prepped for an earlier departure."

"Team Three has." The ambassador placed her hands on her hips. "And besides, safety in numbers. You'll follow our convoy."

"Madam Ambassador…" Gage looked agitated. "I don't think it's wise to change our plans at the last minute."

"For ten million dollars, you can leave with us."

"Wait. What?" Chantal felt her eyes widen at her mother's words.

"It could be fifteen." Elofson smiled. "A good friend of mine lost his leg in Afghanistan. I want to help amputees."

"For fifteen million, I'll race you back to Colombo." Grinning, Chantal nudged Dishan in the arm.

Alexis waved her hand in the air. "Can I come too? I could help to open up the clinic, but I don't have transport."

"We don't have room." Dishan reached for his walkie-talkie.

"I do. You can travel down with us. Hugo." The tycoon extended his hand, and Alexis grinned in delight as she gripped his hand in hers.

"Then it's settled." Fredrik hung back as her mother and the Swedish investor walked from the room. "You owe me." He winked at Chantal. "I'm looking forward to the tour."

"You're coming?"

"Of course. Mr. Elofson is Ambassador Lindberg's guest. I'm to take great care of him."

Crossing his arms, Gage looked away, his surly attitude apparent.

The next hour passed in a flurry of chaos. Chantal and her team returned to the bungalow to check out and retrieve belongings. After packing their equipment, Gage walked over to Chantal's suite to check on her progress. Her security team stood near her open door.

"Is she inside?"

Dishan answered, "Doing one last walkthrough."

Nodding, Gage entered the cool living space and made his way over to the bedroom, where Chantal checked the bedside table.

"Ready to go?"

Jerking, she straightened. "Jeez, you move quietly."

"Part of my job."

"Well, you look the part. Back in your ninja gear."

He looked down at his ballistic vest and the MSD weapon and tools strapped to his belt.

"Where's your big gun? The rifle?" She walked into his arms.

"Hidden away. Where you can't find it." Gage grinned.

"Is it ready for action? Could I… cradle it in my tiny hands."

"Mmm… Sounds tempting. Do you know how to use my 'big gun'?"

"You tell me." Standing on her tiptoes, Chantal stretched up for a kiss, fingers tracing the strap of his combat helmet.

Gage kept it short, listening for approaching footsteps. When he pulled away, he tucked her choppy hair behind her ear. "I don't like this… not following protocol."

"You worry too much. The amount of firepower traveling down that mountain—we have an army. Like twenty men."

"Twenty-two, actually. Excluding that rich dude's protection detail."

"You see? And it's time for us to behave. I'll get you in trouble."

"That's what you're worried about?" he asked.

"Aren't you?"

Gage stepped back. "Where do you see this going?" Confusion lit her big brown eyes, and Gage looked away. "Do we have a future? What you want is different from what I can—"

"Whoa! What I want? What does that mean?" she asked.

"You'll find someone better suited to…"

"To what?" Chantal crossed her arms.

"Uh…to your lifestyle."

"My lifestyle? Do you mean as a chiropractor? As a politician's daughter? Oh, wait…"

"Don't look at me like that."

"Is that how you see me? As a wealthy snob?"

"No… Chants. I think we should take this slow. Perhaps think about the practicalities…"

"Get out of the way." She shoved at his chest.

"You have the quickest temper, and you're overreacting—"

"You're digging a deep hole, buddy. Stop talking and pick up that bag."

"Yes, ma'am."

If looks could kill, he'd be toast.

Gage couldn't resist poking her with a verbal stick. "You're good at channeling your mother—when you're angry."

"You're on a roll! That's not funny."

"It kind of is. I think it's cute."

"This is where we part ways. I'll see you in Colombo." She walked to the door.

Gage paused. Part ways? Did she mean permanently or for the day? Had Chantal just dumped his cautious ass? The thought felt like a hand grenade to the plexus. By the time he'd emerged into the damp air, she was already heading for the reception area surrounded by Dishan's team.

Shoving aside his frustration, Gage followed but stood to the side as Alexis engaged in lively conversation. "Cool jeans!"

"Merci." Chantal looked down at her dark gray skinny jeans, which matched her gray Arc'teryx jacket. Gage approved of the military brand.

"I like your cargo pants."

Alexis smiled and brushed a hand over an army green pocket. "They're hiking pants—loads of pockets, and they're waterproof. They've been a great option in a monsoon. I'm tired of this rain."

To Gage, they looked more like tactical pants. The first

time he'd seen Alexis wear something remotely practical and they matched her sturdy hiking boots.

Instead of waiting in the lobby, Gage handed over Chantal's luggage and headed for Team Five's suburban. Water fell in sheets from the sky, dampening the neck of his shirt. After pulling his jacket from the back, he settled in the passenger seat beside Gannon.

"You okay, man? It looks like someone kicked you in the balls."

"Someone did." Gage rested his head back and watched the parked convoy through slitted eyes as Lucius checked in with Team Three. This trip would be one long-ass ride, and the weather didn't bode well for their precarious descent.

A fancy Hummer rolled past, and Gage spotted the wealthy investor chatting to Fredrik in the back seat. The sport utility SUV parked behind Team Five in the convoy line. What a fucking circus. Gage felt penned in by the numerous vehicles and bodies.

His phone buzzed, and Gage took the call. As soon as they left the lodge, they'd lose the limited reception.

"Martin?"

"Hey, son. I heard you're coming back early."

"Yes, sir."

"How's Connie doing? She must be in agony."

"Uh. I guess. She's still not on friendly terms with Chantal, so…"

"I've been doing some digging and think you're right."

Gage sat up. "About her father?"

"I spoke to a federal agent who worked the assassination twelve years ago. The guy is retired, but he has a theory."

Gage waited for Martin to continue.

"He worked with a profiler who reckoned that Otto Kivela wasn't working alone. Not on his last assignment."

"From what I've read, he always worked alone."

"Yes, but that day he would've been too weak. Of course, the feds overruled the theory as they chalked it up to adrenaline in the moment, but I agree. The elevator didn't work, which means Otto would have trekked up ten flights of stairs—with his gun case and equipment—and then took the shots. In my eyes, not plausible to do both, even if he took his time."

"And they haven't found the accomplice?"

"No. I'm looking into his past—and family. Records are scarce as he's from a small Finnish town on the Russian border."

"And we still don't know who hired him?"

"I mentioned the Sri Lankan connection to the retired agent, and he said that the last wire transfers to Otto's account came from Colombo. Through Interpol, they'd gained access to one of his Swiss accounts. Over thirty years, there were encoded transfers from all over the globe."

"Yet, Colombo stood out?"

"As a flagged origin related to the last payment. I'll call you when I have more intel." Martin hung up, and Gage lowered the phone to his lap. Wyatt led Chantal to the convoy. She glanced at Gage's suburban, and even though she wouldn't be able to see him through the tinted glass, his pulse picked up. God, she was beautiful. Which didn't matter because she was never meant to be his.

The car's atmosphere felt tense as they slowly looped around another precarious turn on a narrow pass. Chantal stared ahead, preferring not to glance over the drop-off right beside her window.

"This was a bad idea."

Dishan fiddled with the windshield wiper settings. "I'm comfortable with the monsoon season, and I've grown up on these roads. Relax, I know what I'm doing." He reached for his water bottle.

Gripping her seatbelt, Chantal nearly climbed onto her seat. "Both hands on the wheel!"

"You sound like my wife."

"Who obviously cares about living!" Wyatt added from the passenger seat.

Chuckling, Dishan slowed and edged around a boulder. "We do have to watch for mudslides—a pretty common occurrence in this region."

"Gee, thanks. How long have we been at this?" Chantal asked.

"Fifty minutes. Three hours to go. At least we're on a tarred road. There are worse passes on the island."

"Always the optimist. Did you hear any news of your baby before we left?"

"Priya arrived at the hospital. At least she's in good hands."

Turning in her seat, Chantal glanced out the back window for the hundredth time. Team Five followed closely in their matching black suburban, and she wondered if Gage drove. Her temper tantrum seemed foolish in retrospect.

He was right to ask the question, "what now?" Which indicated that their night together meant something. That's what scared her—the sense of belonging as she'd lain in his arms.

Wasn't she meant to be cutting relations and riding off into the sunset on her own—like a lonesome cowboy—cowgirl? Is that what she wanted?

And what about what Gage wanted? Was he seriously considering a future with her? How would that even work? Her head hurt, thinking of the logistics. Or maybe she felt car sick again. Chantal rubbed her mouth and stared out the window at the passing palm trees. The road straightened as they emerged from the pass.

"How far is the next town?"

"Not for a while," Wyatt replied over his shoulder.

"I'm feeling car sick, so we may need to pull over so I can throw up." Her hand moved from her mouth to her stomach. "Can't I open the window?"

"No," Wyatt replied. "Bulletproof glass doesn't work with the window down. Focus your eyes on a distant object out front."

Grumbling, Chantal leaned her head against the window. "How am I supposed to do that through this thick fog?"

The rain had finally slowed as the mists rolled in and visibility dissipated with every turn. A vast white blanket cloaked the landscape, and Dishan cautiously closed in on the rear of the ambassador's detail.

Chantal bet that her mom was feeling just as queasy. Chantal got her motion sickness from dear, old mum. She remembered going deep sea fishing in Alaska with her family as a teenager. A cursed trip where both mother and daughter had hung their heads over the side and heaved up their breakfast and previous night's dinner. Daddy had been fine.

Daddy. Had she ever known him? Her gut said "no"' and her heart said "yes." Happy memories remained front and center, but would his dark secrets taint her love. He'd adored her. Of that, she was sure. Was he a stone-cold warmonger?

When a stone pinged against the glass, Chantal sat up and looked around. Not a stone. Her team erupted, and shouts filled the air as a truck appeared from the thick fog, hurtling down the small hill and aiming straight for her. Bullets bounced off the windows, and Chantal screamed.

"Ambush. Get down!" Hard hands pulled her to the floor. Time slowed, and she braced herself as her world detonated in an explosion of metal and pain.

Her steel prison, which could become her casket, slid across the road, flipped and slammed into a ditch. An elbow punched into Chantal's temple as she flew into the roof. Her world flickered and adrenaline coursed through her aching body.

Sudden silence replaced the bedlam aside from the sound of rain on metal. A breeze stole across her warm skin. And then the shooting started back up.

Wyatt's face appeared, and he shouted her name. His voice sounded muffled as he pulled her across the seat. Using her legs, Chantal helped her AIC, and they fell back into the mud.

"Stay here." Wyatt left her sheltered in the ditch, and she lay on her back as he used their battered car for cover. The world spun as Chantal tried to sit up.

"Need to help." Pitching sideways, she rolled to her hands and knees. A buzzing noise filled her ears and darkness floated at the corners of her vision.

"Wyatt…" Chantal saw him pull the trigger. He rested a rifle on the hood and fired into the noisy battle. Men screamed. An explosion nearby shook the ground. And when Wyatt fell back, Chantal gave in to her dizziness and collapsed into the dirt. She turned her head to watch blood pour from Wyatt's broken face.

"Help… help him." The darkness pressed in as her face sunk into the wet earth. An insect crawled across her cheek, and then it was gone, like her last desperate thoughts drifting away in a misty dream.

The well-planned attack took everyone by surprise, on a rough stretch of road surrounded by fields and foliage on all sides. When Gage had caught a glimpse of the targets' vehicles barreling through the brush, he knew that they were screwed—and outnumbered. His only thought—live long enough to get to Chantal.

He prayed Team Five's training would pay off as a pimped-out Land Rover slammed into the MSD armored vehicle. Seconds before the collision, Lucius and Gage had already begun firing at the occupants as Gannon reversed.

At the last second, and thanks to a headshot, the Rover driver veered off target, striking the hood of the MSD suburban, instead of pounding Gage and his team to kingdom come.

"They've blocked the road to the front and rear!" Gannon shouted. "Heavy goods vehicles."

They'd need to evacuate on foot. There was no way that the teams could retrieve both principals and ram their way out of the fight. The agents grabbed their backpacks before throwing themselves into the firefight as they rushed towards their principal's battered transport.

Mercenaries appeared from the brush like a swarm of ants, and Gage peppered them with a semi-automatic spray while assessing the carnage.

The ambassador's convoy took the worst hit from a large truck, which had propelled Team Three's vehicle straight into the embankment. Crushed metal was all that was left. The ambassador's driver tried to bulldoze his way out of danger, revving his engine and shooting forward.

"Incoming!" Gannon shouted.

While rushing for Chantal, Gage took cover as an RPG sailed out of the veiled mist and clipped the front of the ambassador's ride, flipping it in a concussive explosion.

"Fuck!" Lucius yelled.

"Take out the fucker! Gannon!" Gage knew who the next target would be and rose, surging towards Chantal's suburban. Not caring about bullets flying, he leaped over bodies and rolled through debris, mowing down tangos as he charged for his principal.

Wielding an SR-25 Precision Fire Rifle, Gannon took off in the opposite direction, dodging bullets as he dove into the bush. If he stayed alive, the sniper would stop the shoulder-launching shithead from launching another anti-tank missile at Chantal's vehicle.

Trusting his teammate to find the target, Gage slid down the embankment and landed beside Dishan, who fired at will. Blood poured from a head wound, and the soldier cleared his bloodied vision with a swipe of his sleeve.

"Where is she?" Gage clipped in another magazine.

"Behind the tire. Best cover Wyatt could find—our ride is a mangled mess. We're outnumbered—this will be a massacre."

"Not if I can help it. Move away from the vehicle—the fuckers have a grenade launcher."

"This is the only cover we have!"

Gage scrambled towards Chantal. Icy tentacles twisted in his gut as he caught a glimpse of her lying face down in the ditch. A woman shouted in the distance—sounding like Alexis.

"Chants! Honey! Say something." Gage felt for a pulse, and she stirred beneath his touch. "Wake up. I'm turning you over."

"I'm fine. Give me... second."

Bullets pinged against the armored suburban. Rolling Chantal into his arms, Gage searched for injuries, clearing away the mud clinging to her pale face. A knot formed on her brow, and she groaned when he touched the bruise.

"Anything broken?"

"Don't... think so."

"We gonna make a run for it. I'll support you, but I need your help because I'll need my weapon hand."

"Run where?"

"Into the hills."

Chantal gripped Gage's arm. "Dishan... the team. Wyatt was shot."

"He's dead," Dishan called before firing another round. "Bullet to the head. My team is gone—a couple of my men took off, and the rest are dead."

Gage's heart dropped. They'd lost good men. "Roger. I'm exfiling you both to a safer position while the rest of Team Five retrieves the ambassador." Gage adjusted his headpiece and communicated with his team before helping Chantal to her feet.

"Mom. Oh, God, Mom!" Chantal struggled to get free.

"Lucius and Kohen are with her. Relax. We've got her." His team spoke through scratchy comms. Ignoring her protests, Gage half-carried Chantal along the muddy trench, pausing before hitting exposed territory. "We'll take fire, and we need to run as fast as you can. We're heading up that hill. I'll cover you along with Dishan."

"I can do it. Let go of me."

"Chants—"

"You need both hands free. In 3...2...1."

"Jesus—wait."

Ignoring his command, Chantal took off, and he dove into the line of fire, clacking off rounds as he surged across open ground. In his peripheral vision, Gage saw her stumble, just as he lobbed a grenade at the five assailants closing in.

Dishan raced past and dragged her up the slope by her shirt. Gage went to town with his MK-18 carbine rifle. Grateful for the thickening fog, he covered their retreat over the first ridge. Gunfire echoing to his left indicated the firefight surrounding the ambassador.

Gage dropped a charging fighter who got too close while still keeping up with Dishan and Chantal. An RPG round buried itself in the slope to his left, and Gage dove as dirt and rock exploded, rolling him across the wet earth.

His head slammed into a tree, dislodging his helmet. Gage rolled to his back and reached for the head bucket which rolled down the slope, along with his comms.

Chantal shouted his name. Lurching to his feet, Gage staggered towards the shocked pair and shoved them towards a descent. "Go, go, go!"

Plunging into thick foliage, they ran for their lives, falling and slipping over roots and through the mud. When Chantal tired, Gage towed her along. He avoided confrontations and using his weapon, as that would mark their location. Instead, he led them on a winding route through thick foliage, skirting the tea fields.

Finally, the air grew silent, and the rain began to fall in earnest. Chantal's shoulders shook with cold and shock, and Gage knew they needed to rest. He also needed to navigate with his team. Both Dishan's and Gage's direct comms were now missing. Chantal's pallor worried him, and he needed to re-check his principal for injury.

They'd all sustained damage, and Gage knew he'd need to see to his aching shoulder. He'd been shot—which felt like a graze—and warm blood dripped down his arm. The relentless downpour would wash away most of the evidence, hopefully, along with their footprints.

They ran for another twenty minutes, and when Gage spotted a rocky outcropping, he led them to a wide shallow cave to rest.

"Sit."

Chantal collapsed, her chest heaving as her limbs shook apart.

Kneeling, Gage cradled her dipping head and stared into her stunned eyes. "Do you have any double-vision? How does your head feel?"

"Sore and no. A little dizziness. You're bleeding."

He was, and his blood clung to her mud-stained cheek.

"So… so is Dishan," she added.

"A small cut." Dishan kept watch. His rifle shook in his wet grip.

Gage glanced over. "Good job, bro. Your startle response while under fire was on point. Is this the first time you've been in a war zone?"

"Affirmative. I feel like a mess—I guess my training kicked in like it was supposed to."

"You're a great teammate."

"My mother. I need to get to her." Chantal gripped Gage's wrists and tried to straighten.

"Leave that to me. Rest for a second while I call my team." He covered her head with her jacket's hood.

"With what?"

"A satellite phone. Our traditional comms are gone." Gage

swung off his backpack and dug in a side pocket. "Have some water in the meantime." Gage pulled out a flask and offered it to Chantal.

After she'd drunk, he passed it over to Dishan. "Anything?"

"Still clear," Dishan replied, seeming calmer than he had appeared a minute ago.

Turning on the phone, Gage entered the international access code and made the call. Nothing. He tried again, this time venturing into the open and using a different number. There were four phones assigned to Team Five, and he'd memorized all four numbers.

What if his men hadn't made it? The ambassador... and his best friend. The last time he'd seen Gannon, he'd been running headlong into enemy territory.

"Alpha Five, this is Beta Five. You're alive."

Gage closed his eyes in relief at hearing Gannon's voice.

"Beta Five confirmed. Bloody, but mobile. I have the primary principal."

"Roger. We have the Chief of Mission, and we've communicated our distress to the embassy."

"Injuries? Casualties?" Gage braced himself.

"The ambassador has torn up her side but is still mobile, and we've patched her up. Delta Five—Jason—is deceased."

Silently screaming in grief, Gage turned and paced.

Gannon continued; his voice thick. "Aside from their team leader, Team Three is out of action. Five men gone. Alpha Three sustained damage to his left arm in the crash."

Jesus. The only survivor on Team Three was their team leader? Fuck.

"How many locals do you have?" Gage asked.

"Three—along with the ambassador's Agent in Charge. And we've rescued Alexis."

"I have one—Wyatt didn't make it. Dishan is alive and on

overwatch. Text me your coordinates. I'll do the same. Let's meet-up and find the strongest point—a defensible structure—until reinforcements arrive."

"What about the nearest town?"

"What do you think? Because I reckon it'll be overrun with enemy targets. There were close to a hundred men out there. They don't want us getting back to Colombo, and we don't have enough ammo to fend off a mercenary army."

"Roger that, sir. We'll lay low. Watch your backs, and we'll see you soon."

Not ready for company, Gage hung up and scanned the terrain before leaning against a tree and taking controlled breaths.

So many good men lost. Jason's dead—gone. Oh, God.

"Gage?"

Her soft voice had him straightening.

"You broke cover. I told you to rest."

"Yes, but—"

Gage swung to face her. "When I give you an order, you listen!"

Visibly flinching, Chantal hugged herself.

Gage stalked forward and took her arm in a firm yet gentle grip, directing her back to the rock face. "Move."

"Why are you so angry?"

"Because this isn't a game."

"Of course not, I—"

"Jason Webb is dead. My fucking friend—MSD brother—is gone. Six MSD agents in total have lost their lives in a damned ambush; Wyatt's gone. Dishan lost his men, and we've been here too long."

"Gage—"

"So when I tell you to stay put…"

"You're blaming me?" Chantal yanked her arm from his grip. "You think this is my fault!"

"Never. But I'm not losing you. Understand?"

"They… killed… shot Wyatt in the head. I couldn't help him! Just like Daddy." Tears streamed down her cheeks as words fell. Chantal was in shock. "I watched it happen— watched my father's head explode."

Gage reached out. "Chants."

"No! You don't know what that's like!" She clamped a hand over her mouth and stumbled back. "Oh, God. I'm sorry."

"We're walking out of this hell together."

"Gage…I didn't mean… your dad."

"I know. Hey… it's okay." He pulled her in for a quick hug. "We'll be okay."

Gage stroked her back, hoping that wasn't a lie. His chest ached with torturous grief as he thought of Jason—left behind —lying in the mud.

No-one else would die on Gage's watch. They couldn't remain in one place for this long. Pulling away, he gave her the news. "Your mom is okay—for now. She's slightly injured from the RPG attack—probably from shrapnel—but she's mobile, and they've patched her up."

"Oh, Mom." Chantal tried to run her hand through her hair but encountered dried mud instead. "And we're meeting up with her?"

"Yes," Gage answered, directing her towards the forest, and adjusting his pack as Dishan fell in from the rear. "We need to walk our asses back to safety. Are you ready?"

Chantal nodded. "I'm right behind you."

Chantal focused on the warrior leading them through the brush rather than the awful hollowness settling into her bones. He'd lost Jason. She knew that feeling—the emptiness in his heart—the waves of misery pounding in his skull. That's how

185

she'd felt when she lost her father. And she'd blurted out those thoughtless words.

The day's horrors could never be unseen—images now layered on top of old memories. Her shattered mind recalled old violence which melded with the new. Was this her fault? Because of the flash drive?

They walked in silence—more like jogged. Although Chantal worked out three times a week, her yoga routine didn't prepare her for jungle warfare. Both men scanned the land-scape, always looking for danger.

"I don't have it," she stated between breaths. "God, I wish I did. I could've saved them."

Gage glanced back. "You don't have what?"

"The flash drive. That's what they're after, right? That's what our attackers want."

"Of course you don't have it. Stop blaming yourself." Dishan piped up from behind.

"I could have negotiated with Rajin. Tried to track it down."

Gage paused and turned to face her. "We would never have allowed that. Stop finding a way to blame yourself."

"You said—"

"I'm angry, and I've said a lot of things in the last hour. The one responsible for this mess is Rajin—and his army of assholes."

"Are we sure he's responsible?" Dishan asked as they continued their uphill hike.

Gage kept silent, and Chantal examined Dishan's state-ment. Many extremist groups would love to attack an ambas-sador's convoy. Not just in Sri Lanka but throughout the region. Until the U.S. completed an investigation, the motive was unclear.

"What happens now?" Chantal widened her strides to keep up with Gage, while watching her step on the slippery hillside.

The rain came in bursts. Grateful that she'd worn her Arc'teryx jacket, she took turns burying her hands in its warmth as they ventured deeper into the rural territory.

"Once we're together, we'll seek out a defensible structure. And before you ask, we're avoiding the nearest towns. Our assailants brought so much firepower to that attack that we believe they'll be hiding out along the route—look for squirters while hunting our two principals."

"What is a squirter?"

"An individual who's escaped an attack."

Chantal's definition for a "squirter" was an unfit target on the run, breathing through her ass.

"So they aren't chasing us?"

"I'm sure they are. There were enough soldiers. The fog saved our lives, and so did the rain."

"That's why we're running like Rambo up the side of a mountain?"

"Do you need to rest?" Gage shot her a look of concern. "More water?"

Waving a limp hand in the air, Chantal shook her head. "You're still bleeding. Can't I take a look at your shoulder?"

"I already have. It's a graze."

"How do we know where to meet the rest of the team?"

Gage held up a long device the size of his fist. "A GPS Tracker—it's called GoFindMe. Works without cell service. It has a built-in GPS and long-range radio technology."

"Is that a military tool?"

"Nope. Just cool tech."

"Is that how Martin is going to find us?"

"Nope again. We all have personal trackers on a team. And we've activated our distress signals."

"Does that mean they'll send in reinforcements?"

Dishan laughed, and she shot him a glare. "What?"

"You're full of questions."

"I'm a control freak. I like to know how deeply we're covered in ambush manure."

Gage coughed on a sip of water and paused to wipe his mouth. "Ambush manure?"

"Bad guys ambushed us, and now we're in the shit."

"And we'll have to dig ourselves out of the poop pile."

She frowned at his metaphor.

Gage sighed and offered her the flask. "Let me explain. Protocol demands that after notifying the embassy of our 'situation,' they'll start talking DOD support."

"Department of Defense," Chantal confirmed after handing the water to Dishan.

"Yes. But before the U.S. can send in Special Forces, they'd have to get permission from the host nation. Otherwise, it's considered an 'invasion.'"

"It's hard to get that permission," Dishan added. "But, then again, attacking the U.S. Ambassador is an act of aggression against the United States."

Her shoulders slumped. "So we're on our own."

"Probably." Gage squeezed her arm. "Even if we do get support, it could take days. And we don't have time on our side."

Taking a deep breath, Chantal nodded. "We have to fight to get back to Colombo—to U.S. territory. And then we'd wait to find out who's responsible."

"You got it." Gage tried to tuck her hair behind her ear.

Chantal grabbed his fingers. "It won't cooperate. It's a mud mask. I'd give my right boob for a shower—with shampoo."

His eyes sparkled in amusement. "It's cute. And your nose..."

"What's wrong with my nose?"

"It's still completely covered. You look like Minnie Mouse."

"And you're Goofy!" She punched him in his good arm.

He winked as he tucked away the flask and continued

leading the way. Glad to see a glimpse of the old Gage, Chantal focused on keeping up and hoped they'd at least hook up with the rest of their posse before nightfall.

With only a few hours left before sunset, as hope began to rise, torrential rain began to fall, and Chantal tried not to shiver. High altitudes meant cold showers, and soon her breath misted in the shadowed forest.

Glancing back at the ghostly scenery, she tried not to imagine the mercenary hunters closing in from all directions. Picking up her pace, Chantal ignored her burning muscles and edged closer to her two-man security detail.

19

G age stopped suddenly and drew out his satellite phone.
Dishan immediately took point, checking for danger.
Gannon answered on the second ring, and Gage verbally gave
their coordinates. "We're within a klick. Use your GPS
tracker."

Gannon complied, and ten minutes later, Gage crested a
hill and spotted Team Five and the rest of the survivors.
Letting out a relieved breath, he guided Chantal into her
mother's arms.

For the first time, the ambassador showed genuine emotion,
sobbing into her daughter's shoulder. Turning away from the
heart-wrenching sound, Gage greeted the rest of his team.

"It's good to see you standing, bro." Gannon pulled him
into a tight hug, and Gage shuddered out a sob.

His friend's arms tightened. "We couldn't save Jase. I tried.
I fucking tried."

"Hey, man." Liam Dalton limped over, and Gage turned to
face Team Three's Team Leader. The guy looked paler than a
ghost. His blood-soaked shirt hung torn beneath his bullet-
proof vest, and a sling held his left arm to his chest. It was the

look in his eyes—that broken, haunted stare of a man who'd lost everything—all his brothers in one brutal afternoon.

"Oh, man. I'm so goddamn sorry."

"I couldn't… they didn't even get the chance to fight. That fucking truck…"

"We'll find the bastards who did this and make them pay."

"We will." Ambassador Durant joined the two team leaders. "I swear, upon my life. I'll get justice for your team and their families." She stood, rod straight while vowing her support, and Gage's admiration for the ambassador grew. He hated how she treated Chantal, but the woman knew how to fight on the front lines for what was right.

She turned to Gage. "Thank you for saving my daughter."

"Dishan and… Wyatt. They're the real heroes." Gage changed the subject. "Liam, how bad is the arm?"

"It's a dislocation, and it's preventing me from doing my job."

"I can help with that." Chantal moved to his side. "First, let me feel around and get an idea of the exact injury. If there aren't any complications, I'll push the ball of the upper arm into its natural position. Gage, do we have ten minutes?"

"Doubtful." Gannon handed Gage a couple of ammo clips. "And if he passes out. We'll need to deal with his dead weight."

"I won't pass out. Fix the damn arm."

"Take off your vest." Kohen knelt beside Chantal and dug in his pack. "I can give you a shot for pain."

"I don't want to be drowsy."

"I'll give you a minimal amount."

"You've got five minutes," Gage commanded. "Lucius and Gannon are on overwatch."

"I'll join them." Dishan shouldered his rifle and ran behind the agents, disappearing into the forest.

Gage turned away and headed over to the rest of the

group. Alexis lounged against a tree. Hands tucked in pockets. Compared to Chantal, she looked like she'd just completed a casual hike.

"You weren't injured."

"Pure luck and cowardice on my part." She smiled, watching him. "I rolled out that rich dude's car at the first sign of trouble and took off into the trees. When I saw the rest of your team retreating, I circled to join them."

"I'm glad you're okay."

"None of us are okay until we hike ourselves out of this mess."

"Agreed. Keep up because we'll be moving at a rapid pace."

She dipped her head, and Gage called the embassy, before pulling the ambassador's Agent in Charge aside for a quick brief.

A muffled scream had Gage turning to watch Liam curling to his side after Chantal had jerked his shoulder back in place. Looking up, she offered Gage a small smile before standing on wobbly legs. She needed to eat something, and he worried about her head. Still dizzy, Chantal had battled at times with their grueling ascent. All Gage had were MRE's.

"Anyone got protein bars? How many do we have between us?" Gage checked with the agents. "Let's ration the bars and distribute the quotas."

"Roger that."

Two minutes later, they were back on the trail, this time with a destination in mind—a recently abandoned tea factory, four klicks to the East. As they fell into single file, Gage chose to stay close to Chantal and her mother, trailing them over the rough terrain.

Due to her mother's injuries, they fell behind the leading pack who'd slow now and then and wait for them to catch up. The constant downpour had them all watching their step.

Water streamed across vegetation, and rocks loosened down slippery hills. At some point, they'd need to break cover and move through tea fields to get to the factory.

"Are you okay, Ambassador Durant?" Gage helped her around a particularly large boulder.

"I'm the 'Anaconda,' I could hike for days." She grinned at his surprised expression.

"Do you think I don't know about the nickname, Golden Boy? I've known for years."

"It's bad-ass." Gage guided her along the path. "They chose a good name."

"Yeah! So, no resting on my behalf. I have a reputation to uphold."

Gage chuckled and checked on Chantal who stuck to their rear. She looked determined and brave.

"Thanks for helping Liam."

"Glad I could help." Chantal held onto a sapling while Gage helped the ambassador over a fallen log. "I hope to contribute as much as possible."

"Chants, just follow orders. If I tell you to run or get down, do as I ask."

"Kohen gave me a knife—if the worst happens."

"A tango could use the knife against you in a fight. Where is it?" Gage asked.

"In a weird leg band." Chantal lifted her pant leg.

"That's a neoprene ankle wrap designed for knives."

He wasn't comfortable with his principal wading into a fight—especially since it was Chantal. And he decided to set her straight. "You can use the weapon when you're out of options, if your protection detail is dead or incapacitated or if we're overrun. Till then, you follow my instructions."

Chantal grumbled in French, and they continued along the winding path. After thirty minutes of hard hiking, the party stopped to rest the injured. Gage helped to lower the ambassador to the ground before handing her his flask.

"Thank you, Gage. Sit, Chantal—while you can."

"Yes, ma'am." She scooted up and wrapped a hand gently over her mother's waist.

Seeing the tea fields peeking out from below their vantage point, Gage positioned himself near Chantal and scanned for bogies. An incoming storm muted the afternoon light.

"I'm sorry I was so hard on you—back in Colombo." The ambassador ran a hand over Chantal's hair. "I don't want you to leave me. You're all I have."

"Don't you get it?" Chantal looked up into her mom's face. "No matter where I am, I'll never leave you. You'll always be my mom. But I need some degree of separation—I need my own home."

Gage swallowed; her statement had him thinking about what he could offer. Outside of his career, who was he? A roving soldier with a rental in Virginia. He loved his job, but it didn't offer total fulfillment.

The only time he'd ever felt completely at ease was with... he glanced at Chantal. That wasn't possible. They'd known each other for a couple of weeks, and it was the adrenaline talking. Gage thought back to the moment he'd found her behind the suburban—face down in the ditch. He'd switched to panic mode—feeling a gut-wrenching terror he'd never felt before.

Thunder rumbled, and a small movement down the hill had Gage ducking out of sight and he swore under his breath. Gannon glanced his way, and Gage signaled trouble. While waiting for the team to fall into an attack formation, Gage counted the armed targets winding into the forest from a field.

"How many? Have they seen us yet?" Chantal whispered.

"Seven and negative. I need you to retreat out of the line of fire. Dishan?"

"Understood. Do you want us to continue? The path gets steep ahead."

"Just until they're safe. Also, take Alexis. And Kohen as back-up."

"I want to stay and fight." Kohen widened his stance as a rainstorm began.

"Protect our principals. That's an order."

"Fucking-A."

"You're staying behind with me, dick. We've got this. My firing arm is back online." Liam glared at Kohen before leading Chantal and the ambassador into the brush. Alexis hurried to catch up as Dishan and Kohen fell in behind.

The wind picked up as the mercenaries closed in. Gage recognized a couple of the bastards from the ambush. Pounding rain dropped from the sky, preventing conversation.

Gage's team didn't need words to communicate. Finding cover, they waited until the right moment before firing on the unsuspecting targets. Three men dropped under fire, scarlet blooms spreading across their fallen bodies. The rest scrambled for cover, firing back as Gage's team ran and ducked down the hill, closing in on the four remaining tangos.

Gage fired and slipped on a rock as a bullet buried itself in the tree beside his head. His target tried to dive to the left, and Gage knelt, pulling the trigger, blowing out the side of the mercenary's head. A guttural shout to his right indicated that Gannon's bullets found their mark.

The last two men fell under efficient fire, and the team wasted little time in racing back to the group. Gage rushed ahead, ignoring his burning muscles as he accelerated up the steep gradient, leaping over boulders and skimming past trees. Spotting Liam signaling ahead, Gage slowed, but not by much.

"Let's go. The gunfire will have bastards nearby zeroing in." Gage grasped Chantal's hand and pulled her to his side. He wanted her close and didn't care what her mother or his team might think. Enough with the games. All that mattered was being beside her.

The steep path ahead led down into a valley, where thick indigenous vegetation sheltered a rushing river. In the far distance, the river widened and slowed, nestled amongst green tea fields. Somewhere beyond the valley lay the abandoned factory. According to GPS, a two-hour hike from their position.

Alexis surged ahead, and Gannon called to her to slow down.

"I need to pee. I'm running ahead."

"You're like a mountain goat." Chantal paused to watch Alexis hop across a crevice.

"We can't take too much time with this descent." Gage guided Chantal down the same steep path.

"What I said earlier—about not knowing what it's like to see your father—"

"Don't ever apologize for dealing with trauma. Of course, you had flashbacks during the ambush and I'm so goddamn sorry."

"Like I was a helpless kid again, lying on the school steps."

Gage squeezed her hand and she offered him a shaky smile. "I'm fine."

"No. You're not. None of us are okay."

"At least you're by my side. I feel safe with you." Her foot slid and he grabbed her elbow.

"See? I'm safe."

Gage wished it were that easy. With dozens of mercenaries closing in on their scent, how long could his team stay on their feet? They'd fight to the death. Gage hoped to make it to the tea factory before the showdown. Team Five would go to war on his terms.

The slippery mud slowed them down, and once they were on solid ground, Chantal straightened and let go of Gage's hand. Alexis disappeared ahead, the rain cloaking her from sight. Gage's attention constantly switched between the environment and their principals.

Falling behind, Dishan supported the ambassador as she stepped, wobbled, and slid to the side.

"Dammit." Gage turned back. "Don't move; let me help your mom."

"Thanks." Chantal grasped a nearby branch as Gage backtracked to help Dishan. He'd just leaned down when he heard the trees snapping from above. The hairs on the back of Gage's neck stood to attention, and he straightened as the hillside dissolved into a muddy waterfall, snaking down the hill.

"Landslide! Run." Dishan thrust the ambassador back towards Liam and waved his arms frantically at the group. "Run!"

Adrenaline leaped as Gage registered Chantal's flash of terror. And then she was gone—the earth giving way beneath her feet, dragging her down the mountain in a deadly avalanche of rocks and trees.

20

G age's horror switched to primal anger. Shedding his pack in one swift move, he rushed towards the mudslide. No-one or nothing would rip Chantal away.

"No!" Gannon shouted, but Gage didn't care. Launching himself at the brown river in a suicidal leap, he braced himself for the rough descent. The powerful tide swept him along a chaotic path, and Gage focused on keeping his head above the mud—a challenge when his heavy tactical vest weighed him down.

Something slammed into his back, twisting him sideways as the avalanche gained speed. A fucking tree. Trying to spot Chantal, he raised his knees and leaned back, guiding himself with outstretched arms.

"Chants... Chantal!" He caught a glimpse of her shooting around a bend. Gage tried to sit up, instead, he slammed into a log, and his strapped rifle became snagged, ripping him to a stop and flinging him to his stomach. Gage refused to give-up, needing to get to Chantal. If she ended up buried, he'd need the location.

Ducking his head and freeing an arm, Gage parted ways

with his primary weapon, allowing the sludge to pull him the rest of the way down the hill. Mudslides weren't often survivable and meant certain death for the majority. Gage had to live long enough to save his woman. If he lost Chants…

As they hit the valley, a tree limb punched him in the side, and Gage shouted as it tore away skin. Pain surged, burning down to his hip as he rounded the same bend where he'd last seen Chantal. Catching another glimpse of her in the distance, he watched her tumble beneath the surface as the landslide dissected the river, creating a dirty whitewash of circling rapids.

Shit, his Kevlar vest might suck him under. Gage used his arms to row closer, relieved when the muck around him gathered speed, and he held his breath as he hit the icy flow of the mountain stream.

Chantal's body tumbled over and over, caught in a dizzying death-wash. She fought for breath—for life. Her lungs hurt, and her head spun. Opening her eyes, she looked for light and saw the flash of the sky. Chantal kicked her legs and swam against the swirling current. Breaking the cold surface, she sucked in a quick breath as the riverbank rushed by.

"Chants!"

Had she heard her name? Unable to look back, she focused on swimming closer to land. Everything hurt, and her limbs felt weak from fighting the tide. And God, she was so cold.

One last push. Fight!

Her father's voice whispered in her head, echoing the times he'd taught her to ride a bike, ride a horse, dare to stand in front of an audience.

C'mon, stubborn girl!

Releasing a battle cry but sounding more like a strangled

duck, Chantal kicked with all her might, using her tired limbs to stroke towards the shore. Her frozen hands brushed past the bank, and she willed herself to grab at the reeds. Trying once, twice. Spotting an exposed tree root, Chantal lunged, and held on.

Someone shouted, and she looked up as Gage swept past, using powerful strokes to swim to the bank.

"Gage!" She twisted without letting go, watching as he disappeared around a bend. "Oh, my God. Oh, shit!"

Shoving aside fear for her own life, Chantal dragged herself to safety, collapsing, before crawling downstream. She tried to stand and fell to her knees. "Gage!"

"Chants." His answering call had her wailing in relief.

"Where... where are you?" She kept crawling, speeding up when she saw a flash of movement ahead. He'd made it out of the water and lay on the wet embankment, his back towards her.

"Gage!"

He didn't move, and Chantal sobbed out a breath. Once she'd made it to his side, Chantal collapsed and tugged at his wet shirt, trying to pull him onto his back. CPR. She could do this. Groaning and then coughing, Gage twisted to face her. She watched his chest rise and fall and she sagged in relief.

"Honey. Oh. God. You're alive." Strong arms pulled her onto his chest, wrapping her in a trembling embrace. He shook... wait, she also shook. Her teeth rattled, and his skin felt like ice. They needed warmth. The wet clothes would kill them quickly. Gage sat up, cradling her against his chest. He cried out in pain, and she tried to pull away.

"No. Not letting go. You need to get warm."

"Let's get off the... wet sand. Find shelter. Dry our clothes." It still rained, and they wouldn't survive the night in their current state. The team wouldn't find them anytime soon.

They'd been carried deep into the valley, and Chantal knew that they were on their own.

After a couple of tries, they were on their feet and clearing the bank. Leaning against each other, the pair teetered and lurched through the brush before stumbling into an old field. Chantal fell to her knees, bringing Gage down like a felled tree. Blood soaked through his wet shirt, and Chantal tried to locate the wound beneath his bulky bulletproof vest.

"Leave it... shelter first."

Glancing frantically around, Chantal stood. Her knee throbbed, and she favored the other leg while studying their surroundings in the fading light. It looked like a neglected tea field—weeds grew amongst wasted bushes, and Chantal squinted through the gloom.

"Wait here." She took off, limping across the field as Gage rolled to his knees.

"Chants! What the hell."

Staggering and tripping through muddy furrows, Chantal zeroed in on her target. Gage's panicked shouts closed in from behind, and she turned to watch the stubborn warrior reel up beside her.

"Told you to wait..."

Her lips shook with the effort. "I'm not walking all that fast. Old hut ahead, and I need to check—"

"My job! Behind me. Now."

Not having the strength to argue, Chantal did as he asked.

She kept close as he circled to the trees and sidled up to the mud-clay walls. The thatched roof looked neglected—fragile beneath the canopy of trees. Moss clung to the exterior, and as they rounded to the front, Gage paused and studied the broken steps.

"No track marks. The door is open," he whispered before easing to the entrance. He'd visibly relaxed, which meant that they were visiting an abandoned plantation. Was that a good or bad thing? Finding citizens would mean a connection and assistance. But that also held the risk of leaking intel spreading to mercenaries in the area.

The survivors in the ambush were sadly outnumbered—at least for now. The better plan was Gage's response in staying off the radar until help arrived.

She followed him inside and paused to take in their dark surroundings. Holding her frozen hands to her chest, Chantal willed her body to stop quaking. The hut wasn't all that warm, but it was dry. The only furniture left was an old sofa, a stove, a chair, and a battered desk in front of the small window.

"Look! A wood-burning stove." Gage pointed at a biomass cookstove connected to a chimney. "We need dry wood. Hold on. Get out of... clothes."

"A pot." Chantal pointed at a rusty looking container near the stove.

"Good... for boiling water." Gage disappeared into the rain.

He left her standing in the dark space, and she stripped down, disappointed to see the knife missing from her ankle holster. Two minutes later, Gage returned, clutching a pile of logs. "There's an old woodshed... out back. Saw it earlier."

Unstrapping his vest was a challenge as his fingers wouldn't work. Chantal stumbled forward and helped. As she eased off his vest, he groaned, and she gently lifted his shirt over his shoulders. Next came his pants.

"Gage." She couldn't see much in the gloom, but she'd felt his torn side and warm blood on her cold skin.

"I'm fine. Nothing broken."

Still, she worried. Folding her arms over her wet bra, Chantal crossed her bare legs and waited to see how he'd start a fire. Gage pulled a lighter from a pocket, and she chuckled on a shaky breath.

"Still have my handgun... I need to dry it out. Left my

pack but never go without a knife and lighter—or firelighter."
He packed the wood in the stove, using his knife to shave some
kindling. "Hope… chimney is clear."

She did too. Otherwise, they'd smoke themselves out of
their shelter. She watched the wood spark, and under Gage's
competent care, the fire blazed to life. While she waited, she
used the chair to hang their clothes near the stove.

He dragged the sofa closer to the flames and pulled her
down beside him. They waited to warm up, shivering in each
other's arms.

"Your side."

"Can wait. The bleeding stopped."

Chantal felt exhaustion pulling and rested her head in the
crook of his neck. Time passed, and her shivering slowed. His
body warmed, and she settled into his sheltering embrace,
careful not to place her weight on his injured side.

Gage seemed comfortable enough and rested his chin on
her head. The dusk turned to dark, and in the intimate glow of
the fire, they were the only people left on earth.

Finally, she stirred and sat up. "While our clothes dry, let
me look at your injury."

"What about you? You're limping and winced when I
squeezed your arm."

"I'm battered but functional. I hurt my knee, and I have a
bruised elbow." Easing around, Chantal used the firelight to
examine his ribs.

"Something tore you up in the water."

"A damn tree. My Kevlar vest saved my life by protecting
my back and chest."

"It's not too deep; the graze is shallow. But you're bruising
badly."

"I didn't break a rib. I'm fine."

Chantal poked and felt around, and Gage swore soundly.

"Hold still."

"You're a sadist." His jaw ticked as she felt along each rib.

Happy with her examination, she rose and checked on their clothes. Her eyes fell on Gage's sheathed knife, and Chantal reached out.

"Careful! That blade is sharp. That's a Ka-Bar."

"Isn't that what SF soldiers use?"

"Yes—It's a U.S. Marine Corps Fighting Knife. Mine's not a standard issue."

"What do you mean?"

"Martin gave it to me when I graduated basic training—back when I was a grunt."

She smiled and touched the aged leather sheath. "It's sentimental."

"And vintage—from World War II. It still has a perfect stacked leather grip, and the blade cuts like butter. We've both looked after the fixed blade over the years. The Ka-Bar is my prized possession."

Chantal loved the sentiment and felt glad that he hadn't lost the knife in the water.

"You've killed with this knife?" Stupid question—of course, he had—she'd seen him fight fearlessly. He'd sliced down mercenaries with well-aimed bullets. Gage was a honed weapon.

"Many times. Your knee is swelling."

"There's nothing I can do about it."

"I need to sort out my Glock and check the perimeter." Gage moved carefully, easing himself into a standing position. He must've picked up on her concern because he grasped her shoulders and offered a reassuring smile.

"Bad news is that we're separated from the pack. The good news is that we've floated a good distance. We're way ahead of the bad guys, and from what I can remember—co-ordinates wise—we're pretty far from the nearest village."

"How is being isolated a good thing?"

"Because for tonight, we're off the radar. No-one's venturing out in the dark in this deluge. That's suicide. I'll still keep watch, but we're invisible. Even if the mercenaries hunting us saw us slide down the mountain, it would take hours of hiking in unstable terrain to find our location. And they'd be blind in the stormy night. No tracks, no light, no solid ground."

Chantal liked those odds, and gently wrapped her arms around Gage's waist, avoiding his injury. Unable to resist the solid agent, she kissed his chest and felt him pull in an unsteady breath.

"As much as I'd love to stand here all night, with you in my arms, I need to prepare for the morning. When the sun comes up, we'll hike to the rendezvous point, and until I can get to my teammates and their firepower, we'll have to be overly cautious. I have fifteen rounds in the Glock. Every bullet counts."

"Such an optimist." Chantal stroked his bristled cheek, and her pulse stuttered at the tender look in his eyes. The only sound was the pitter-patter of the rain against a small window. The rustic firelight softened Gage's features. Shadows danced over his grim face, making him look mysterious... dangerous.

She asked the question which had niggled ever since they'd crawled to the bank. "Who else was swept away? Did you see anyone fall before the slide pulled you down the mountain?"

His throat moved as he swallowed. "I think everyone else was spared. I... I wasn't caught up in the mud."

"But..."

"I couldn't leave you. No matter what the outcome. You weren't..." Gage frowned, trying to form the words. "You weren't going to suffer or die alone."

"Wait—you dove after me? Because I'm your principal?" Chantal couldn't imagine anyone taking that risk unless...

"Nothing to do with my job."

Mind reeling, Chantal stepped back and viewed him with

new eyes. He'd thrown himself off a mountain and into a violent river filled with mud, trees and debris. For her?

"Chants—"

"Your gun. Um… you need to clean your weapon. I should…" Crossing arms over her chilled stomach, Chantal turned to the fire. "I should turn our clothes."

"You're still shaking." Warm fingers ran over her neck, and Chantal closed her eyes. She loved his touch—like a trail of fire across her skin.

"You have the prettiest neck." Firm lips touched her shoulder. "We both danced with death today—in a spiraling tide. I nearly lost you."

His words from earlier—at the bungalow—which seemed so long ago, circled in her exhausted brain. *"Where do you see this going?"*

A question she hadn't yet been able to answer. This wild warrior, who would leap off mountains and risk a watery death for her… what lay in his heart? And was she ready to discover that secret?

Her future shimmered like a mirage on the horizon. What happened to her plans, her five-year goals? Leaping into the unknown wasn't Chantal's modus operandi. Planning and plotting out her journey was the safer choice. A relationship with Gage fell into dangerous territory. And he didn't know about her painful secret.

Stepping out of his embrace, Chantal drew in an unsteady breath and moved towards the fire. She couldn't look at him. He drew her in with that magnetic heat and made her forget herself. Gage made her forget about a lot of things.

Turning the garments, she heard him shift and move to her side. He reached for his gun and moved away—to the desk under the small window. Then he returned and picked up his damp shirt before tearing a scrap of material off the bottom.

"What are you doing?"

"I need to dry out the dismantled parts. The rest will air-dry. Rest awhile. I'll be at the window."

She took his advice and stretched out on the sofa, watching him stand by the desk and work on his gun. Now and then, he glanced out the window. Her eyes drifted shut, and when she woke, she found his large jacket draped over her bare skin. It felt warm, and she stirred, pulling it close and gazed at the flickering logs in the stove. She should rise and get changed back into her dry shirt.

The front door stood open, and the wind stirred the subdued flames. She was alone. Panic stirred and her muscles locked.

"Easy. I'm here." Gage entered in just his boxer briefs and boots, his gun held by his side.

She let out a relieved breath and turned to her back.

After placing the weapon on the chair and shaking out his wet hair, he closed the door and strode over to the cooker. "I added more wood about ten minutes ago, and I'm boiling water from the river. He pointed at the pot. We don't have much firewood left. I couldn't find food. Critters aren't out in the storm."

Moisture droplets glistened on his tanned skin, and Chantal admired his carved physique. His side looked raw and painful. "You remind me of a wet dog, coming in from a muddy walk."

"Woof." Gage shot her a saucy wink before turning and warming his back.

"You went out like that?" She gestured towards his wet gray briefs, trying not to linger on what lay beneath. He'd also risked hypothermia by not taking his jacket—instead he'd covered her in the dry warmth.

"Perimeter check. No-one is out there. And if I'd come across a target, they'd be more worried about my gun."

"Your lethal weapon?" Grinning, her gaze drifted back down.

Chantal didn't expect Gage to waggle his hips like a male stripper, and she broke into laughter. "I think you're in the wrong line of work."

"Boom shaka boom…" Gage shimmered her way.

"You'll hurt your side, and you'll get me all wet."

"Now we're talking." His smile widened.

"You know what I mean." Turning serious, Chantal sat up and crossed her arms.

"Hey, it's okay. I'm a weirdo, and I'm trying to distract you."

"From the bullets and mayhem? I'm worried about my mom."

"Chants." He crouched beside the sofa and cupped her jaw. "She's with good agents. Heroic men who will die to protect her."

"I'm sorry about Jason."

Gage turned his head and stared at the floor. His jaw ticked, and she felt his acute sense of loss.

"We lost many brave agents today. It's a heavy blow for DSS and their families."

The brutality of the attack haunted her. "I feel like it's my fault. They were after me. My mother."

"Never." His gaze returned to hers. "The ones at fault are the evil fuckers that stormed the convoy. And by ambushing the ambassador—that's an act of war against the United States. With that many enemy combatants, there was never a safe outcome. Casualties on both sides are expected when facing such huge odds."

"We should've cancelled the symposium—you were right."

"No—those mercenaries showed organized determination. They would've found another opportunity."

"Do you think it's Rajin? Or another militant group?"

"I can't say." Gage stood with a wince. He walked over to the window and stared out into the rainy night. "But we'll find out eventually. The DOD... the Whitehouse... the Department of State... they'll all be gunning for answers."

"And will hopefully rescue our asses?"

"As I said before, that will take more time than we might have. Evading the enemy is all we can do."

"I don't want to think about tomorrow." Chantal also didn't want to think about her future. Not while locked in another cocoon with Gage. A golden sanctuary filled with warmth and temporary peace. Standing, she discarded his jacket, and then her bra and panties, and walked over to the shadowed man standing by the desk. Tracing the line of his damp briefs, she pushed between him and the desk.

"Chants—You're naked."

"You can keep vigil—staring through that small window. I'll play." She sat on the desk, positioning herself near the edge, and opened her legs, hoping he'd step between her thighs. The bulge in his underwear took shape, growing under her gaze.

After a moment's hesitation, he complied. "I need to stay focused."

"You said it yourself. We're safe for now. If you're hurting, we don't have to—"

"I want to be inside you." He groaned as her fingers stroked him through the fabric. "I don't have... protection."

"I'm clean, and I'm... I'm on birth control."

"I get tested on every deployment. I'm also clean and I haven't been with anyone for—"

She pushed down his boxers and gently fisted his solid length. His head dropped back, and she rubbed a thumb across his tip before circling and stroking. Grabbing the table's edge, he thrust into her moving hand, and a savage growl escaped as she shifted, positioning him on her wet opening.

His gaze shot to hers. "Are you sure?"

Mouth dry, she nodded and welcomed his delicious invasion. As he buried himself deep, she wrapped her legs and pulled him closer. She needed this raw moment—skin on skin in a secluded hut. Cut off from the world and cradled in each other's warmth.

Would this be her last night on earth? Would the mercenaries find them in the morning and gun her down in the Central Highlands of Sri Lanka? And Gage would sacrifice himself in the firefight. All to save her.

Heart pounding, Chantal curled a hand around his neck and held on as he slowly pulled out and plunged back in. Her body clenched, holding him tight, and they both moaned at the perfect fit.

"God, you're amazing." His hands drifted down to her lower back, and he held her in place as he stroked her to pleasure. She didn't want the moment to end. He felt too perfect, and Chantal buried her face in his neck as he breached all her defenses.

Her body ablaze, she allowed her release to carry her to the point of no return. Gage shouted her name. Chantal arched her neck, feeling tears roll down dusty cheeks as he shattered and pounded out his pleasure. The orgasm lasted forever, pulsing and expanding as they both held on. And then he pulled her close, swiping at her tears and muttering sweet nothings into her hair.

In the tender moment, she held tight, and they remained that way, still joined and suspended in eternity. She loved Gage, and the thought terrified Chantal. What if she lost him? What if he died trying to rescue her? And if they survived? What then? Would he walk away? Would she?

"What's wrong?" He cupped her face. "You're scared."

Unable to find words, Chantal nodded.

"I'll protect you." His sworn sincerity shone from fiery eyes, and her heart sunk. She didn't want that—to be responsible for his death. Memories of her father's assassination invaded the moment—a dead parent and fallen bodyguards.

She'd protect Gage—at all costs. Regardless of their uncertain future, in the rainforests of Sri Lanka, he'd remain by her side. And God help anyone who got in their way.

～

"Wake up." Crouching carefully beside the sofa, Gage stroked her cheek. "Easy."

Chantal jerked awake, and he felt a flash of regret. Perhaps he should've left her to sleep.

"What's wrong?" Chantal sat up. "Did they find us?" Her knotted hair stood out at all angles, and Gage suppressed a grin.

"We're safe. There's something you need to see. Here's my jacket and your socks."

"Gage… what's happened?" Chantal slipped her arms into the deep sleeves as he pulled on her socks.

"Trust me." His hand couldn't resist sliding up her calf to her bare thigh. Forcing himself to rise, Gage stepped back and extended a hand. "Boots next."

Even though the fire still glowed, Chantal shivered as she slipped her fingers into his. Gage led her to her boots and then the door. They stepped out into the quiet night.

Chantal paused on the top step. "The rain has stopped."

"So has the wind. And the clouds have cleared. Look up." Pulling her to his front, Gage slipped his arms around her waist and pointed at the starry sky. "Look up."

"Lyra." Her awed whisper had him bending and kissing her tipped-back forehead.

"I forgot about the meteor shower."

"I remembered what you said about the peak times for viewing. I'm guessing it's around four in the morning. Let's get comfortable."

They sat on the crumbling steps and waited for their eyes to adjust.

"Are you warm enough?" Gage cradled her between his legs.

"You're toasty." Chantal snuggled into his thighs, and he slid a hand into the jacket and cupped her breast, enjoying the feel of her nipple against his palm. He lazily played as they watched the celestial event. Every now and then, she arched her back with pleasure and leaned back for a deep kiss.

A possessive sentiment had him devouring her soft mouth. Their easy intimacy was like nothing he'd ever experienced before, and Gage communicated his desperate need for this woman.

When they returned to watching the sky, she sighed. "Isn't the universe incredible? And unpredictable. Those streaks of light are all rocks and boulders hurtling through space. We live on a giant marble, never knowing when it could collide with other marbles. Suns explode... stars collide... black holes destroy entire solar systems."

"And yet there's also order in the universe—on this planet," Gage added. "The cycle of life. A seed germinates and grows. Reproduces and pollinates. Eventually, the plant dies and returns to the earth. Death can be predictable." Unable to hide his grief, he continued. "The unpredictable part is knowing when it will happen. For some, it happens sooner—others get to live a long life." Gage stilled, and Chantal turned to cup his face.

"Jason was so young, and I'm so sorry."

"I can't stop breaking down that ambush—figuring out how I could've saved him. Perhaps if he'd stuck by my side..." Gage allowed the guilt to roll through his tired bones. "And Wyatt—if I'd gotten to you sooner. I couldn't have saved Team Three, but maybe—"

"Don't do that to yourself," Chantal cut in. "You'll go insane."

"MSD Teams are well-trained, and we've prepped for this scenario for years."

"Gage, the enemy came from all sides. It's a miracle that any of us survived."

"All I could think of was getting to you. When I saw your suburban roll into that ditch…"

"And you saved my life—and Dishan's—and your own life. Without your bravery—without Jason's bravery—we'd all be lost."

She'd be lost. God, what if she'd died? Grateful to have her in his arms, Gage looked back at the stars, and they watched the streaks of light in silence. He'd never forget this night. Gage realized that he'd fallen for Chantal.

Thinking back, he recalled the moment he'd first known it was love—when she'd been on the symposium stage, fighting for the rights of her patients. After what she'd lived through, she still always put others ahead of her own needs.

Most people would scurry to safety after being almost choked to death—they'd book a flight to the States. Not Chantal. Her determination to attend the symposium and fight for her cause spoke of her rare soul.

"I can't lose you." Gage pulled her to his chest. "I just found you."

"We found each other. What happens tomorrow?" Chantal shifted.

Gage had to be honest about how he felt. "I want us to build on what we have."

"You want a future. With me?"

"It's complicated right now, but…"

They only had tonight, and Gage wanted to be as close as possible to Chantal. As much as he'd love to bury his cock in

213

her heat, they both needed rest. Gage had to be ready for the unpredictability of battle.

"There's something I haven't told you."

The misery in her gaze had him pulling back to study her shadowed face, and he didn't like what he saw. "Let's go inside and talk."

"No—I prefer the dark. What I'm about to tell you—you may change your mind about us."

Gage couldn't imagine walking away from this courageous woman.

"The night on campus—when I was stabbed. I had internal damage that needed repair."

Gage squeezed her arm in reassurance as she stared past his shoulder.

"The damage to my uterus—the surgeons did an excellent job, but… I needed a hysterectomy, which they performed laparoscopically."

"Oh, honey."

"I lied to you earlier about birth control. I didn't know how to tell you—I can't have children." Blinking rapidly, she folded her arms.

"I'm so damn sorry." An evil son of a bitch had taken away an eighteen-year-old's choice to have a family, and Gage wanted to hunt down the elusive piece of shit. Instead, he wrapped Chantal in a firm embrace.

She resisted. "What are you doing?"

"Uh… trying to hug you."

"Why?" She pushed at his chest. "That's not what you should be doing!"

Gage raised his hands and leaned back. "What should I be doing?"

Shaking her head, Chantal swiped at a tear. "Deciding if I'm what you want?"

Gage didn't know what to say, and she must've picked up

on his confusion.

"I probably shouldn't be asking—not this soon—but don't you want kids?"

He answered honestly. "Not at the moment. Especially with my job and—"

"Don't you want to be with a healthy woman who can—"

"Don't finish that sentence." Gage touched her cheek, her skin cold beneath his touch. "You're never less than. You're always more than. More than I could have dreamed. More than I've ever known. More than I deserve."

"And what about five years from now?"

"Do you want children?" he asked.

"That's a silly question given my circumstances!"

"Because you have options—like adopting or finding a surrogate."

Chantal stood, and Gage did the same. "We're not even dating. We shouldn't have this conversation."

"Don't compare our connection to a random couple who just started dating." Gage felt pissed. "That's like comparing the Grand Canyon to a pothole."

"Because we're on the run, and adrenaline fuels this 'connection.'"

"That's bullshit. I'm always living on the edge and stress defines my career. The moment we met had nothing to do with adrenaline. And I immediately knew I was in too deep."

"I'm giving you time to think about a future with me—if you'd be happy with a childless reality."

"I don't need to think about—"

"The reason why I broke up with my first serious boyfriend in Algeria—he couldn't come to terms with my injury. He wanted at least three children. And I didn't break up with him —it was the other way around."

"The sandaled asshole sounds like a fucking prick."

"He had every right. He wanted a family."

"I won't change my mind."

"I wouldn't blame you. Think about a legacy."

"I have and—"

Sealing his lips with her hand, Chantal covered his heart with her other palm. "It's time for sleep. We have an early start."

She slid by and entered the warm shack. Gritting his teeth in frustration, Gage took one last look at the night's sky. No more streaking lights. All he could think of was the weight Chantal had carried for the past decade—that's what he'd seen in her beautiful eyes. A gaze filled with grief and longing that branded his soul for eternity. This night together had changed Gage on a cellular level.

And she expected what—to continue on her solitary path —to push Gage away?

What happens tomorrow? Her haunting words had him scanning the tea fields one last time. He prayed that at least he'd do his job and protect Chantal. Keeping her alive was all that mattered.

21

Rajin didn't like the news. The ambassador bitch and her daughter had escaped the ambush. Harris seemed confident in tracking down the women. His soldier was a loyal dog, trailing their scent.

But Rajin couldn't remain on Sri Lankan soil. He trusted his network, but one betrayal could lead to his arrest, and without that USB, he had little leverage over the president. He glanced at his Rolex before taking a seat on a leather sofa. A maid walked by.

"How long must I wait? Are they done packing?" His loafer tapped against the coffee table impatiently.

"I'll check, sir." She rushed towards the stairs and Rajin admired her shapely ass. He'd fucked her a few times—along with the rest of the female help. They all bore the marks. Rajin wasn't a gentle lover. He'd tried with Pearl—his dedicated wife. But she'd never seen the monster below the surface—the man who got excited with thoughts of torture and death.

That's why he'd recorded his "interrogations." Watching them gave him endless pleasure—especially when he tied up a paid whore and screwed her while watching the tapes of his killings.

And now, his cherished cassettes were gone—stolen by the one person he'd trusted. The one person who'd taken everything—his sanity, his career and his child. He'd loved his ex-wife. When they'd first met in India, he'd fallen for the beautiful traveler. Pearl had sat beside him at an outdoor café and they'd struck up a conversation.

The pale beauty with the short hair stood out on the busy street—her hair had glowed like a halo in the sunlight and her intelligent eyes had captured Rajin's heart. Abandoning his meetings for the week, he'd trailed after the pretty tourist and charmed her with fancy dates in Mumbai.

Marrying her had felt victorious and he'd hoped his new wife would cure him of his sick urges. She hadn't and his secret cravings destroyed their bond. Letting go of Pearl was one of the hardest decisions he'd ever made—knowing he could never be a decent husband to the mother of his child. But he'd still loved her. And she'd discovered his secrets and betrayed that love.

Pearl would pay, and once he found her, she'd see who she'd married. Beauty and the Beast. Except when he was done with her, no-one would want her. She'd become the Beast. Even her own daughter would fear her mother's face.

Rajin's servants carried his luggage down the stairs and he stood.

"Is everything packed? My toiletries and razor? All the clothes?"

"Yes, sir." The butler bowed and Rajin headed for the door. He'd never return to this beautiful land—not while the hunt was on.

Harris would take care of the ambassador and her child. For Rajin, it was time to find Pearl.

~

The sun shone. Both fully dressed, in their soiled but dry clothes, Gage and Chantal readied themselves for departure. They both moved easier, thanks to a little rest. Chantal was ready to get back to her mom and hoped she had the energy.

Feeling famished, she salivated at the thought of food, but at least they'd drunk water—boiled water. Not ideal, but that's all they'd had. If they could make it to the tea factory, they'd have provisions. The old pot could still be useful, and Chantal decided to bring it along.

"Wait." Gage caught her arm as she opened the door. "I want you to have this." He presented his knife. "Do you still have the ankle holster?"

"Yes, but I can't take your Ka-Bar."

"Why not?" He bent and rolled up her pant leg.

"Because if I lose it..." Chantal reached out and tried to stop him. "Gage—you said it yourself—it's your most prized—"

"No. You're my most prized... well, not possession. Treasure." He slipped the knife into its new home and fiddled with the Velcro strap. "The Ka-Bar is large, but it will hold."

"I can't—"

Standing abruptly, Gage gripped her shoulders. "If you're taken, you'll let that knife do what it's designed for—killing the enemy." His hands tightened. "Wait until the time is right to make a move."

"Don't think that way—that won't happen." Her pulse raced as she circled his wrists.

"Last night after you fell asleep, all I could think of was Rajin and his methods of torture—tying bags filled with gasoline around his victim's heads. Beating the bottoms of their feet with a steel bar. Breaking bones to extract information." A vein ticked at Gage's temple.

Chantal nodded. "I know what he's done—I've seen the footage."

"I'm sure Rajin is behind the ambush, aiming to eliminate the enemy. But he wants the location of the USB drive, and he might use torture to get it."

"I don't know where it's hidden."

"We know that, but he doesn't. And he won't stop until all the players are wrung dry."

Chantal shuddered at the image his words conjured.

"They won't expect you to be armed. Promise me—you'll fight to live if I—"

Pulling him in for a rough kiss, Chantal stopped the morbid words. They'd have a long hike to the factory and would need to cross the river at some point, but they were walking away from this nightmare together.

When Gage finally drew away, he pressed his lips to her forehead. "Let me show you how to use the knife. He bent and pulled it from her ankle sheath and positioned it in her hand with the blade pointing backward along her wrist. "Never show your weapon. Keep it concealed and when you strike out, use slashing and stabbing movements. Stab someone by pulling back and hooking your opponent. Like this."

Gage took the blade and showed her a few basic moves— hooking and pulling the knife towards him.

"That would cause much damage."

"That's the idea—before your attacker realizes his predica- ment. Now practice."

She cupped the hilt and concealed the knife along the length of her forearm.

"Easy. Watch the angle—don't cut yourself." Gage twisted the handle.

For the next ten minutes, he taught her three moves— nothing too complicated. The strikes sat close to the body, and Chantal concentrated on the subtle angles and the right grip.

"We should go." Gage placed the knife back at her ankle before taking her hand. Chantal welcomed the warmth of the morning sun, feeling grateful for the firming earth beneath her feet.

Their green surroundings looked like an emerald carpet. Gage's sharp eyes continuously scanned for danger. They moved fast, and Gage looked for cover at every turn. As the morning wore on, the air turned muggy, and Chantal's knee pounded as they traversed hilly ground before rewinding to the river and following it.

Instead of focusing on the pain, she thought about her revelation from earlier. Telling Gage about her infertility had felt terrifying, and she wondered how it might affect their relationship. After years of therapy, she'd come to terms with her condition. Not entirely—she'd never get over the loss. But she'd learned to tamp down on the bitterness.

Chantal had always wanted children, and her inability to conceive led to feelings of failure, shame, and guilt. It also led to difficult conversations with a potential partner—which was why she hadn't dated much since her injury.

The truth was that she felt flawed—like she'd never measure up. Months of therapy didn't erase the shame. She'd never be able to share a child with the man she loved—a child that would share their DNA and their quirks. All Chantal could do was offer her love. Would that be enough?

Perhaps she should encourage Gage to move on—find a future with a woman who'd give him a family. Was it selfish to hold onto her warrior? The love of her life?

When they reached a serene junction, they removed their boots and waded through the rocky shallows to the other side. Thankfully, the icy water only came to Chantal's knees, and after crossing, she tried to balance as she used her jacket to dry off her feet. Damp feet would mean foot rot, and she wasn't about to explore that blistered path.

Gage stepped up to help. "Do you need to rest? You're battling with that knee."

Gritting her teeth, Chantal shook her head—wanting to get to her mom. "I wish we could drink the river water."

"Not without boiling it. Most of the natural supply is unsafe in Sri Lanka—we'll soon be at the tea factory. Let's find cover in that small grove ahead, and we'll rest for five." He glanced at the pot. "I could start a fire to boil water, but the smoke would draw attention."

"I'm fine."

"You're not." After they'd booted up, he guided her ahead. "And we'll both soon be dehydrated. I'll have to make a fire if we don't get to the team."

"God, I miss food. I hope your team has saved some MREs for us."

"Me too." His fingers stroked down her back, and she suppressed a shiver. Her body tingled from the contact.

When they finally paused in the small thicket, Chantal dropped the pot and collapsed beneath a tree. Gage walked the perimeter before doing the same. Shoulder to shoulder, they sat as she caught her breath. Her knee pounded along with aching limbs and Chantal clenched her shaking hands into fists and imagined a meal and a soft bed waiting at the end of this journey.

Gage kissed her head. "I can smell a trace of your perfume." He kept his lips in place.

"That's surprising, considering the knotted mess on my head."

"That fragrance is familiar... calming... what do you wear?"

"It's a French perfume— L'Artisan Parfumeur Premier Figuier. It has notes of fig, rice, coconut, and sandalwood."

Gage sniffed her head like a basset hound, and she laughed.

"Fig, of course!" He pulled her close. "A year after my father's death, after Martin had rescued me from a foster home future, the Department of State sent him to Greece for two years. He took me along, and I enrolled in online classes. Martin worked as a DS agent at the U.S. Embassy in Athens."

"Sweet gig!"

Gage chuckled. "He loved that deployment. And it was a special time for a kid who'd lost everything. We spent a vacation on the island of Evia—fig trees everywhere. Our rental cottage had some growing in the yard, and I spent many an hour doing my homework in the shade of a fig tree. You smell like my best memories—a time when I learned to smile again."

Not knowing how to reply to such touching words, Chantal stroked his cheek and studied his rugged profile.

The dappled light filtering through the leaves drew her attention. "The Central Highlands are beautiful, and in other circumstances…"

"Is that still part of your grand plan?" Gage asked as he scanned for danger. "To take a vacation and travel?"

Chantal shook her head. "I thought about what you said— that sometimes a bad person is just a sad person. My mother is difficult, and she's always had that 'red' personality, but after the shooting… she's battled with depression along with the pain. I needed a break and I hate myself for wanting to turn away. The 'vacation' idea was just me—figuring out how to run from my problems. And then this thing between us grew."

Gage grinned. "This thing, huh?" He nudged her with his shoulder. "You're willing to abandon all those post-its and planners for me?"

"Hey! Don't diss the planner. It's a comprehensive goal setting and tracking system."

Gage laughed. "You're cute when you're defending your organizational tools."

"You don't believe in life-mapping?"

"My job throws me from post to post. And deployments are all about tactical charts. In my downtime, I go with the flow."

"You're an untamed nomad." Chantal squeezed his leg, knowing his restless nature stemmed from losing his parents. No roots meant not having to care.

"And you're an organized one."

Turning thoughtful, she agreed. "I guess... since the day of my father's assassination. My life changed irrevocably. I don't like the unknown."

"The unknown is unavoidable—and adversity whittles you into a stronger version of yourself."

"Is that what happened after your parents died?" Chantal slipped her hand into Gage's broad palm, and his fingers curled and held on.

"Yeah. The future had felt terrifying. Martin taught me how to live again—how to smile and how to be a kid. His guidance gave me courage."

"He's a good man."

"The best." Gage brought her hand to his lips. "But you're right. Although I excel as an agent—I'm a drifter. I lost my roots a long time ago and I guess that's why this job works for me."

Chantal let go of his hand and stood. "And after this deployment. You'll disappear back to Washington with your team."

"For work, yes." Gage rose. "You and I will talk when this is over. For now, let's get moving."

That wasn't the answer she wanted. What choice did they have? Stolen moments on the run? She wanted more, with a man who'd altered her in every way. Gage branded her with his unrestrained charisma and heroic charm. How would any other human compare?

"One more thing." Gage brushed a hand over her waist. "You're allowed to have a break—a vacation—from a stressful life. Taking that time away, might strengthen your relationship with your mother. Don't carry so much guilt."

Easier said than done.

A twig snapped, and Gage shoved her behind him as he pulled his weapon. Tracking the invisible threat, he altered his stance, and Chantal held her breath.

22

"Don't shoot!" Hands raised, Alexis emerged through the beams of sunlight and shadow. She looked as tired as Gage felt. Dried blood coated the side of Alexis's face, and her hands trembled as she stepped around darkened foliage. Her mud-caked clothing looked stiff and damp.

Stepping over a gnarled root, Chantal moved to her friend, and Gage blocked her with his broad frame.

"What are you doing? Lower the gun."

"She may not be alone—this could be a trap."

"I haven't been kidnapped," Alexis called. "I'm just relieved to see you both. I've felt disorientated since being dragged down the hillside in a wall of mud."

"The landslide got you too?" Gage asked.

"Yeah! I shouldn't have gone ahead. I heard your shout and it was too late. How many were swept down the hill?"

Gage lowered his weapon, and Chantal hurried over to her battered friend.

"I think it was just the three of us. I can't be sure." Gage watched the women embrace before scanning the trees for hidden dangers. "We need to keep moving. Are you strong enough to walk?"

"I am—an annoying head wound. I've had worse in the past—on a climb. Do you have any water?"

Chantal shook her head. "We found a shack last night and boiled a pot. Nothing today, though."

"We'll soon be joining the team. When last did you drink any?"

"I constructed a rain trap last night using my jacket's hood. I should've filtered it, but I didn't have a sturdy container, though my stomach feels fine."

Gage nodded down the valley and gestured for them to walk.

Instead, Alexis unzipped one of her pant pockets and pulled out a protein bar before tossing it to Chantal. "You guys must be starving. Eat."

"What about you?"

"I've eaten one this morning. I'm always prepared."

Chantal handed Gage half the granola bar, and they set off, winding through tightly knit trees.

Gage eyed the blonde. Crumbling clay still coated her plaited hair.

"I'm guessing you didn't hit the river."

"What do you mean?" Alexis asked, crushing damp wild-flowers beneath her feet.

"We both were swept into the river." Chantal smiled. "And almost drowned."

"I had luck on my side." Alexis touched her hairline." I knew I had to keep my head above the mud, and I remembered sliding on the periphery of the sludge. And then, a branch slammed into my head. Next thing, I woke on a crumbling bank. I stumbled around and found a small hollow in a hillside. It kept me dry till morning, but it was a miserable night. I haven't been that cold since Everest."

"Wet clothes will get you every time." Gage grasped Chantal's elbow and helped her down a slippery incline.

He liked having her close—feeling her body heat near was reassuring. The next hour would be the riskiest as the terrain ahead flattened out into stagnant tea fields. Having little cover was unavoidable, and Gage's adrenaline picked up as he scanned the first clearing.

"Wait here. I'm doing recon." He threw out the order, ignoring Alexis's quip about Chuck Norris.

"And keep your voice down." He shot her a stern look.

If Alexis and her games endangered Chantal, she'd answer to him. As an experienced climber, she could aid his team, and they needed to be on the same page.

"Gage!"

He turned back at Chantal's whispered shout.

"Be careful." Walking over, she slipped her hands around his waist.

Pulling her in for a swift kiss, Gage savored her soft lips and stroked a thumb across her brow. He could hold her for hours, and after they'd survived this mess, he'd do that. Take his time exploring every inch of this beautiful woman.

Not wanting to let go, Gage reluctantly pulled away and looked down at her worried face. A scratch marred her pretty cheek and dirt smudged her chin. Plucking a small leaf from her hair, he swallowed, realizing how deep his feelings ran for the ambassador's daughter. He loved her with his entire being. Gage didn't like the foreign feeling. If he lost her…

"What's wrong?"

He felt his frown deepen.

"Hey, third wheel here! I want to wrap up this adventure." Alexis pointed to the fields. "Can we plate the lovey-dovey shit for now?"

"Go!" With a quick squeeze, Chantal stepped back, and her arms fell away.

"Stay hidden." He forced his mind back to their mission and turned away.

～

"You've turned your 'lethal weapon' into a sap."

Crossing her arms, Chantal turned to face Alexis. "What do you care? Feeling jealous?"

"Whoa. Easy. I'm not trying to be a bitch; it's an observation."

"No, seriously. Why does it bother you?" Tilting her head, Chantal tried to read further into Alexis's defensive expression.

"You're trying to start an argument."

Chantal lowered herself against a tree and rested her knee. "You don't make connections easily—even with me. You don't want to care. But I think you do."

"You don't know what you're talking about." Alexis's expression flattened, and she turned away.

"You're right. I don't, because you won't let me in. I hardly know anything about you, except for your hobby."

"Maybe I'm a boring person." Alexis pocketed her hands and brushed a boot over damp leaves.

"A solitary existence isn't a bad thing, except you're a human. A social being who needs—"

"Love?" Alexis scoffed as she faced Chantal. "You're the expert on love? Did you learn from your mother? Or has your flash romance with your bodyguard shown you the way?"

"That's not fair." Chantal tightened her crossed arms, raising her shoulders.

"Love is for fools. Even those that truly love us will hurt us in the end."

"And who hurt you?" Chantal asked.

Shaking her head, Alexis stared into the canopy. Her eyes

shone, and her lips twisted. "I hurt myself. I'm a disappointment."

"To whom?"

"My father." Her expression turned cold as she sat beside Chantal.

Their shoulders bumped, and something thorny jabbed Chantal in her side. "Ouch."

Shifting to a more comfortable position, Chantal offered a sad smile. "I know all about being the perfect daughter—that's why I led an ordered life. I wanted to meet every one of my mother's high expectations." Rubbing her temple, she sighed. "I'm done with my prison of guilt. I want a happy life filled with laughter and warmth. I want to find the girl I used to be."

Expression turning hard and resentful, Alexis narrowed her eyes. "Your privileged existence isn't exactly a prison."

Leaning back, Chantal frowned. Her head buzzed and blinking, she tried to focus as Alexis stood.

"I don't feel so good. I think something bit me."

Alexis crouched. "You mean like a snake?"

Chantal tried to nod.

"You gotta watch for the poisonous buggers. They sneak up on ya."

Chantal's face met the earth. A beetle scurried by, and a breeze blew her hair across her face. Her eyes closed as her world slowed.

23

"Come quick! It's Chantal."

Gage froze, and his heart paused at Alexis's words. He'd been gone ten minutes, and he'd kept close to the women —within shouting distance.

"What happened?" Breaking into a run, Gage rushed towards a frantic Alexis.

"Something bit her. I think a snake. I thought she was joking. But when she collapsed and—"

"Where?" Stumbling over a root, Gage spotted Chantal lying in the leaves. "Honey! Oh, God. No!"

"It doesn't make sense. Unless she's dehydrated. She's not waking up!"

Alexis's babbled words barely registered. His brain screamed, and Gage tried not to lose his shit.

"I placed her in the recovery position. She's not responding. Does she have a pulse?"

Skidding to his knees, Gage dropped his gun beside him and touched her cool face and colorless lips with a shaking hand. "Chants, honey?"

He needed to check for a pulse and consider his options. If

he ran with Chantal in his arms, how long would it take them to reach the factory? He could find a nearby village. He vaguely knew where they were. Gage tried to think back to his last intel on coordinates. First, he needed to find out what the fuck was wrong with her. Chantal lay too still. Feeling a pulse, he bent to watch and listen for breath.

His gun skittered across the forest floor, as a sharp pain to his left shoulder had him swinging for the threat. Alexis flew back and landed; a syringe clutched in her hand.

"What the fuck?"

"You're faster than I'd thought." Alexis looked at the vial as he shook his head to clear the encroaching fog. "You'll need the full dose." She lunged, and Gage tried to counter, immediately recognizing her as a trained martial artist. His movements felt clumsy, and yet his forearm made contact with hers, blocking the jab.

Grabbing her arm, he twisted, and she dropped the injector. Rolling, he threw her to the ground, narrowly avoiding a strike to the eye. The bitch held on, and a punch to his throat had him twisting her beneath him. As he pinned down a wrist, he spotted the pot and grabbed it, hammering the syringe beside them, smashing the contents into the earth. He needed his gun. Gage raised the pot, his arm feeling heavy and slow.

Alexis responded with a head butt, the blow disorientating his reeling mind. The world spun, and Gage fought the narcotized sludge dragging him into a dysfunctional coma. Too late, he blocked another blow, toppling to the side, and Alexis kicked at his leaden limbs and shimmied to freedom. His relaxing grasp let go of the pot and it rolled down a slope.

"You asshole. Look what you did! There was one fucking syringe." Had her accent changed?

"Chant... Chantal. Is she dead?" Gage battled to form the words as he held onto consciousness.

"No. But she will be. I want her to be awake when I kill her."

"Who... are you?" He scanned their periphery, looking for the Glock. The earth tilted like he was on a carnival ride. His limbs refused to work, and Gage screamed silently, living his worst nightmare.

Crouching out of reach, Alexis swiped at her bloodied mouth. "Jona Kivela. At your service."

"Kivela... Otto." Raw fear for Chantal overwhelmed Gage as he fought to stay awake.

"Yes. My father is a famous assassin, but I've eliminated more men—and women. A decade of killing, and I beat his strikethrough number. That's dedication." Alexis stood and walked off, bending to pick up his handgun. "It will be a shame to kill your lover. Chantal's death is unavoidable—it's personal."

"Chantal... is... your friend."

Alexis spat on the ground. "Don't say that!"

"Please..." Gage's thoughts drifted, dispersing the panic that kept him lucid. "Kill me... not her."

"Rest, warrior. Count yourself lucky—I only kill my assigned targets. When you wake, we'll both be gone, and she won't be coming back."

The drugs won, and darkness replaced light. Gage's last helpless thought was of an unimaginable world without Chantal.

～

"Get up."

Something cold nudged her on the cheek. Eyes drifting open, Chantal watched the sole of a boot descend before it tapped her forehead.

"I don't have all day."

"Alexis?" She sounded different. Harsher, somehow.

"I gave you a light dose. So, get the hell up before I kill your big, bad boyfriend."

"Gage?"

"Yes, bitch. I'm giving you sixty seconds."

Chantal stirred and raised her aching head. Struggling to focus, she licked her dry lips. When she saw Gage lying a few feet away, Chantal clawed at the mossy ground, trying to pull herself to his side.

"There's no time for that. He isn't dead, but will be if you don't listen."

"Gage! Oh, God. Gage."

"You're crying." Alexis swore in another language. "Enough with the waterworks. He isn't going to save you. I have his Glock." Bending, she waved his gun in Chantal's face.

"Why? Alexis, why?" Chantal focused on crawling to the fallen agent.

"My name is Jona—Because you've made my life a living hell."

"At the... rehab center?"

"No, stupid. By not dying that day at your school. You and your bitch mother should not have walked away."

"You were... you were there?" Confusion swirled. They'd caught the assassin. Chantal stroked Gage's stubbled cheek, praying he'd stir. But that might get him killed. Chantal needed to leave Gage to save his life.

"I was the one that pulled the fucking trigger."

Alexis's words didn't make any sense.

"You would've been just a kid."

"Same age as you. Otto was my father. We lost our daddies on the same day." Alexis looked away. "I killed both yours and mine."

"Your father died in jail—of cancer."

"He died too early because I was scared to follow through

STRIKETHROUGH

with my first kill on my own. I needed him by my side—he should've rested and stayed behind. In my stupid teenage brain, I thought he was invincible."

Chantal took a moment to choose her words carefully. How did she negotiate with a killer? And what did Alexis hope to accomplish by Chantal's death?

"Sounds like you loved your father very much—like I loved mine."

"Your father was a dirty bastard. Henri made his billions from the sufferings of others."

"No—"

"He provided funding and weapons to both the Tamil Tigers and the Sri Lankan government during the war. Henri's money built safe houses used for the interrogations and torture of the very victims you try to help."

"You're a liar!"

"That's why he was killed—for playing both sides and profiting from death. Your mother must've known he was a monster. Eliminating your father—a satisfying hit. Well, it would've been if I'd removed all three targets."

Chantal turned away, and dry heaved. Nothing came up.

"The man who attacked you in the clinic—he worked with your father. He was the one to discover the deception. A Sri Lankan government official hired my father to remove your family from existence." Alexis nudged Chantal's head with the gun's muzzle. "The daughter of the assassin will kill the daughter of a traitor. Ironic, since my father always wanted a son."

"Please... Alexis. You don't have to kill me." Chantal looked up. A ray of light lit up Alexis's blonde hair, and she looked angelic in the dappled sunlight.

"I have to finish the job, and I've never failed. Next will be your mother. On your knees."

Limbs trembling, Chantal obeyed as the gun pointed at her head.

"I liked you—a lot. In another life, we could've been good friends. But there's no glory in defeat." Alexis stepped closer.

Gage's hand snaked out and grasped at Alexis's ankle. His drugged attempt failed but caused enough of a distraction. Chantal launched herself and plowed into Alexis's stomach.

Both women fell hard. Alexis slammed the butt of the gun onto Chantal's shoulder. Responding by slamming her forehead into the bitch's face, Chantal rolled away. She wouldn't stand a chance against a trained assassin with a gun, but she could save Gage by getting as far away as possible.

Chantal ran. Thanks to the drug still coursing through her blood, she stumbled and teetered. A gunshot rang out, and the bullet slammed into a tree beside her head.

Gage shouted her name as Chantal righted herself and rushed through the trees. She tripped, tumbling down a slope, and rolled to grazed knees before stumbling into a tea field.

Another bullet whizzed by and hit the earth. Chantal dove to her stomach before scrambling along the maze of small trees, which sat at around four feet.

The unplucked branches provided thick concealment, and ignoring the rough ground on her scraped hands and knees, Chantal crawled through the field, finding cover from a previously unknown nemesis.

24

Panting against the dizziness, Gage tried to push himself up. His heart hammered in terror when he thought of Chantal—in the fields—being chased by a fucking assassin.

Alexis—Jona—was well-trained but had made one fatal mistake. She hadn't given Gage the full dose of whatever drug she'd probably bought on the black market.

And now, he'd hunt. Snapping Jona's pretty neck would be a satisfying revenge—especially if she hurt his woman. The best he could do was get to his knees.

Roaring in frustration, Gage crawled from cover and rolled down the hill. His damn legs wouldn't work, and he couldn't slow his descent. His head slammed against a rock, and blood poured from a sliced-up cheek. Another shot sounded as he rolled to his stomach. Had Jona found her?

If he lost Chantal, his soul would crumble to dust.

"Hold it together. She needs you."

Hardening her resolve, Jona ran silently through the mazed

field, watching for movement. She'd waited for over a decade for this moment—when she could complete her first assignment. Once she'd killed both mother and daughter, she'd be able to move on with her life. And do what?

Would she knock off new targets? Hadn't she been doing just that when she wasn't stalking the Durant family? Was that the life she wanted?

Soon she'd retire to a small island and sit on a deck and watch the ocean. Could she hang up her weapons and ignore the corrupt cockroaches who she'd terminated over the years?

Chantal isn't a cockroach. Neither is her mother. The silent words slammed past her adrenaline, causing her to pause.

"Voi Saatana." It felt good to swear in her native language.

Jona didn't allow herself to even think like a Finn when she took on a new persona. She'd lived as Alexis for months and slipped comfortably into the role. Helping the injured at the clinic brought purpose to Jona's life, and she was sad it was over. When she retired, she'd find volunteer work at a charity. Would that make up for the blood on her hands?

Jona glanced down at the Glock, which she gripped so competently—she'd transformed from the tiny blonde village kid who'd followed Papa through snowy woods. A child who grew up on the precipice of nowhere—in a rotting cabin on the Russian border. And now she was somebody—a warrior who killed the unjust.

A bush stirred—twenty meters to the left. Shifting direction, Jona hurdled over a line of small trees, catching a glimpse of Chantal's boot. Fifteen seconds later and Jona sprung on the woman. Immediately grabbing and twisting at her hair, Jona shoved a knee into her back.

"Got ya. No use fighting."

Not listening, Chantal squirmed like a pinned butterfly but was no match for Jona. A female assassin needed to be on top of her game. Not only did Jona dispatch all types of targets, including capable men, but she dealt with fellow mercenaries who would love to see her bleed.

The deception game required hours of physical training, and Jona's strengths were speed and her hand-to-hand expertise. Papa had taught her well. She could fight before she could walk.

Chantal's head hit the ground—once, twice—with the help of Jona's fisted hold. Swinging and rolling, Jona came to rest in front of the defeated woman and placed the gun at Chantal's head.

"Look at me." Jona waited.

"Fuck you."

Jona smiled at the mumbled words. "That's what I like about you—you never accept defeat. You're always trying to find a solution—save every patient with that trusty planner. Squeeze out every drop of your precious time. I admire your discipline and your desire to place others first. Like with Sunny —you saved that little family. That's what delayed your death. You're so damn likable."

Raising her head, Chantal's defeated gaze punctured Jona's cold heart. "So were you." Chantal let out a ragged breath and weakly pushed herself to her knees. "I liked your prickly attitude. I should've seen the threat."

"You trust too easily." The gun shook, and Jona gritted her teeth.

"I do. But I don't love easily. I love Gage and wanted a life with him." A tear rolled. "What did I do to you? Tell me, and I'll make it right."

Jona shook her head. "Your saintly attitude kills me. You can't save yourself; I'm sorry, Chantal. It's time."

Hands fisting in the dirt, Chantal raised her chin. "Don't hurt Gage. He'll search for you—for vengeance."

Her finger lay on the trigger, and Jona tried to ignore

Chantal's direct stare. This woman was Jona's first truly innocent target. She'd known that all along.

Papa had known, and he'd still wanted the girl dead. He'd told Jona about all his kills over his lifetime—the tarnished enemies that deserved their afterlives in the underworld —Tuonela.

As a child, she'd believed his heroic tales where he slew evil adversaries. As an adult, she knew better. Sometimes, good people perished.

Or did they? Papa wasn't here—standing beside Jona. No-one stood beside her. Her future became clear—it wouldn't change. Jona would always stand on the periphery, no matter where she lived. Family... love... connection. Not meant for her—Jona Kivela was born to kill.

Gage yelled Chantal's name as he stumbled their way. Too late.

Decision made, Jona pulled the trigger.

25

His chest felt like it would burst as he shoved to his feet and staggered after the women. Spotting Jona in the distance, Gage sped up and fell in his haste to save Chantal. The drug felt like syrup in his veins.

Gage saw Jona raise the gun as he pounded through the field. Chantal knelt before the skilled slayer, and her shoulders straightened defiantly. Too far off, he was out of time. Gage felt it in his bones.

Jona shifted her stance—straightened her elbow at the last second. Even as he flung himself across uneven ground, Gage knew he'd failed. With one last futile shout, he called out to his love and closed his eyes against the horror.

The gunshot echoed across the valley, shattering his soul. Gage's foot caught on a root, and he flew, landing and sliding to a final stop. Twenty feet away. Tea shrubbery blocked his view, and Gage rose to face a killer.

Two pairs of eyes turned his way. Chantal still sat on her knees, and Jona pointed the gun to the side. Her gaze returned to Chantal as Gage cautiously approached.

"I couldn't do it… Jumalauta!" Screaming in anger, she aimed at Gage. "Not one more step."

"Okay." Raising his hands, he felt beads of sweat trail down his neck. Weaponless, he needed to get close enough to tackle the crazy bitch.

Tears ran down Jona's cheeks as she glanced back at Chantal. "Why can't I kill you? I can't fucking shoot you. Not now and not back then."

"Let's talk…" Chantal volunteered in a raspy voice. "You don't have to do this."

"This was supposed to be easy and… and… shit! I hate you. I'm supposed to hate you." Tears rolled down Jona's dusty cheeks.

"But you don't hate her." Gage slid closer.

"The perfect billionaire's daughter. Why couldn't you be shallow and spoilt?" Jona paced, her gun still trained on Gage.

She stood too far from either of them, and he prayed that Chantal wouldn't go for the weapon. Torn with conflicting emotions, Jona wavered. Like a wolf honing in on its prey, Gage went for the verbal jugular.

"Is Chantal the first friend you've ever had? I don't think Otto was a friend—or even a kind father."

"Fuck you."

"Did he break you? Repeatedly? With his words and actions?" Gage asked.

"You know nothing about my life."

"I bet he took a sweet, young girl and beat her into a fighting machine."

Eyes glistening, Jona shook her head.

"I know what it's like to be alone. Where was your mother?"

"Whoring around the village. She had many lovers." Jona spat.

"And your father taught you how to protect yourself. He was gone often?"

"Stop trying to play on my sympathies—poor little Jona. I'm the one with the Glock. Asshole."

"Fine." Gage took another step. When he found a gap, he'd break her neck. He wanted to do more and knew if he looked at Chantal, he'd lose his mind.

"Saatana! Watch out." Jona glanced across the field, and Gage followed her gaze.

His gut clenched. Their chance at life and freedom had evaporated. Eight mercenaries appeared, melting from the forest and heading across the fields. Five of the men carried rifles. It would be too late to run, and Gage couldn't take on eight men—maybe four.

"Take Chantal. Protect her!" Jona pulled Chantal to her feet and shoved her towards Gage.

What the hell?

"If you want to live, play along." Jona waved the gun in his direction as she swiped at her wet cheeks.

Dragging Chantal into his arms had him almost sagging in relief. At least they both stood and still breathed. And he'd regained most of his strength. "Are those fuckers also your friends?"

"I trust no-one. Don't do anything foolish." Jona moved behind the couple and raised the gun at their heads.

"Are you okay?" Gage whispered in Chantal's ear as he pulled her tightly to his chest.

"Don't die trying to protect me. Promise?" Her body trembled in his.

"I can't promise that. Not as your lover or as your agent."

"You don't stand a chance. Let me help—your knife."

"No. They'll take it from you—quickly and brutally."

"I love you."

Gage barely heard her whispered words, but he felt her

choking sob vibrate through his chest. He would die a thousand times for this woman. And if Gage sacrificed his life for hers, he'd make it count. He wouldn't leave her alone to face these barbarians. When she drew back, he ran a thumb across her cheek and pulled her to his side.

"Chantal Durant. Nice to see you again."

By her cry of distress, Gage knew that the brute addressing her could only be one man—the bastard who'd wrapped his thick hands around her neck.

"We haven't met. I'll be your executioner." Gage smiled grimly.

"Cocky words, coming from a weaponless chump." The older thug looked amused, and Gage sized up the biggest threat on the field—aside from Jona.

"Howdy." The big man nodded at the assassin. "I'm surprised that Miss Durant still lives. You're such a bloodthirsty girl."

"I'm not a girl, Harris—you'd do well to remember that. You know how many I've killed."

Harris. Gage now had a name.

"Yes, you're a terminator."

"How did you find me?" Jona asked.

"Pure luck. We heard the gunshots and followed the racket."

"And here we are." She shrugged. "I work alone."

"Yet you helped us arrange the ambush. I've been tracking for two days. We can't have loose ends."

Jesus. Jona worked with Rajin. How had Gage missed this connection?

"I agree. You continue and find mama bear, and I'll kill the daughter." Jona winked.

"I have a better idea. Since this pretty chiropractor is still alive, I'll use her to find the USB drive."

"I don't know where it is." Chantal stared mutinously at the ugly shithead.

"I might believe you—but your precious mother knows. I'm sure of it, and there's one way to find out."

Gage shoved Chantal behind him. "Touch her, and I'll take you apart. Limb by limb."

"You won't be around to see what I'll do to her. I like torture. It gets me all hard."

"You son of a bitch." Red edged around Gage's vision.

"Do you like pain, sweet thang?" Harris called out to Chantal. "I can make you scream—send your body parts to mama dearest. Do you remember the last time I touched you?"

Gage's rage swelled like a scorching tide—blazing through his veins. His breath burned as he lunged forward.

Five weapons swung their way.

"You're done, boy." Harris waved a satellite phone. "A spy at your embassy tells me that your local SF buddies have just landed. Meaning, I'll retreat. I got what I came for." He nodded at Chantal. "Her mother will concede defeat when she hears I have her daughter."

"If you take her, you're depriving me of a valuable kill," Jona called from behind. "You know what Chantal Durant's death means to me."

"She's mine." Harris narrowed his beady eyes.

"No-one gets near." Gage pulled Chantal to his back.

"Harris, then make it up to me." Jona pushed. "I need someone to kill. Leave me with her lover."

"Nah. Kill him." Harris nodded at his men.

"Wait!" Chantal struggled in Gage's hold. "Don't hurt him. I'll do whatever you want."

"Fuck that." Gage gripped harder.

"Give me the MSD agent." Jona sounded mutinous.

Harris shrugged. "Fine. But my men will work him over first."

A mercenary surged forward and slammed the butt of his rifle into Gage's stomach. Letting go of Chantal, Gage retaliated, lunging for the man's weapon. Another rifle slammed into his side, and he kicked out.

Twisting the firearm from the asshole's hands, Gage turned the weapon on his attackers and pulled the trigger. Hearing a click, he knew it was a misfire—probably due to defective ammunition—of all the luck.

Instead, he used it like a spear, jabbing the nearest target in the chest. Four men immediately pounced, striking, and he fought blindly, exchanging well-placed blows.

"You can have me! Leave him." Chantal threw herself into the fight, and Gage grappled to stop her. Meaty arms gripped her around the waist and dragged her away. Harris.

Gage clashed against the hammering fists and weapons. A blow to the back of his thigh toppled him. With another strike to the head, he collapsed under an onslaught.

Jona's voice cut through his dizziness. "Take her, but I want this kill."

"You don't want to come with us?" Harris asked suspiciously.

"I'm hunting the mother; besides, do you have room in the chopper?"

"No. Not even for all my men. I'll leave a couple with you. Don't get caught."

"You're not my boss, Harris."

"I'm running this assignment. You work for Rajin." Harris pulled Chantal further away, and Gage crawled to stop him. His wrist pounded in time with his throbbing gut. Blood dripped from a split eyebrow, clouding his vision.

"Act like a hero and I'll throw her out of the bird."

Still eight against one, and if Gage fought to the death, he'd sign Chantal's death warrant. They'd toss Gage's body in the river, and his team would never find her, assuming they'd both died in the mudslide.

And if Harris contacted the ambassador, she'd never know who took her daughter—or know of Alexis's deception. Gage needed to stay alive to save his woman.

Chantal's last desperate glance broke his heart as Harris pulled her away. Gage screamed in rage as they disappeared from view.

"The big, fancy federal agent isn't so tough." A skinnier man spat on the ground, circling Gage like a hyena.

"The odds aren't in his favor. Do you have a cigarette?" Jona asked.

"You're not gonna cap him?"

"He's unarmed and not going anywhere. I'll kill him when I'm ready."

Not if Gage got to her first. She cleverly sat out of reach.

"You're skinnier than I thought." The other man eyed Jona. "I expected Godzilla—the way Harris speaks of you. You don't look like a bad-ass bitch."

Gage rolled to his back and watched the three cut-throats through gritty eyes. He couldn't wait to make a move—every second counted. Three armed against one unarmed; Jona had skills, but the other two? The way they moved indicated adequate but not necessarily excellent training. Gage's first kill would be the strongest of the two.

A helicopter crested over the ridge, flying low before landing on the next field.

"Don't even think about it." Jona shot Gage a warning look. "Even at the top of your game, you wouldn't get there in time. She's gone, and you'll die before you're on your feet."

She was right, and his heart squeezed with impotent rage. Breathing deep, Gage took measure of his injuries. His ribs were bruised but still intact. Aside from the dull ache, none of his limbs screamed in pain. He could fight.

The chopper ascended. It was too late. Chantal was gone, Harris had pulled the plug on Gage's heart.

Jona waved her cigarette. "Do you have a light?"

Nodding, the rangy man produced a Bic lighter, and she leaned in, puffing until it glowed. Ready to engage, Gage pulled in a slow breath.

"Thanks, dickhead." Jona moved fast, planting the cigarette in the scrapper's eye while smoothly pointing the Glock at his friend and firing.

Veering back, her first victim fumbled to raise his rifle. Gage was up and barreled into the man's chest. Ripping the weapon away, Gage clocked him across the temple before firing a round into his chest.

"Nice work but too late." Jona nodded at the distant chopper which flew in the opposite direction. He wanted to collapse to his knees.

His newly acquired weapon already aimed at Jona's head, Gage hid his raging grief and stepped back and circled the remaining target. "I'll find her. I would love to stay and chat, but..."

"You have to rescue our girl." The handgun hung loosely at her side.

"Fuck you," Gage yelled. "You wanted to wipe Chantal from existence."

"I did, and I'm sorry. Here's your Glock—a 19C Gen4. Impressive and versatile. I'm a SIG girl myself, but this is fast and accurate." She placed the gun slowly on the ground and backed off. "I like the reversible magazine catch—I'm a left-handed shooter."

"Why did you help kill these tangos?"

"Because I want to save Chantal."

"Like I'd trust that sudden change of heart."

"You don't have to trust me. But the longer we stand here and chit-chat, the further away Harris gets."

"Yes, time for me to go." Gage aimed down the barrel and watched her raise her hands. Her cocky attitude grated. "You're not scared of dying. I can see it in your eyes."

"In my profession, I thought I'd be dead a long time ago. Besides, from what I know of you, you won't shoot an unarmed woman."

"I'm not that same man." She must've seen his exquisite anguish because she tensed and raised her arms higher. "I know where they'll take her. Without me, you'll lose her forever."

Gage didn't move, ignoring his throbbing wrist as he held the barrel steady.

Jona pleaded her case. "I could have killed her a hundred times. I didn't. Let me help."

"If we don't find her… if we're too late… I'll end you."

"Noted."

"And you don't get a weapon."

Jona shrugged. "Fine, I don't need one."

"And I get to search those pockets." The rifle still raised, he pointed at her cargo pants.

Jona unbuttoned them.

"What are you doing? I meant I'd frisk you."

"It's easier this way." She slipped off the pants and tossed them at Gage. "There are two knives—one in the right and one in a back pocket."

Gage moved further out of range and unzipped numerous pouches and hidden pockets.

"I had those trousers specially made." Jona grinned. "Waterproof and tear proof."

Gage pulled out a carbon fiber knife and gave her a WTF look.

"What? It's lightweight."

"And you have a pocket survival kit." He pulled out a pouch. "A compass—nice. But, no gun?"

"I don't carry a gun unless I need to—especially when hiding in plain view."

"And I see only one knife." He slipped the contents into a jacket pocket.

Confused, Jona frowned. "I must've lost the other along the way." She turned in a circle and lifted her tank top. "See… nada. No need for a cavity search—I don't stick sharp objects up my butt."

"Your smart mouth will get you killed one day. Did you honestly slide down the mountain on your ass to complete your mission?" His hands trembled as he searched, and he tried not to think of Chantal at the mercy of Harris.

"I did… leaped in when I saw the mud take Chantal. I knew she'd be separated from the herd."

"An easier target… You could've died."

"A chance I'll always take—I'm not scared of death."

"Your grand plan failed." Gage examined an LED flashlight.

"It did. I grew a heart. Don't get too comfortable; I'm not all that fond of you, so don't piss me off."

Gage threw back her emptied pants and bent to pick up his Glock. After holstering the smaller weapon, he retrieved the second rifle and secured the additional ammo, which he'd use for the first. And then he searched the men.

"Bingo." He waved a satellite phone before calling the memorized number, all the while keeping an eye on Jona.

As soon as Gannon answered, Gage spoke. "Are you at the factory?"

"Not me. Dishan and I are in the field—looking for you. We left the rest with the principal."

"Have you spoken with Martin? I hear there are SF teams on the hunt?"

"Yeah. Sri Lankan—Army Special Forces Regiment. We

gave them our coordinates. Apparently, Islamic extremists are the suspects."

Gage paused and forced the words past his aching throat. "Call Martin—we need to mount a rescue operation. Rajin has Chantal at an undisclosed location. And there's a leak at the embassy."

"What the fuck?"

"I failed, and…" Gage blew out a harsh breath. "Rajin is behind the ambush. He wants that drive, and he'll use Chantal against the ambassador."

"How badly are you hurt?"

"Nothing broken. Where are you?"

Gannon gave the coordinates, and Gage hung up the call and pulled the compass from his pocket. He gestured for Jona to walk ahead as they moved to the East.

His body ached, but at least he could walk. A shoulder and his wrist were the worst injuries. Blood still oozed from his brow and cheek, and his stomach clenched against the metallic scent—a reminder of his beating and defeat. They'd taken her. Stunned and sickened, he rallied his strength, and fell into the interrogation.

"I need details. Your obsession with Chantal and your rela-tionship with Harris and Rajin."

Jona paused to look back, and Gage nudged her forward. "Keep walking—and talking. Multi-task like your life depends on it."

"On one condition—They can't arrest me."

"There are no promises, and that's not up to me."

"If incarcerated, I can't help you in the field. And that's a waste of precious time. You can't tell the embassy who I am."

Gage silently agreed, but once he rescued Chantal, Jona would need to answer for her crimes. Keeping silent, Gage waited for her to talk.

"Henri Durant was my first kill. I was just a kid trying to

walk in my father's shadow. He hated that I was a girl—that's why he named me Jona. Which is technically a unisex name, but there aren't many female Jonas in Finland."

Her accent took hold as she drifted away from her Alexis persona. She also carried herself differently. Still confident, but revealing a harsh substance beneath her elaborate act.

"And over the years, you've become a chameleon."

"I have." Jona seemed proud of the fact. "Which takes much work—months of dedicated research."

"Does anything about you ring true?"

"I enjoy mountain climbing."

"And you kill for money. You must be a wealthy woman."

"I do, and I am. But I choose my targets carefully—I kill corrupted turds. Evil fuckers who deserve my wrath."

"Unlike Chantal."

"She has a good soul, and I didn't want to see past my heartache. I let my father down, and..." Jona paused. "He should've retired and rested—gone for chemo. I wasn't ready for the Durant assignment. I got him killed before his time."

"From what I've read, the cancer was advanced. I don't think chemo and rest would've helped. What about Rajin—and your brutal friend?"

Gage pointed ahead, and Jona continued to walk.

"My father worked with Harris on occasion. He even came to our home over one Christmas and liked to see himself as my other mentor. I trained with him in Russia when I was fourteen—a brutal month-long camp. He may be from Texas, but he speaks fluent Russian and prefers their harsh winters to his ranch. Harris likes to test his limits but has a narrowed vision. And he's gotten lazy over the years. He now hires minions for his dirty work."

"And he is Rajin's minion—like you."

"I don't work for Rajin. I've never worked for anyone but myself."

"Yet, you participated in our annihilation."

"And I changed my mind. A girl can do that." Jona tugged at a tea leaf on a passing shrub.

"You let Harris into the center—the day he attacked Chantal. That's how we missed the bastard. He had inside help."

"I slipped him in through a side door, and I..." Jona rubbed her neck. "I didn't like what he did to Chantal. I thought he'd scare her a little—find out what she knew. He went too far. I wanted to ignore his brutality, but..."

"But what?"

"When I saw her curled on the floor—and her terror." Jona shook her head in apparent disgust. "I justified his actions—and mine."

"Do you know what's on that USB drive?"

Her shoulders straightened.

"You won't tell me?"

"A quick tip—don't trust the local forces."

"How high up does this go?" Gage asked, knowing the answer.

"To the top."

"The president participated in torture." It wasn't a question, and his terror for Chantal grew.

"They've sent a team to the States to eliminate Pearl and bring back Rajin's daughter. He won't stop until he's recovered both items of value. That evidence is his death sentence."

"Who did they kill on that USB drive?"

"The British reporter who disappeared a while back."

"Jeffrey Benson?"

"That's the one."

"Where will they take Chantal?"

"I'm not sure—"

Gage grabbed an arm and twisted Jona around. "You said you knew where she would be."

"I will. Over the past weeks, I've planted a tracking device —a couple—on Harris."

"We're relying on black market trackers?"

"I already tracked him to two locations. The data is stored in the cloud. Dickhead, let go."

Gage shoved her away. "Remember what I said I'd do if you fail."

"I won't forget."

Movement in the distance drew Gage's attention, and he squinted through the afternoon light.

Spotting Gannon and Dishan, Gage nudged her along. "I won't lie to my team. You'll come clean."

"You promised—"

"I promised fuck-all. My team will rescue Chantal—no matter what anyone says. We'll be first on the ground, and my men will know the risks."

Gannon sped up and raced along a furrow. "You look like hell, man! Like you fought Thanos in the depths of fucking hell!" He pulled his friend in for a hug, and Gage groaned and then squeezed his friend hard.

"Easy. We'll get her back."

Gage nodded as emotions pulled him back to the last time he'd seen her face. They had work to do before he could save her, so Gage stepped back and faced his friend.

"You found Alexis." Gannon turned to Jona, relief evident on his face. "I was worried."

Before he could close in, Gage pulled her out of range. "This isn't Alexis."

Gannon frowned as Dishan joined them.

"Let me tell him." Jona shot Gage a pleading look, which he ignored.

"This is Jona Kivela, and she tried to kill Chantal."

26

Jaffna Peninsula, Sri Lanka.

They'd walked for just over a mile from the chopper landing site, and Chantal stumbled to keep up. Approaching the thirty-five-hour mark—aside from half a protein bar—she hadn't eaten.

Desperately thirsty and exhausted from her two-day ordeal, Chantal's weakening body felt uncooperative. All she cared about was Gage. Staring numbly ahead through eyes swollen from tears, she prayed he lived. He'd lain bleeding, beaten and surrounded the last time she'd seen him. He had to have found a way. Gage wouldn't give up on fighting for his life or for her rescue. The alternative would destroy her heart—her soul.

They'd flown north and had stopped once to refuel. Chantal guessed—from what she'd seen on the approach—that they were on the outskirts of a coastal town which looked familiar. The humidity cloaked her in damp heat. Jaffna sat on the Northern tip of Sri Lanka.

Chantal's stomach sank as she realized how far she sat from Gage—200 miles away. After landing beside a small mango orchard, they'd exited the chopper and wound their way past shacks and family farms.

The locals retreated when spotting the armed mercenaries, and Chantal knew that no help would come anytime soon. Could they smell her terror? Her heartache? She'd find a way to escape, and scanned the landscape, deciding on the direction she'd run.

Distant cars indicated a main road beyond the farms. Chantal chose to believe that Gage had survived and would find her.

She hoped before it was too late—before Harris played his cruel games. Her mind flashed back to his hands around her neck, and Chantal rubbed her collarbone as they slowed to a stop. The derelict building before her looked grim. A rusted, tin roof covered the single-story structure. Set into one wall sat three huge ventilation fans; their rusty propellers turning slowly.

Harris knocked on a cracked window, and dust fell from the rotten and blistered frame. Stepping back, he waited, and a frail hand appeared, slipping a key into the barred security door before swinging it open. An elderly man stood aside, and Harris shoved Chantal into the gloomy space. She looked around the room as he barked commands at his men.

A sweet, cloying smell assailed her nostrils, and she eyed three women crouched in the corner, unmasked and sorting buckets of dried tobacco. The ventilation pipes running along the ceiling and the machinery taking up much of the space, confirmed her belief that this was a black market tobacco plant.

Sri Lanka had just placed a ban on tobacco farming, which threatened farmers' livelihood, and some turned to illicit production.

From the stacked cigarette crates in the corner, she guessed that this operation took care of production from field to end-sale. The lucrative, low-cost crop had a high sale value, and the government would struggle to stamp out tobacco use in Sri Lanka.

"Please, help me," she begged in broken Tamil—in a whisper—while Harris saw to his men.

The women refused to make eye contact.

"He will kill me. Please. My name is Chantal Durant. Call the American Embassy—in Colombo. Tell them—"

Harris approached, and Chantal flinched as the large man stepped up beside her. Harris shoved her up a passage, and the elderly farmer turned away—another blind eye. Tired of being pushed around, Chantal shoved back. Grabbing her hair, Harris slammed her, face first, into a brick wall.

"You wanna fight me, girl?" He rubbed against her back. "I like a fighter."

"Don't do this. My mother won't stop until—"

"No-one is coming for you. This will be your resting place, and once I'm done torturing you—for your dear mama's pleasure—you'll be unrecognizable."

Closing her eyes, Chantal thought of Gage, wishing she could be anywhere else. The time at the pool when he'd swiped her sandwich. The way he'd felt beside her—solid and reassuring—the teasing silence and the peace in that moment. Harris stroked her hair, and she shuddered.

"I love your fear. It's palpable—like thick syrup coating my skin."

The hands that touched her were those of a true psychopath—the serial killing kind who enjoyed a victim's suffering. Chantal couldn't show emotion in front of this monster, so instead, she took deep, calming breaths.

Finally, Harris pulled away and grabbed her by the shoulder. Her heart hurt as he led her through a courtyard and down cracked steps. An older building sat to the rear—reinforced with iron bars on one tiny window. The solid wooden door stood open, and panic took over. This hovel would be her prison... her crypt... her grave.

Thanks to a harsh shove, she stumbled into the dank, humid space. And then Harris dragged her to a corner and shackled her ankle to the wall. Chains and a cuff hung from the cemented ceiling and walls, and icy shock seeped through the terror. An iron bed frame with a stained mattress and a thin blanket sat in the corner. Chantal wasn't the first captive in this horror hell—who'd come before her?

Teeth chattering, and knowing she needed strength for this new reality, Chantal turned to her captor. "I need water and food."

"You have to work for a reward, sweet cheeks."

Harris turned and left, extinguishing the afternoon light by closing the door and turning the key. Grateful he'd left, Chantal sank to her knees. Water pooled where she sat, and she stood back up, re-situating herself in a drier spot. The chained shackle gave her some leeway, and once she'd settled, she immediately pulled out Gage's knife and worked the lock, looking for weakness in the rusty links.

In all their arrogance, they hadn't searched her for weapons. She remembered Gage's words in the shack. Choose the right moment. If she chose wrong, they'd overpower her and take the large knife. She couldn't leave it on her person— they may take her clothes and reveal the secret.

She'd recognized this prison and seen it on the camcorder recording. Would they torture her the same way? What damage would occur? She may be blinded by petroleum—her lungs burned. How many bones would Harris break? Would he... would he rape her?

Don't cry. Don't cry. You're tough and capable. He's a savage coward who won't win. He won't break you.

How long did she have before Harris returned, and what was he planning? She'd break down an escape attempt into manageable sections. Chantal decided to dedicate equal amounts of time to the cuff's chain, the lock, and the bars on the window.

She used the knife to saw at a link and worked the blade, fast and hard. When it slipped and sliced her ankle, Chantal held back a sob and started over. Now and then, she'd listen for sounds. The walls and door were too thick, and she'd need to move fast to conceal the knife when the key hit the door.

Sweat gathered and dripped down her damp back. Her arms burned, and her fingers blistered; still, she worked the problem. Shackled, she had no hope and Chantal needed freedom in order to fight.

The room grew dark, and her head spun, and Chantal never paused. When the key finally turned in the lock, she slipped all evidence of weapons under the filthy mattress. The dark—so absolute, prevented her from identifying the shapes that entered the room.

The door closed, and she clutched at her knees, hearing heavy breathing fill the small space. More than one person stood before her. Shuffling noises had her silently edging towards the wall. Chantal held her breath, wanting to scream out her terror and fight the ghostly demons.

Without warning, the first punch came, toppling her to the rough floor. A bright light blinded her against a boot striking out and another fist. Chantal covered her head. Stinging blows replaced the initial fists, and Chantal reached out, grabbing for what felt like a bamboo stick which then whipped at her fingers.

Crying out against the thrashing whip, she gave up and curled into a ball. The burning slaps of the rod pushed her to plead and shout for them to stop.

The beating ended when a rough hand grabbed her by the

neck and dragged her to her knees. "Say cheese." A distorted voice echoed in the empty room, and light still blinded Chantal as she blinked through the tears.

"Day one, Madam Ambassador. Tomorrow gets a whole lot worse." Her jailer threw her against the wall, and her head bounced.

Chantal slid sideways and came to a rest in the same damp puddle. The light extinguished as she wrapped an arm around her shuddering body. A finger touched her cheek, and she yelped.

"You get to drink." Water dribbled over her mouth, and she opened her parched lips, greedily trying to catch the trail. Bruising fingers twisted her face towards the ceiling, the rim of a cup shoved in her mouth. The flooding water had her coughing, and someone laughed.

"Stop..." Chantal sputtered, trying to pull away. The stream choked up her throat and nose, and she fought, grabbing at a thick, hairy wrist.

"What? No more water? Fine."

Free of his hold, Chantal curled back into a ball. The door opened, and they were gone.

Tomorrow gets a whole lot worse.

How much would her battered body take? Chantal slowly sat up and groaned. Her fingers traced along welts covering her back and arms. Her cheek and ear bled where the tip of the rod had caught open skin. She tested her bruised jaw and felt along her ribs. Lost in a vortex of evil, Chantal finally crawled to the bed. Her chained ankle hung awkwardly over the edge as she tried to settle.

Keep up your strength. Rest for a few hours and then work on the window.

She could do that. Closing her eyes, she imagined lying in Gage's arms—cocooned in safety—his breath trailing across her shoulder as he slept. Remembering how his fingers twitched against her skin as he dreamed, Chantal touched her stomach and channeled his warrior strength.

27

G age sagged against a pillar, an empty water bottle crushed in his fisted hand. His bruised body screamed as he waited for ibuprofen to kick in. Not that the meds would make much of a difference. Kohen had patched up Gage's head and cheek, sealing the lacerations with glue and steri strips.

Now, they stood outside the tea factory, surrounded by Sri Lankan Special Forces while awaiting exfil. Ignoring his exhaustion, magnified by worrying grief, Gage focused on his team and mentally cataloged their capability. With or without them, he'd be heading up the rescue operation.

His MSD team would still be the first choice, but as a rule of thumb, the host nation would have to weigh in and give permission. They couldn't allow American Federal Agents to run rogue in their country.

How would the Sri Lankan President work around this shit-storm? Would he block rescue efforts? Was Rajin in touch with the president, and did he know about Chantal's kidnapping and how that would serve in his favor?

Regardless, the Minister of the Interior would give Gage's

team the green light, and if they didn't, the U.S. Embassy would ask for forgiveness after the rescue.

The attack on the ambassador worked in America's favor. If Sri Lanka refused to assist in rescue efforts, it could be construed as a further act of aggression.

The ambassador sat to the side, on an empty crate, surrounded by his team. She looked as broken as he felt. Confessing that Harris had taken her daughter and that he'd failed had been the hardest moment of his life.

Gage rubbed his forehead with the back of his hand, remembering the ambassador's horror and heartbreak in the deserted warehouse that sat behind him. Her rage at Alexis— Jona. She'd wanted to destroy the younger woman for killing her husband and attacking her child. Despite her injuries, the ambassador had lunged for the assassin, promising retribution.

The only thing that saved Jona was her cooperation. She'd given up the location of her rented apartment, and Martin sent a team to retrieve her laptop and devices. Then she'd handed over her passcode to access her intel, and they'd gotten a bead on Harris's location.

Gage wanted an assault team in place before morning. That would mean a rushed mission, but he knew that Chantal had limited time. Stomach roiling, he covered his mouth and imagined the horrors she could be facing as the sun set on Sri Lanka.

"Can I join you?"

Gage jerked to attention as the ambassador limped over. The rest of his team watched from a distance.

"How are you feeling?" she asked, giving nothing away.

"Physically? I'll live. You need to sit back down and rest."

"Can you rest?"

Gage folded his arms and looked out over the lush green landscape. "Madam Ambassador, if you hobbled over to pile on the guilt, it won't work. If Chantal... if anything happens." He couldn't finish that thought. "My life would be worthless."

"That's not why I'm here." She leaned against the pillar, echoing his earlier stance. They stood in silence.

"You care for her."

Gage wouldn't answer. He'd walk away from his MSD career before losing Chants. She was all he cared about, and he'd made peace with the possible consequences. Gage fucking loved her.

"I can see that you fought tooth and nail for my daughter."

Gage searched for the right words. Eventually, he settled on the truth. "I've never been in love, and when I met Chantal, I fell hard. She swallowed my soul. I couldn't deny my feelings for the principal—for your daughter. That led to mistakes in the field—I'll shoulder the blame. I've never lost a fight or a principal. And yet in the past two days—I've lost friends, brothers, and the woman I love."

"And you're hanging by a thread."

That was an understatement.

"When this is over, you're welcome to file a report on my inappropriate attraction for my principal. Just so you know, I acted on those feelings at the lodge."

"I've been a bad mother." The ambassador rubbed at her shoulder. "All I ever wanted was Chantal's happiness. Jona Kivela shot my husband, almost killed my daughter, and set me down a path of agony and self-pity. The pain consumes me."

Gage offered her a conciliatory smile.

"I don't need sympathy. I get little rest, and the only person who soothes my injuries is my daughter. I'm no longer that same, kindly mother. I'm a grumpy bitch—that's what debilitating misery does to a sane mind. I'm a snapping turtle."

"Chantal is good at soothing injury. Both body and spirit." His heart hurt. "You're too hard on yourself. Your reputation as a fearless and fair envoy is legendary."

"At the expense of my child. I've lived, devoid of emotion, for so many years. Will I get the chance to make it right?" She turned to face Gage, standing taller with tightening lips. He didn't like her pallor and moved closer in case she fell.

"I trust you with my daughter's life. You will be the one to find her and bring her back to me."

"I will die trying," Gage promised.

The sound of rotor blades in the distance had her turning. He recognized Mi-17 and Bell-212 helicopters as the Sri Lankan Air Force rescue birds approached. Gage helped the ambassador over to the rest of the team.

Gannon stood to the side with Liam, watching over Jona. Gage didn't feel regret about placing her behind the sniper rifle that killed Henri Durant. Ambassador Durant deserved the truth, and Jona would pay for her crimes. And if she gave them incorrect intel—Gage would kill her.

The flight to Colombo ran fast and smooth, and the ambassador insisted that they run the rescue op from her residence—especially if there was a leak at the embassy. She refused medical care or a hospital bed, insisting that she wouldn't rest until they'd rescued her daughter. Gage said the same. Aside from eating and rehydrating, he wouldn't stop until he'd found Chantal.

They gathered in the fancy boardroom. Gannon led Jona to a seat, and she surprised everyone by getting straight to work on her retrieved laptop. She highlighted Harris's team and their weaknesses, identifying all of the mercenaries. She knew which were right or left-handed. What weapons they preferred and who fell asleep on night duty.

The dossier she pulled on Rajin, Harris, and their men impressed the hell out of Gage—years of gathered intel. He'd never seen such keen observational skills in the field, and he guessed her thorough training came from daddy-dearest.

Jona pulled up a new excel workbook before pausing. They

all looked her way as Martin's phone buzzed, and he stepped from the room.

"The worksheets are color-coded and alphabetically ordered." Jona smiled sadly at the confusion at her statement. "Chantal taught me how to use Excel sheets the right way—when I first started at the clinic." She chuckled dryly. "I liked her militaristic approach and that love of order. Her damn planners, though."

Gage fisted his hands and stared out into the night. "We have to move faster. I want to do this tonight."

"Gage." Gannon sat forward. "We can't be reckless. Let's learn the layout first. A rushed attempt could get her killed."

"Plus, according to his tracked location, Harris is in the Jaffna region. The only way we're getting there fast is via a bird," Kohen added.

He was right. Military transport would be the quickest infil plan.

"And we don't have the immediate support of locals?" Liam asked carefully. "The Sri Lankan President had no choice but to step in and help a trapped U.S. Ambassador. How will he feel about a kidnapped 'American civilian'? One who, according to her intel," Liam pointed at Jona with his pen, "is being held hostage to secure his dirty secret."

Gage ran a hand over his face and winced at the ache in his wrist. Martin stepped back into the room, looking ashy. The way he fisted his phone had Gage rising to his feet.

"That hostage is my daughter, and I'll do anything to save her." Ambassador Durant leaned forward, directing her next words to the now pale RSO. "We'll secure private transport if necessary. Find us the resources. And—" Suddenly recognizing his distress, she paused. "Martin, what's wrong?"

"We got an alert—for an email sent to the embassy's website address. It's a video."

"No." Gage knew in his gut where this was heading, and he

braced himself against a chair. Gannon stood and moved to Gage's side, eyeing his team leader warily.

"I'm sorry, Connie—you shouldn't see this." Martin walked to her side. "Why don't you rest for a bit. I have a medical team here to take a look at your injuries."

"The MSD boys patched me up in the field and did an excellent job. I'm not going anywhere."

"Connie—"

"Play the fucking tape."

Gage wanted to toss the chair across the room. His eyes burned as Martin opened a laptop and tapped away. He connected to the widescreen tv before glancing around the room. "They wrote out their full demands in the email and attached the video—filmed on a device. Most likely, a phone."

Martin glanced at the ambassador, who'd circled to Gage's side. Her hand curled around Gage's bicep, and he covered her fingers with his.

"I'm staying right here." She raised her chin.

With a slow nod, Martin cranked up the volume and tapped the space bar. The shaky image showed little light. Footsteps stopped at a wooden door. Gage couldn't be sure but heard a key in a lock. The screen grew even darker, and the image stabilized. Scraping noises. Shuffling.

Gage held his breath. The image blazed to life, and Chantal filled the screen—huddled against a concrete wall. The videographer stepped back as a masked man lunged and punched her in the face.

He had Harris's height and build. The ambassador cried out, and Gage caught her as she stumbled back. The fucker kicked Chantal and caught something thrown his way. A rattan cane?

Gage turned the ambassador away from the flogging, his eyes still glued to the screen. Chantal tried to fight, and the cane whipped at her hands and her head. When she curled into a shuddering ball, Gage swore his revenge at the screen. The lashings didn't slow as she begged for mercy. The bastard grabbed her by the neck, and the camera zoomed in on her terror.

Blood coated her face as the voice-modulated asshole spoke. "Say cheese. Day one, Madam Ambassador. Tomorrow gets a whole lot worse."

He threw Chantal like a rag doll against the wall, and the image went black.

Stomach rolling, Gage couldn't remain in the room. He handed the sobbing ambassador off to Gannon and headed outside. The warm coastal air didn't help the nausea, and Gage collapsed onto the bottom step and stared out onto the lawns. He could almost smell her soft perfume, and memories of their first kiss replaced the reeling images of her beating.

He'd have to watch the recording again, and again, to study her prison and the layout. Bile rose, and Gage huffed out a ragged breath.

"You'll kill him. The man who hurt her. Promise me."

Gage stood and faced the ambassador. "I'll wipe Harris from existence. Ideally, his will be a slow death."

"Good." Although still shaken, she smiled grimly. Martin stood just behind.

"Have you eaten, Madam Ambassador? You should—"

She raised a hand. "My chef is making sandwiches for all." Her mouth twisted. "Chantal's favorite—Chicken salad on whole wheat."

Trying not to lose his shit, Gage looked away.

Ambassador Durant stepped closer, her brow creased. "As far as Rajin is aware, who else knows of the USB contents? Of the president's involvement in the killing of the journalist?"

Walking up the steps, Gage considered her question. "His team and... Jona Kivela."

"And as far as he's aware, Jona is still on his side?"

Gage agreed. "Harris believed she would execute me. When the rest of his team—the men Jona and I killed—don't check-in, it will cause concern. Still, if he thinks I'm alive, he may think that I also killed Jona. He wouldn't jump to a betrayal. That's why we need to rescue Chantal tonight, before Harris gets suspicious."

Only the survivors of the ambush knew the full story, and they all sat in the boardroom. Gage considered a leak.

"If one of the SF soldiers who rescued us was a bad egg… "

"They could say what they observed—a blonde woman, matching Jona's description, stood with your team," Martin added. He turned to the ambassador. "What are you thinking?"

She looked back at the occupants in the meeting room. "Can we trust Dishan Farook?"

Gage nodded. "He'd give his life for Chantal—but his wife has just given birth, and he wants to be by her side. He's torn."

"He can't go anywhere until we have Chantal. Martin, get President Sameera on the line."

Martin pulled out his phone, and both men followed the ambassador into the meeting room. He handed over the phone once he'd connected the call and the ambassador greeted the Sri Lankan President in Sinhalese.

They exchanged pleasantries as Gage sat back down. He guessed that the president asked about her health after her rescue. The White House and DOD—The U.S. Department of Defense—would be breathing down his neck and pushing for a full investigation. Pacing, she switched to English, and her tone changed.

Deliberately placing the call on speaker, she sat. "Mr. President, you're aware of my daughter's kidnapping and my request for assistance."

"Yes, and mounting such a rescue takes time. I can't say for sure—"

"I have the thumb drive."

All eyes jerked her way, and Gage shoved to his feet, rage replacing his fear. Jona cocked her head and folded her arms.

"I... I'm not sure what you mean."

"The missing USB. I've seen what you did—how you tortured that journalist."

"You're mistaken—How dare you accuse me of torture!"

"How about murder? I've made copies."

President Sameera's heavy breathing filled the room, and the ambassador waited.

"What do you want, lady?"

"If you continue to support Rajin and prevent the rescue of my child. If she dies at the hands of Rajin and Harris, I'll release the footage to the media."

"You're blackmailing me?" His muffled shout indicated his lost temper.

"If you help to retrieve Chantal Durant, I'll destroy the evidence."

"You'll hand it over."

"Mr. President, you know how I work. We've spent many hours together. I'm a woman of my word, and you have little choice but to cooperate. I don't negotiate with terrorists—even for my daughter's life. The USB drive stays with me. Mercenaries attacked my convoy and took my daughter. My government wants answers. Who will they blame? Will it be Rajin or you?"

"If you come after me..."

"Instead of helping Rajin Bandara, it would be wise to distance yourself from the man. He no longer holds power over you or your presidency."

"But you do."

"All I want is my daughter—safe and whole."

She waited for a reply, and when one eventually came, Gage relaxed. But only marginally. With the president's cooperation, they'd secure transport—two military choppers. Ambassador Durant hung up and turned to the tense room.

Gage was the first to speak up, his words coated in reckless anger. "You've had the thumb drive all along? Even after the attack on Chantal at the clinic? You couldn't be bothered to unravel this clusterfuck before we reached a point of no return?"

"I lied—I don't have the damn drive. The president doesn't have to know that. As far as he's concerned, we hold power in this negotiation. You now have the means to bring her home."

The slow clap in the room had the team swinging to Jona.

"Well played, Ambassador Durant. Let's hope Rajin doesn't find the flash drive before we rescue Chantal. He has men hunting for Pearl and his daughter in the States."

"We're aware." Martin retrieved his phone and left the room. "I'll check in with Pearl."

Pearl Bandara wasn't Gage's priority. Only Chantal. Only ever Chantal and he wasn't done with the ambassador.

Gage pulled her aside. "Can we talk? I want answers to a couple of questions."

The ambassador quirked a brow. Gage guided her to an adjacent room.

He didn't wait for permission. "Were you aware of your husband's dummy corporation? Of his 'contributions' during the war?"

"That's none of your business."

"Is that why you took this post? To right his wrongs?" Gage asked in a hushed tone.

"I don't have time to be interrogated."

"Your husband's death has everything to do with your daughter's predicament. I'm questioning your integrity. There,

271

I said it. Do you have the USB drive and how involved were you in your husband's dealings?"

"You have some nerve."

"I'll protect Chantal at all costs. If your actions endangered her in any way…"

The ambassador sat beside a small table and sighed. "I knew Henri spent a lot of time in Sri Lanka. I didn't know why. I asked to go along on a trip and he conceded. We went sight-seeing, but I also spent too much time in the hotel room while he disappeared for days. I… I decided to explore on my own and fell in love with Colombo and its people. Over the years, I questioned Henri's business dealings, but I never found evidence."

Gage unfolded his arms.

"I took the post in Sri Lanka because all those years ago, I connected with the country and its people. And I don't have the damn drive. If I were in possession of such dangerous evidence, I would've put Chantal on a plane at the first sign of trouble."

"I believe you." Gage helped her up.

"Your feelings for my daughter have kept her alive. I saw you leap into the mud slide. Your protection in the field went above and beyond. Without that personal investment, my daughter may have died. I won't be reporting your conduct— I'll be commending your bravery."

"If you change your mind, I'll understand."

"Find my child and bring her home."

Gage led her to the kitchen, and they all grabbed a sand-wich and a Coke.

"C'mon brothers. Eat up quick." Gannon addressed Team Five, "We have a mission to plan—let's rescue our brave prin-cipal and bring her back home."

28

Chantal paused to examine her bleeding hands before switching from the window to her chain. She knew, if she slept anymore, she'd waste time. She began a fresh count to five hundred, and would switch tasks unless she made progress with either the bracelet around her ankle or the chain link.

It took an agonizing moment to lower herself to the ground. Her body screamed with exhaustion and relentless pain. Was this how her mom felt every day?

And Chantal had wanted a break—thought about walking away? What kind of daughter was she, to abandon her impaired mother, to run off and "find herself"?

Except she'd found herself—with Gage. Each moment they'd spent together was etched in her shattered mind. For the hundredth time, she analyzed their last moments together. And Alexis… the way she'd looked before pulling the trigger and deliberately firing past Chantal's shoulder. The defeat and sorrow reflected in her gaze.

Chantal tried to imagine Alexis doing the same with Gage —sparing his life. She still thought of the assassin as Alexis, because they'd worked alongside each other for so long. Sawing away at the chain, Chantal asked the hard question. Would Alexis help Gage? She was an assassin who'd killed Chantal's father.

How could Chantal not have seen the danger? She'd shared secrets, goals, and dreams with a deadly stranger—a woman who'd most likely killed the man that Chantal loved. Tears fell, and she wanted to scream—release the grief which sat trapped in her chest like a caged animal. If he hadn't survived…

Pausing to feel her progress, Chantal stilled. She needed light, and although the room brightened a fraction as dawn approached, she couldn't see the chain in her dark corner. She scooted towards the center of the room and re-examined her handiwork. Hope stirred. Chantal fingered the sliced link. If she could bend it, she'd be free.

The next step may waste precious time. Hammering the link would be the best option, and she could use the handle of the knife, but that would draw attention. Chantal crawled to the steel bed frame and felt around for a way to anchor the link as she twisted with the knife. She settled on a rusted corner, and minutes ticked by as she jammed it between the metal.

A distant laugh had her stilling. She recognized Harris and fumbled with the knife. What would she do, once free of the shackle?

Gage's words came back to her.

"If you're taken, let that knife do what it's designed for—killing the enemy."

Hoping not to break the knife, Chantal inserted the tip in the link and twisted it with all her might. The blade slipped, and she swore, trying over and over.

Please, Gage. Help me.

The Ka-Bar slipped again and nicked her wrist. Chantal

bent over and rocked. "Don't leave me. Please give me this—help me. God, help me."

Sucking in the dank air, she tried once more, jamming the knife through the link with all her might. And she heaved out a long breath and wrenched the handle slowly. When the blade stayed in place, and something gave, she shoved the knife beneath the mattress and wiggled the link out of the bed frame. Shaking fingers traced the widened gap, and she fiddled with the chain.

Harris laughed again—this time closer, and Chantal twisted and pulled at the chain, knowing he was close.

"C'mon... c'mon... c'mon." And then she was free.

The door rattled. Chantal dug under the mattress, before scrambling onto the bed, and covering her leg and lower body with the nasty blanket. Pretending to be asleep, she hid her hands as the door swung open.

"Wake up, Shweethard. Daddy's home." Harris stood silhouetted in the early light, clad in boxers and a t-shirt, his rifle swinging by his side.

God. He was drunk. Heart thumping, Chantal readied herself. Her opponent outweighed her. Was it foolish to fight him? She could pretend to be unconscious due to injuries and lack of food. It wasn't a stretch. Her weakened defense was a major disadvantage.

How fast and how far could she run? Chantal watched him through lowered lashes, and the gloom covered her deception. Harris turned and shut them inside, locking her back in her prison.

They'd landed a couple of miles away, and it had taken too long to reach the target location. Team Five had circled to find cover amongst fields, and Gage felt like he was crawling out of his skin. Rushing the rescue mission would lead to mistakes, and he couldn't endanger Chantal or his agents. So, he took his time.

The sallow half-moon helped to hide their movements as they closed in on the targeted buildings. Occasionally a grove of palms separated the fields, and the shacks, providing concealment.

Half a mile out, they came across the first sentries. One of the mercenaries slept—an easy kill as Gage slid up and snapped his neck. The man looked familiar—one of the soldiers who'd ambushed them in the Central Highlands.

Four more men fell silently as the agents closed in. When buildings emerged through the gloom, the team spread out, surrounding and infiltrating the ramshackle dump. Thanks to a government drone, they knew the layout, and Gage approached the main building.

The remaining guards were drinking and loitering near a burn barrel. The flames lit up the targets, and Gage slipped off his night-vision goggles as his men closed in like raptors, ending lives silently.

Kohen slid around a wall. Thirty seconds later, someone yelped, and Gage swore before changing direction to back up the medic.

The large man wrestled with a mercenary; his hand clamped over the tango's mouth as they crashed into a stack of old crates. Gage joined the fight and slid a knife through the enemy's ribs. Once... twice. The body went limp, and they both stepped back.

"Do you know what silence means?" Gage snapped on a whisper.

Kohen looked unapologetic, and Gage shoved past the bearded dick, raising his M4 and heading for the courtyard.

His team could've chosen "shock and gore" over "stealth and stalking," but that would've meant certain death for Chantal. Gage hadn't yet seen Harris, and that fact worried him. Had the asshole bugged out? Had he taken Chantal to another location?

～

"I shaid, fucking wake up!" Harris placed his weapon near the window and kicked the bed.

Keeping her breathing even and her body relaxed, Chantal felt him touch her hair.

"Pretty baby. Time for me to play before you smell of piss and shit. Today we'll be taking your toes. Maybe an ear."

Her mind recoiled and she forced herself to lie still. He stunk of stale beer and sweat, and as he leaned down, she clenched the Ka-Bar beside her hip. Like Gage had taught her, the blade sat against her wrist, concealed beneath the blanket. Harris needed to be closer, and she hated the thought of one chance at escape. A man's shriek drifted through the window, but Harris didn't seem to notice.

Lips traced her injured ear, and his putrid breath lingered on her cheek. "Do you have a boo-boo? I kissh it better."

Chantal couldn't hide her reaction when he bit down hard. The sharp pain had her jerking away, and Harris chuckled. His fumbling hands ripped at her clothes, and Chantal bucked and tried to twist away.

"That's it. Fight me." His meaty fingers clutched at a breast.

A distant crash rent the air, and Harris froze before replacing his hand with his hairy knee. The crushing weight made her gasp as he straightened and listened for noises.

Ignoring his weight, Chantal freed her hand, taking advantage of the distraction. The only place she could strike was his leg, and she went for the back of his knee.

Harris moved fast—too fast and caught her wrist just she made contact.

"Fucking hell! You slut bitch—you cut me."

When he crushed the handle in her wrist, Chantal cried out and let go.

"You like knives? You wanna play with knives?" Harris wrenched the Ka-Bar from her grip and pressed the tip to her neck. "Where did you find the knife?"

Gunfire in the courtyard had him cursing and surging off the bed for his gun. He picked up the rifle and turned to face the door, and Chantal lunged, sinking her second blade—Alexis's blade—into his shoulder and then his arm. Harris staggered and swung out, catching her with his fist. Chantal screamed as she fell to the floor.

"You're finished, bitch. You hear me?"

"Chants!" The door shuddered.

Gage. He was alive, and he'd found her.

"You'll be a dead fucking hostage." Harris tried to raise the gun, impaired by his useless firing arm. Thanks to her chiropractic training, she knew where to strike to cause optimal damage. Alexis's blade wasn't as large as the Ka-Bar, but it required little effort. This time Chantal went for his Achilles heel and sliced through tendon and tissue.

Harris's rifle dropped and he roared as she rolled away. He fell to the blood-soaked floor and the Ka-Bar skittered across the ground. When Harris grabbed her ankle. Chantal jabbed at his hand, but he caught her arm and twisted. She dropped her weapon and glanced at the Ka-Bar—just out of reach.

Harris fell over her to grab it with his good arm. An explosion shook the building, and debris and men blew into the room.

"One more step, and I'll kill her." The knife pressed beneath her ear.

"Chants, don't move. Not an inch."

She tried to smile at her brave agent outlined in the swirling dust, looking tall and undefeatable as he aimed his M4 at Harris's head. It was over. Either Harris would sink Alexis's knife into her flesh, or he'd die trying.

29

As they converged on the courtyard, a mercenary fired from the shadows and Gage aimed and took out the threat. The man fell just as Chantal's scream alerted them to her location. Gage switched to berserker mode, abandoning his training as he rushed the door. "Chants!"

Gannon wrestled him away. "I'll use an explosive breach. Hang back!"

"Fucking hurry! I'll do it."

"We need steady hands." Gannon knelt beside the door and pulled out the putty. He worked quickly and stepped back.

"Clear!" Gannon yelled, and the door blew inwards. Gage followed, rushing into the small space. His heart paused as he took in the carnage. Blood pooled on the rough floor, and Harris lay across Chantal with a blade to her neck. Gage recognized the knife as his own and savage regret surfaced.

"One more step, and I'll kill her."

Gage gave direction. "Chants, don't move. Not an inch."

Harris's head sat partially hidden, and too close to Chantal's. Thanks to his SF and MSD training, Gage could make the shot, but if either of them shifted.

He couldn't look at her, not while making the most crucial kill of his life. Harris thought he held all the cards, not realizing who he faced. Gage wasn't an average soldier and he wasn't mercenary-trained. With MSD precision, Gage tapped the trigger. The top of Harris's skull blew apart, and as his body slumped, Gage rushed forward.

"I... didn't move." Her trembling voice was balm to his soul.

"I need Kohen!" Gage dragged the dead asshole to the side and removed the rifle before snatching the Ka-Bar from Harris's hand and handing it to Gannon.

"He used my knife on you." Her blood-soaked clothes had Gage calling again for the medic as he fell to his knees beside her. Chest heaving in fear, he hesitated, not knowing how to assess injuries through all the gore.

"I used... used the Ka-Bar on him." Chantal tried to sit up, and Gage cupped her shoulders, pulling her spine to his chest.

"Be still. Let's get you checked out." He cradled her in his arms.

"I'm okay."

"There's blood all over the walls—the floor—the bed."

"Some of it is mine—but most of it is his." Exposed skin revealed angry welts and extensive bruising.

"Chants, my God. Look at you." Terrified he'd hurt her, Gage's hand hovered over her damaged cheek.

Kohen crouched beside them and swung off his backpack. "Where's the blood coming from?"

"Harris." Chantal grinned up at Gage. "I remembered what you taught me. I had two knives—Alexis dropped one in the tea field when she pounced. I'm a bad-ass." Her smile dropped. "I think I've damaged your Ka-Bar—on the window bars and cuff."

Chantal pointed at her ankle, and Gage's stewing rage came soaring back. They'd shackled her to the wall.

"I don't give a fuck about the damn knife."

"Well, I do." Her voice shook. "You saved my life in so many ways. Having your Ka-Bar with me?" Her eyes filled. "A part of you was by my side… it gave me courage."

"I love you." They both said it at the same time and both laughed. Their shared wince had her laughing even harder.

"See? A man without a knife is a man without a life." Kohen checked over her damaged hands.

Gage rolled his eyes. "Could you be any more of a knife guy?"

"And I'm a woman, Kohen, so your quote is a little sexist."

The medic grunted.

Relieved to see a sparkle in her eyes, Gage stroked a hand over her hair. "Let's get you to the hospital. Your mother is waiting."

"Will you come with me?" Her frown indicated uncertainty.

"Of course, Chants. I'm not going anywhere." And he meant every word. Gage couldn't imagine walking away—especially when she needed him the most. And what about after the excitement? How would they make their relationship work?

Ignoring the uncertainty, Gage maneuvered her into his arms and stood. Her hand fisted on his shoulder, and her soft moan indicated acute agony. Gage wanted to kill Harris all over again; instead, he gritted his teeth and carried Chantal from the nauseating chamber.

30

National Hospital, Colombo.

The reunion with her daughter had been short-lived. Connie and her detail met them at the National Hospital. Chantal had been rushed from the helipad on the roof to the third floor after Gage's men radioed ahead, coming in hot on a military chopper. Hours later, her daughter lay in a safe and comfortable bed with Gage by her side.

Connie cradled her third cup of coffee and watched the couple from the door. Their heads touched as Chantal whispered with the team leader. His easy smile indicated his affection as he tucked Chantal's tangled hair behind her ear. They both looked like they'd survived a war—or a plane crash. The MSD agent had better not break Chantal's heart.

The lash marks on her daughter's arms and neck had Connie turning away. She'd give them more time.

"Mom?"

"I can come back later."

Gage stood. "Ambassador Durant, I'll—"

"Call me, Connie."

"Uh…"

"Unless you're planning to ride off into the sunset." She glanced at Chantal. "For good."

"No, ma'am. Our orders are to remain in place until it's safe for—"

"I'm not talking about your MSD role in Sri Lanka."

"Mom! Stop." Flushing, Chantal pulled her sheets to her chest. "My relationship is not your concern."

"Your 'relationship' with a federal agent."

"I love Chants and—"

"Because my life is always about your job." Chin raised, Chantal crossed her arms.

Why, when it came to her daughter, did she always say the wrong thing. Connie knew how to negotiate and appease. She was all about unification and uplifting communities. Yet, with Chantal, she'd done the opposite—stopped her from living.

Gage touched Chantal's almost empty IV bag. "I'll get someone. Do you want anything more to eat?"

"Another cheesecake mousse?"

"I'll beg a nurse." He kissed her on the forehead.

"Just flex those man-muscles."

Waggling his brows, Gage asked, "You want me to flirt with the staff?"

"It's the best mousse I've ever eaten."

"Then I won't come back without one. Gannon is in the passage if you feel nervous."

"I have my mom and her entourage. And can you talk to Martin about Alexis—Jona—I want to talk to her."

"That's not wise." Connie didn't want her daughter anywhere near the assassin who sat in a holding cell in the local prison.

"I agree with your mother."

"I'll find a way to see her."

"Why, Chants?" Gage folded his arms.

"Because Alexis was my friend, and I'm trying to under-stand how I missed her malice. She killed my father. I need to know every detail from that day."

Connie commiserated in her daughter's grief. "Perhaps we should keep that chapter of our life closed. We've both worked so hard to heal."

"Mom, have you spoken to her?"

Connie shook her head. "Not since your rescue. My entire focus was on finding you."

Gage turned to Connie. "You should be resting. Did you see a doc?"

"Too many. They've fiddled for hours and have given me something for pain. And we all should be taking it easy. The debriefings start tonight—DC time."

"I'm all too aware." He walked to the door and slipped past Connie. "I'll get that mousse."

"Call Dishan and let me know how his wife and baby are doing?" Chantal called to Gage.

"Will do, honey."

Connie watched Gage work his way along the busy passage, discomfort evident in his stiff gait. Bracing herself, she turned back to her defensive child. "I like him."

"Doesn't seem that way."

"What do you want, Chantal? Tell me." Connie stepped into the private ward and closed the door. "When you were gone... my heart was ripped from my chest. You're the most important part of my existence."

Chantal fiddled with the corner of her sheet, and Connie eased into a chair.

"I remember one summer. You'd just started horse riding, and your thick and unruly hair matched your rebellious spirit. I bought you a 'Charles Owen' riding helmet, and Henri found you the perfect Hanoverian Warmblood. You loved that horse."

Chantal's mouth turned up. "Rosaline. She never liked you —do you remember how she'd nip your shoulder?"

"Oh, I remember." Connie chuckled. "Rosaline was a bitch, but she adored you and kept you safe."

"That helmet you bought was way too tight. You told me I had a big head." Chantal smiled.

"All that beautiful hair—which you cut off after Henri's death. I was so angry that you'd chopped off those long locks. I haven't changed. I should've stepped back and allowed you to mourn in your own way. I always wanted things to stay the same."

"But they didn't."

"No." Connie thought back to the day she'd lost her husband and her blessed existence.

"What about daddy's other life?"

"Until it's proven, I won't believe that my husband was a warmongering traitor."

"They found a dummy corporation. There must have been red flags…"

His deception would break both their hearts. Connie rose and pointed to the bed. "Shift up."

"What are you doing?"

"Snuggling with my child. When was the last time we lay in bed and chatted about life?"

"On Sunday mornings, when I was a kid. You'd make pancakes with berries and whipped cream." Chantal draped an arm across Connie's stomach.

"We'd read that dreadful series together."

"Tolkien? You said you loved it!"

"No, dear. Fantasy was never my genre. You loved the dragons and wizards. After Henri's death, you walked away from the fantastical, and I lived a nightmare—too caught up in healing to see my child's pain."

"Mom…"

"This isn't you—this ordered, obsessed shadow of a girl who was all about the light. I know that much of your despair stems from your hysterectomy."

"What are you saying?"

"I'm glad you're finding your way back to your old self. The last few weeks—you're glowing, even amongst this turmoil. It has everything to do with that overprotective team leader. And you need more. Find your truth and your happiness—without me."

"What about your shoulder—your arm?"

"There are plenty of qualified therapists to help. As long as you promise to visit—often."

"I may not leave. My patients need me, and I'm thinking of extending my studies."

"In what field?"

"Prosthetics. I want to qualify as a prosthetist and work with younger amputees all over the planet—not just in Sri Lanka. I'd like to see to both their chiropractic and prosthetic needs—in one visit. Perhaps, set up more rehab clinics."

"As long as you're doing what makes you happy. Do you not like being a chiropractor?"

Chantal considered the question. "I do. I can greatly improve quality of life, but I want to do more. Along with our prosthetist and translator, I sat in on a conversation with a six-year-old little girl in Hatton who'd lost both legs three years ago. I'll never forget her words—she said that after she'd lost her legs, the ground became her world. The mud and the sand were all she knew. In monsoon season, her hands and arms were always caked in mud. She'd never sat in a wheelchair or worn an artificial limb. It shouldn't be that way and I want to help to raise these kids from the ground."

Connie kissed her daughter's soft hair. "You're smart enough to conquer the bionic world. And sweetie, talking about mud, you need a shower. An actual shower."

"Mom!"

"I'm getting my ass off this bed and finding you some shampoo. And a good conditioner."

"I smell like victory." Chantal grinned. "Like Rambo and Rocky combined."

"You smell like a stinky smart-ass." Straightening with a groan, Connie hobbled to the door.

Gage stepped inside, balancing three bowls of mousse.

"Hand them over and come with me."

"Madam Amb—Connie?"

"Chantal needs pajamas and soap. Toothpaste. Face wash. Body lotion." Connie listed off items, and Gage handed over the desserts and pulled out his phone to tap out the list.

Smiling at his earnest dedication, Connie led the way, appreciative of the time she'd spent with Chantal. Now, if they could just find Rajin and bring him to justice.

Cradling his cellphone, Gage walked over to a waiting room and sat. Earlier, he'd retrieved Chantal's toiletries, along with the ambassador and her new local detail. However, Gage had insisted on bringing along Gannon and Lucius. Ambassador Durant's security lay in shreds, and Gage took deep, steadying breaths, thinking about the tragedy and grief—the deaths of so many good agents.

Now, it was time. Tears leaked from bloodshot eyes as he pulled up the number from his emergency contact list.

The ambush was already making headline news across the globe, and Gage ignored the flashing images rolling across the television in the corner. Aside from the chatter on the box, the room sat quiet. Just him and his sorrow as he prepared to make the call.

Jason's mother had to have seen the news, and although the U.S. hadn't released the details and names, she would be praying for good news, that her son wasn't one of the dead agents.

Gage couldn't allow a stranger to knock on her door—to tell her the opposite. Jase was all she had. After his father had left them, she'd raised her son as a single mom, and God... she'd done a beautiful job.

Gage wanted to vomit as he stared at the screen. Looking exhausted, his teammates entered the waiting room. Gannon sat beside his friend and rubbed Gage's back. Someone sniffed, and Lucius dropped his head into his hands.

Jason's mother picked up, and Gage closed his eyes. "Mrs. Webb."

"Tell me my baby is okay. Agents died. My boy wasn't one of them. Say it! Where is he?"

"I'm so sorry." Gage swiped at a damp cheek as her wails reverberated through his brain. They all waited and mourned her loss as she sobbed out her grief.

When the line went silent, and she asked the details, he told her all he could. How bravely her son had fought and whose lives he'd saved. The words wouldn't take away her heartbreak, and Gage knew that in the coming days, she'd swing between grief and anger. She'd blame the team, the ambassador, and the State Department. All a natural part of the mourning process.

Still, Gage felt responsible. A team leader needed to protect all his men, even in dire situations. He also knew that if he'd chosen differently, Chantal, the ambassador, and the rest of the men would not have survived.

Before hanging up, Gage made sure that Mrs. Webb had

support. Gannon contacted one of her neighbors to sit with her. Finally, when he hung up, he looked around the room.

"Let's get supplies to Jase's mother. Groceries, money, fucking whatever she needs. Lucius, can you make some calls?"

"Yes, sir. I'm sure the ambassador will call her and do the same."

Gage agreed. "All of you go back to the hotel and get some rest."

"What about you?"

"I'm where I need to be."

The guys filed out, and Gage rubbed his hands through his still-muddy hair. Dirt and blood came away in his palms.

"Son?"

Gage looked up.

"I couldn't leave the embassy until we had this fucked-up mess under control." Martin stood a few feet away, his face gaunt with a mix of worry and relief.

Gage rose, ignoring his aching body.

The older agent rushed forward and pulled Gage into a firm embrace. "I'm glad you found her in time. You still look like shit."

"I feel like shit, and easy on the bear hug. My ribs."

"Damn, I forgot. You need to see a doctor."

"Nothing is broken. I was one of the lucky ones."

"Lucky and brave. You saved a lot of lives and... no! I recognize that look on your face. Don't you dare blame yourself. You fought off an army." Martin glanced down the passage at the loitering security detail. "Where's the ambassador?"

"With Chantal. Helping her take a shower." Gage narrowed his eyes. "What's happened?"

"Latest intel indicates that Rajin jumped the border. He has friends in high places."

"Goddammit! He needs to pay for what he's done."

"Well, thanks to the attack on the ambassador, he's now number one on America's shit list. Not to mention Sweden. Hugo Elofson and Fredrik Blomberg were both found dead at the ambush site. The Hummer was peppered with bullets."

More casualties. Gage rubbed his arm. "Rajin wants that USB drive, and he also wants his daughter."

"I have protective measures in place, but Pearl Bandara's safety is now out of my hands. The FBI is getting involved."

"And what about Chantal's safety?"

"Hard to say. Too soon to know, but the heat is raining down on Rajin."

Gage glanced around the empty room and leaned in. "President Sameera?"

"That's why I say it's too soon—the asshole is untrustworthy. Listen, son, you need sleep. We have a rough, few weeks ahead filled with debriefings. You'll need to be ready for a grilling."

Gage knew the drill and tucked away his phone. His mind felt fuzzy, and he almost swayed on his feet.

"Are you still messing around with Chantal?"

"'Messing around'?"

"Because, if that comes to light…"

Maybe it was the exhaustion or his bone-weary grief, but Gage reached his limit. "Then they can sack me. Dole out their damn punishment because I fucking love her and will live with the consequences."

"You love her?"

"Every hair on her adorable head."

"Love as in the whole nine yards?"

"As in, I've never truly loved before, and she's my damn world. I'll move mountains and give up everything for her."

"What a mess." Martin rubbed his eyes, and Gage braced himself for an argument.

"I've waited a long time for you to find someone. That's the way I felt about your aunt. She was everything." Martin straightened his shoulders. "Okay. I'll have your back. If Chantal is what you want, I'll do whatever I can to help. But don't break her heart!"

"Yes, sir." Gage grinned in surprise.

"I love you, son. And I only want what's best for you."

"You saved my life so many times." Gage choked out the words. "I never want to let you down."

"And you saved me—a man without roots. After losing June, I went mad with grief. I'd never walk away from her family, and she adored you. Your parents loved you dearly, regardless of what happened with your father. I just hope that I did them proud."

Gage locked Martin in another hug. For the first time, he wondered about Martin's future. And about his own. They had each other, but they needed more—Martin needed a good woman in his life. It was time to break old habits and start fresh.

31

One week later.
Welikada Prison, Colombo.

"Are you sure you're up for this?" Gage asked, his concern evident.

"I'm fine—just a little tender." Chantal lied, but she needed to have this conversation. She stood with Gage in a dark passage. The rest of the team remained on guard outside the walls, and Dishan waited in an adjacent courtyard.

Team Five insisted on accompanying her, regardless of their debriefings and orders. Chantal's heart twisted, knowing they mourned the loss of their teammate. Local and U.S. teams had retrieved the ambush victims' bodies, and DSS would fly Jason's remains back to U.S. soil.

Gage looked restless, and she knew he was concerned over their surroundings. Welikada Prison was the largest prison in Sri Lanka. Regular prison clashes resulted in numerous deaths.

They weren't exactly standing in a safe environment and although filthy and overcrowded, they'd kept Jona Kivela out of general population as she awaited extradition.

A correctional officer waved them down the hall, and Chantal pulled in a deep breath. Her knees shook as she followed the officer to a set of doors. Gage cupped her back; his presence was reassuring.

"You don't have to come in with me."

"Are you kidding? I'm not leaving your side."

"She's cuffed and poses no threat."

"Never underestimate a trained killer like Jona. She's lived with death since a child. Her father stamped his training regimen into her bones."

"Then let's go." Chantal opened her hand, and Gage grasped it firmly as the door slid open.

Alexis sat at one end of a steel table. Chantal battled to think of her as Jona Kivela and still saw the façade—the "friendly Californian volunteer." A mistake she couldn't correct. They'd spent so many hours together. Perhaps this meeting would reveal the cruel assassin who'd shot Chantal's father in cold blood.

Their eyes met. "From what I can see, Harris hurt you —badly."

"Does that please you?" Chantal's voice shook, and she rallied against the weakness.

Gage squeezed her hand and pulled out her chair. He didn't sit but instead stood guard, watching Alexis's every move.

"No. I always hated Harris's need for inflicting pain. He never killed quickly."

"Yet, your actions have caused me years of pain."

"They did. I didn't know you, and built a biased image in my head based on my father's account of your family. Rich American princess spoiled by her corrupt parents."

"I am rich and spoiled. I have a generous bank account." Chantal saw Gage stiffen. "I'm not ashamed of my wealth—it's a tool for helping others."

Alexis nodded. "I started having second thoughts when I discovered how many prosthetics and wheelchairs you'd purchased for the center. You also funded the extension. When I dug deeper into your philanthropy, I discovered that you've donated to multiple charities for the disabled. And then when you helped the orphan—Sunny. His happy little face haunted me. He's so excited to have that job—to find safety. To save his sister. You did that."

"A drop in the ocean. I want to do more." Chantal folded her arms, her sleeves rubbed at inflamed welts. "You killed my father."

"I did. Ask me anything, and I'll tell you what you want to know. Your daddy wasn't a very nice person. And the contract paid well."

"For all three of our deaths."

"Henri was an easy kill. Corrupt filth stained your father's hands. My conscience got in the way when it came to you and your mother. My aim was off, and I paid the price."

Chantal leaned in. "I saw my father as a humanitarian who taught me how to care."

Gage moved closer to her side.

"There's plenty of evidence that says otherwise, both in Sri Lanka and in other battle zones. Your father was a war profiteer who sold weapons and intel to both governments and rebels. That was his greedy mistake—playing both sides."

"I'm discovering that he's a monster."

"If you're still in doubt, I have additional evidence tucked away."

Chantal sat back. "I've seen what he's done—and his profiteering breaks my heart."

"Did you stab Chantal on her campus? Was that your second attempt on her life?" Gage's expression held cold fury.

"No—it was too soon. After my father died in prison, I stayed in the States. I was just a teenager, learning the business of killing. On a fake Finnish passport, I married an American kid for a Green Card. He was a twenty-one-year-old loser—a surfer in California. I dedicated myself to learning the American culture and went to a voice coach and claimed to be a wannabe actress. I became a chameleon and morphed into an American. But I was obsessed with you and your mother, so I followed your lives online. When I heard about your college attack, I knew what had happened. The client had hired a new hitman to finish the failed contract."

"To kill the ambassador and Chantal?" Gage widened his stance.

"And that couldn't happen. That was my revenge—nobody else's. So, I hunted and tracked down Chantal's assailant. The dumb fuck wasn't too bright. He liked teenage girls and it didn't take me long to isolate the asshole and cancel his contract."

"You... you killed him?"

"Count yourself lucky. I tortured the hitman first and discovered that he was preparing for a second attack. In your hospital room."

"Who's the client?" Gage asked.

"I can't give a name. An old partner of Henri Durant, but he's dead. A mysterious heart attack." Alexis winked. "He kept getting in my way and now won't be coming after Chantal. You're welcome."

"I hate you—for what you've done to my family. And yet you've saved me twice."

Alexis shrugged. "Three times if you count the initial hit. I could've easily shot you on those steps. I had plenty of opportunities to kill you at the center and I kept making lame excuses."

"How do you live with yourself? All those victims?"

"Fifty-two contracts. I only go after the evil pricks—traffickers, molesters, gun-runners, mobsters. And, of course, despot billionaires. My father wasn't as selective."

"Why are you so chatty?" Gage raised a brow. "It isn't wise to share."

"Let's just say, I might be receiving a 'get out of jail free card.' I have gathered a lot of intel over the years on many criminal organizations—useful for specific agencies." Alexis turned to Chantal. "You won't get justice for your father's death. And I won't apologize for taking his life."

Confusion hammered through Chantal's brain. Along with heartbreak and betrayal. Betrayal of her father and betrayal of a friend.

"Where is Rajin Bandara?"

"The last I heard from Harris was that Rajin was fleeing the country. I'm guessing he's hunkered down somewhere, but he won't give up on finding Pearl and his daughter. He's determined."

"You helped Rajin and Harris to plan the ambush."

"I tried to guide them away from the foolhardy plan, but Rajin was determined, and so I used the ambush to my advantage."

"You never thought about giving us a heads-up?"

Alexis almost looked ashamed. "I couldn't get near you or your mother. It seemed like an opportunity."

"An opportunity that killed six men. Brave warriors who had families and loved ones back home!" Feeling ill, Chantal stood. "We're done."

Alexis stretched a shackled hand. "I'm broken. Thanks to my upbringing. I'm a psychotic bitch."

No kidding.

"Let's go." Gage lightly cupped Chantal's elbow.

"But I cared about you. I didn't want that. The irony is that you revealed my warped soul. I so badly wanted to be Alexis—the happy-go-lucky girl from the West Coast. I loved helping amputees, and I hated how I felt. I despised your likable nature and your kind words. I was your friend."

"You're Jona Kivela, and you've taken many lives in exchange for money." Chantal stepped away from the confused woman. "And you changed my life forever. Goodbye, Jona. You were never my friend, only a wolf, waiting in the wings to finish the job."

Chest burning and vision blurring, Chantal allowed Gage to lead her from the room. Jona called her name, and she kept walking.

"I'll make it up to you! I swear."

Gage turned and stalked back to the table. "If you come within ten miles of Chantal, I'll rip you to shreds. Forget that she exists."

Jona's eye's glistened, and tears gathered. "I can't forget her."

"I. Will. Destroy. You." Gage snarled; his words heavy with violence. "Wherever you end up, I'm keeping tabs. If you think you're a good hunter, you haven't seen my tracking skills. If you want to live, take my advice."

"Promise to protect her!" Jona shouted as he walked back to Chantal. "Protect her! She's all I have."

The guard closed the door behind them, and Chantal welcomed the escape.

"What the fuck was that?" Looking agitated, Gage paced the passage.

"I guess we got the answers we need…" Shellshocked, Chantal leaned against a cement wall.

Looking like he'd tear apart the building, he swore soundly. "Jona is legitimately obsessed."

"Do you think she'd hurt me if she got out?"

"I don't know what to think."

Hating his turmoil, Chantal walked into his arms. Gage stilled and pressed his lips to her hair, his hold gentle on her battered body.

"I'm not afraid."

"That makes one of us," he muttered. "If Jona is released…"

"Then we'll deal."

"How are you so calm?" Gage pulled back.

"Because I have you. Don't I?" Her forehead creased, and Gage stroked the frown with his thumb.

"If you'll have me."

"Can we take our time, doing 'couple' stuff? I have to ask though, what about… what about kids? My feelings for you are already established, and I need to walk away now if we're looking at different paths."

"You know, Martin is an incredible dad. I call him an uncle, but he's so much more. Without his love, I wouldn't be here—I'd be in prison or stuck in a dead-end job I hated. We're not blood relatives, but he's family—my family—a father. I don't care about bloodlines or DNA. I know that's what bothers you—not having children of your own."

"I never want you to have regrets."

"Are you kidding? I have this incredible woman wrapped in my arms, and I'm hitting way above my paygrade. She's kind and courageous. Graceful. Brave. Super intelligent." Gage kissed her head. "She smells amazing."

Chantal giggled.

"After all she's lived through, she was still brave enough to face the person who killed her father—the killer who held a gun to her head."

Pulling him closer, Chantal sheltered in his protective warmth.

"She knows how to bring a knife to a gunfight," Gage added.

"A Ka-Bar!" Chantal mumbled.

"Agree. A big-ass Ka-Bar. Like a ninja goddess. I should be pinning her to my side."

A prison guard cleared his throat, and Gage got the hint, steering Chantal down the passage.

"Speaking of pinning, when do you leave for DC?"

Gage stiffened. "In a couple of days." His deployment would be over, and she knew he was reluctant to leave her.

The Department of State had recommended that Chantal move back to the States until the dust settled in Sri Lanka and they could assess the threat levels. Chantal wouldn't disappear indefinitely. Perhaps for a few weeks. It was time to share her plans.

"I want to come along."

"Are you sure? Virginia of all places?"

"To be with you, yeah. I'm guessing dating will be a challenge with our hectic schedules. You could be anywhere in a month, so while you're in DC, we'll spend quality time together."

They emerged into the courtyard and headed towards Dishan; Gage pulled her in for a quick kiss. "So we're riding into the sunset together?"

"As long as I'm riding a business class seat."

Gage laughed. "Gee, thanks. I'll be flying on the government's dime—guess where I'll be sitting."

"I knew my flying miles would be good for something." Chantal winked. "I'll make a plan."

Gage slowed and turned. "About that... I know you can afford ..."

Chantal cocked her head. "Say what you're thinking. How about I fill in the blanks? You're uncomfortable with my wealth."

"A little. I don't want you…"

"Paying for your shit?" She grinned.

Gage looked uncomfortable.

"Let's get this boulder shifted out of the way, before it causes problems. Firstly, as an alpha-male, I'm sure you want to pull out that wallet on our dates. And I know you're paid a decent wage and can take care of yourself. Danger pay and all that. I won't turn you into some boy-toy."

"I didn't say that."

"If I want to pay for something and it makes you uncomfortable, then say something. I could've easily offered to buy you a business class ticket but knew you wouldn't accept. I'm not flashy with my money—aside from paying for comfort. I like to work on a plane—whip out that laptop—and I'd prefer to do that in a cozy seat. I'd also love to have you by my side, but we don't have to sit together."

"I know you're not 'flashy.' And, even if you were, it's your money to spend as you wish. I just… I don't have much to offer at the moment. I'm still racing around the globe. I have no furniture—a crappy apartment—and you deserve everything."

"'Deserve.' I'm not fond of that word, which is saturated in entitlement—and greed. I have everything I want. I'm alive. I'm able to make a difference through my work. I'm standing beside a good man with a generous soul who risked everything for me—a man who loves me. And I'm so excited about our journey, even when we'll work in opposite regions. Besides, I don't need much furniture—you've seen my cottage. A bed and a sofa, and I'm happy."

"I do have a comfortable bed in DC." Gage grinned, pulling her close.

"I'll have to test it out. That might take some time, and I'd need your help." Chantal winked.

"A thorough assessment. I'm on board."

"What are you guys doing?" Dishan yelled from across the yard. "Let's go!"

"Ignore him." Chantal laughed. "He's sleep-deprived with the new baby."

"I'll give you sleep-deprived." Gage poked her in the side as they left the prison grounds, starting their new adventure.

EPILOGUE

Christmas Day, two months later.
Quantico, Virginia.

"Connie, grab the salad tongs. They're in the drawer next to the sink." Gage leaned over and placed the large salad at the center of the table. He paused to look around his new home. So, maybe his whirlwind romance with Chantal had moved a little fast.

He'd ended up spending the rest of the year in Virginia, commuting between DC and Quantico as the investigation into the Sri Lankan attack dragged on via multiple debriefings.

Gage spent every spare moment with Chantal and wanted more—a cemented life with the gorgeous chiropractor. A home. Not just any home—a place they'd chosen together. Technically, they'd moved into their own place, but...

"You used my first name without a reminder. Finally." The ambassador tapped Gage on the arm with the tongs and grinned. "Your secret salad dressing had better be impressive."

Gage mock-bowed. "The least I can do since Chants cooked the roast chicken and all the side dishes."

"Talking about secrets..." Chantal walked in from the lounge. "Did I see you kissing Martin in our driveway?" She looked festive in her red swing dress and a white apron. Gage couldn't wait until they were alone—he'd slide up that dress, slip aside her panties and...

"You're imagining things—are you spying on your mother?" Connie's cheeks flushed.

"Mom... what happened since I've been gone? Are you guys getting frisky in embassy closets?"

"Chantal! Hush. Martin will be back any minute."

"He's fine—wading through my last-minute shopping list." Chantal stepped closer. "I'm glad to see you're happy."

Looking uncomfortable, Connie reached for her wine glass. "It's still very new. The ambush made us realize how much we cared. Although, we both have our hands full with a country in transition."

President Sameera had taken Sri Lanka by surprise and resigned from his position—just before the next elections. The intel on the missing USB drive wasn't the only scandal touching his presidency which had begun to topple like a house of cards. Gage only hoped that the next leader worked for all Sri Lankans and loved his island nation.

"Leave your mom alone." Gage pulled Chantal closer. "Give me a kiss instead."

She complied, and Gage tasted the wine on her lips. Three months ago, he'd never dreamed of a 'family' Christmas with the woman he loved. Now, they owned a house together filled with furniture, love, and a giant Christmas tree. Gage had never bought a tree before Chantal. He'd always been travel-ing, and if Martin and Gage happened to be at the same place, they'd find a restaurant to celebrate the holiday season.

Gage and Chants had taken their time choosing the tree

decorations. They'd even made a couple of ornaments. When they'd hung the baubles, Chantal had spoken about her last Christmas with her dad. Her recollections came with a mix of fondness and heartache.

Gage hated that accusations now tainted her memories with her father. That bothered her. The war victims that Chantal helped could've been hurt by her father. And now, her friend, Pearl, ran from a monster. Along with her daughter, she'd disappeared with the DS agent who'd escorted her to the States.

Chantal's worry for her friend had Gage investigating every angle. The sad fact was that Rajin was now a ghost who was last spotted in Switzerland. The Federal Department of Home Affairs had blacklisted the war criminal, but not before Rajin emptied his Swiss account and flew out of Zurich on a fake passport.

Gage hated loose ends. Jona was now an informant for the CIA. She might wiggle out of prison time. Thanks to his spook contacts, Gage would always be monitoring her movements. And Chantal had great plans—to take the prosthetic world by storm—combined with her chiropractic degree and work with victims all over the planet.

Her clinic in Colombo would be her home base. Gage worried over her safety—and thanks to their work, he couldn't always be by her side. With American agencies pursuing Rajin and with Harris out of the picture, Chantal was no longer a high-risk target. Still, Gage insisted that she hire a couple of bodyguards—at least until Rajin was caught. Gage had referred a few men for the job—fellow veterans who now worked as security professionals.

The front door opened, and Martin stepped out of the cold. "I'm bringing home the bacon! And dessert." He waved two bags in the air. "I could only get smoked as the freezers were empty."

"That'll work." Chantal grabbed the bacon packet and rushed to the kitchen. "I'll sprinkle this on the roasty parmesan potatoes. We're eating in fifteen." Gage watched her pull out a pan and smiled at the organized and clean counter. He would've waited until after lunch, but this was the right time— while his methodized angel bustled around the kitchen. Chantal reached for a knife, and he approached and pulled the bag of bacon out of her reach.

"What are you doing? I need that."

"Careful with that knife, my ninja princess." Gage took her free hand.

"I'd never hurt you." Chantal placed the knife on the counter, and he knelt before her.

"Gage!"

Martin and Connie stood in the doorway as he pulled the ring from his pocket. His hand shook, and Gage focused on her beautiful face.

"I know you'd never hurt me, which is why I want to make you my wife. Your compassion and that gentle heart tangled me up in knots on that very first day. Three months with you feels like a lifetime of joy. You're my anchor—my organized nomad. The person who I want by my side—even when we're oceans apart. You're starting your prosthetic adventures and I'll soon be re-assigned. But we can make this work." Gage stroked her soft hand. "Will you take pity on this lonely MSD soldier? Give him the gift of your love?"

Her eyes shone with tears, and Chantal nodded before kneeling beside him. "Tu es mon tout—you're my everything."

Gage slid on the ring and pulled her into his arms.

"I guess this calls for champagne!" Martin opened the fridge as Connie pulled them both in for hugs.

"Thank God, you proposed. Keeping that secret nearly killed me."

"Mom, you knew?"

"I asked Connie's permission." Gage grinned. "I nearly crapped myself. Not much scares me, but asking a U.S. Ambassador for her daughter's hand in marriage? Heck no!"

"He survived the grilling." Connie grinned. "Now. How about grilling that bacon and serving my famous roasty potatoes!"

"Our roasty potatoes." Gage quipped. "It's now our family recipe. And before we eat, time for one last family hug!"

The End.

Thank you for reading! If you enjoyed Strikethrough, consider leaving a review.

ACKNOWLEDGMENTS

I wanted to write about diplomatic agents and their bravery in this new series. I have friends who work as Special Agents for DSS, and often times, this branch is overlooked by the general public for their bravery in the field. From rescuing kidnapped girls in Nigeria, to stopping extremists, to protecting U.S. and local personnel in unstable environments, the men and woman of DS are always on alert and working to save lives.

I also wanted to highlight the challenges in a country recovering from civil war. I read numerous books about the Sri Lankan war, and the hard journey back to normalcy for many. Tolerance is the key challenge in many countries which house diverse ethnic and religious groups.

In the past, I've worked with many Sri Lankan friends and colleagues and their kindness and welcoming attitudes have built fond memories. I loved visiting Colombo which I did often during the war. Those were cautious times and it was hard to miss the fear and terror hanging in the air.

Finally, I'd like to thank all those that contributed to Strikethrough with their research and patience. Derek, thanks for your help on the DSS side of things. I've learned so much about the United States Diplomatic Security Service, although at times, I thought my brain would explode.

To my gorgeous family—love you all so damn much. Colleen! You're a terminator. To my editor, Joan Turner, at JRT Editing—thanks for all that you do, and making Strikethrough shine. My cover artist—Jaycee DeLorenzo—I love this cover!

ALSO BY LOUISE DAWN

Check out the rest of the MOBILE INTELLIGENCE SERIES series!

Heart pounding romantic suspense. Highly trained covert SF soldiers who will fight to the death for the ones they love.

SIREN IN THE WIND ($0.99) - Book One

An MIT Team leader on the hunt tracks down a woman, hiding from dangerous enemies.

STAIN ON THE EARTH - Book Two

A Special Forces Medic watches over a flight attendant exploring dangerous territory.

FIRE IN THE KNIGHT - Book Three

She's getting lost in Morocco, and he's finding her.

JADE IN THE SNOW - Book Four

A sniper trying to forget will fight for a woman in the crosshairs of a determined killer.

KITE ON THE ROCKS - Book Five

Friends to lovers face dangerous foes on a collision course with fate.

Also, check out the STRIKE ZONE SERIES!

The Strike Zone Series follows a group of Diplomatic Security Agents and the women in their lives. Romantic suspense with a political thriller edge.

STRIKING BLOW (3.99) - Book Two

A Federal Agent shelters a mother and daughter from a war criminal on the run.

ABOUT THE AUTHOR

Louise Dawn writes heart pounding romantic suspense. She's also a graphic designer and fine artist in Utah. Louise loves traveling and has lived in many countries before choosing the States as her home. Her passion is reading and writing fast paced stories simmering in romance. If you enjoyed this book, consider leaving a review. It's appreciated by authors both new and established.

Chat with her on Facebook:
facebook.com/authorlouisedawn
Follow her on Twitter:
twitter.com/louisedawnwrite
Or check out her character's development on Pinterest:
pinterest.com/louisedawnwrite/boards/

www.ingramcontent.com/pod-product-compliance
Lightning Source LLC
Chambersburg PA
CBHW020250200626
46816CB00001BA/227